I0659346

DIVINATION AND ROT

A PENELOPE PHAIR MYSTERY

ALEX P. BERG

Divination and Rot, Penelope Phair #3
Copyright © 2021 by Alex P. Berg
All rights reserved. Published by Batdog Press.

No part of this work may be reproduced or transmitted, in any form or by any means, except by an authorized retailer or with written permission from the author. For permission requests, please visit: www.alexpberg.com

This is a work of fiction. Names, characters, places, and incidents portrayed in this novel are a product of the author's imagination.

Cover Art by: Ravven (www.ravven.com)

If you'd like to be notified when more Penelope Phair novels are released, please sign up for the author's mailing list at: www.alexpberg.com/mailing-list/.

CHAPTER ONE

A persistent trickle of sunlight filtered through my eyelids, pestering me and refusing to leave, like a mosquito several hours removed from its last meal. I blinked a few times and turned toward the source of the light, an east-facing window whose blinds hadn't been totally cinched. I could blame Moss for the oversight—it was her guest bedroom I was sleeping in after all—but that would be a gross absolution of personal responsibility and an ungrateful snub of my host, neither of which was my style. Besides, I'd slept through worse: heavy rain, mid-day sun, howling winds a few knots shy of hurricane status, so I couldn't exactly blame dawn's first stretch for waking me.

I was honestly surprised I'd slept at all.

With a groan I rolled off the mattress and sat up. A debilitating yawn nearly inflicted upon me a case of lockjaw, but eventually it passed and my cheek muscles unclenched. I stood and crossed to the suitcase I'd left on the floor next to an empty dresser. Moss had told me I could unpack my things, but I hadn't wanted to take her offer. I figured the longer I forced myself to live out of the suitcase, the greater my motivation for finding an apartment of my own.

I plucked a knee-length nightgown from the pile of personal belongings in my already too messy suitcase and threw it on before heading into the remainder of the apartment. A twinge of jealousy crept up my neck as I passed through the living room en route to the kitchen, but I swatted it away with practiced ease. Growing up, I'd never lived in the lap of luxury. My parents had made ends meet, but there hadn't been a lot of slack in the cord, if you catch my drift, and that was before they divorced and my father turned into a hopeless drunk. When I'd ventured out on my own, I'd gotten by on restaurant tips and the occasional bonus check from the roller derby league, which was enough to buy a cup of coffee and maybe a little sugar to go in it. Thanks to my meager earnings and New Welwic's absurd housing costs, I was accustomed to living in a closet that I shared with whatever boyfriend I was seeing at the time. That made Moss's abode all the more shocking.

Technically, it wasn't an apartment. It was one of those newfangled condos. There were a total of three bedrooms—three!—in addition to two bathrooms and separate kitchen, dining, and living rooms, the latter of which was big enough to house a three piece sofa and a grand piano. There weren't actually any instruments in the living room, but there was a three piece sofa set, leather-upholstered with glossy lacquered legs, as well as one of those huge department store radios that was more furniture than electronic device. I wasn't entirely sure how Moss afforded it all, but unless there was an orders of magnitude salary difference between patrol officers and detectives, it wasn't from her work at the department.

Once in the kitchen, I scanned the countertops in search of

the coffee maker. I found numerous appliances off the bat: a toaster, a blender, even a stand mixer, but the percolator eluded me, as did the ground beans I'd need to make the drink. As I fought off another yawn, I delved into the cabinets underneath the counter, but the shelves played a practical joke on me. Row after row of pots and pans laughed at me, hiding their earthy counterpart behind their backs while they mocked me for my early morning chemical dependance.

"Need something?" said a mellow voice at my back.

I startled, banging my head on the underside of the counter. I pulled back, grimacing as I rubbed the back of my skull. "Just looking for the coffee."

Ginger Moss was everything I wasn't, at least physically. Whereas I was tall and powerfully built, with a wide frame and a little extra weight in places I wished it wasn't, she was five foot three in shoes, with a slim physique and an angular face. Unlike my giant mass of dark, frizzy hair, which was particularly voluminous first thing in the morning, Ginger's blonde locks were long and flowing, like delicate silks blown by a gentle breeze. Though I had her beat on bust size, hers nonetheless looked bigger thanks to her smaller ribcage. At least I could claim the superior derriere.

Ginger wore a similar gown to mine, though hers was made of black satin rather than navy jersey. She pointed to one of the cabinets I'd already gone through. "I use a press. Top shelf, to the right."

"A press?"

"Yeah. A press pot?" Ginger lifted one of her thin eyebrows. "Don't tell me you've never used one? I thought you used to work at a diner."

"Maybe that's the problem," I said. "I'm looking for some-

thing big enough to steep two gallons at a time, not some bour-
geois personal brewing contraption."

Moss scoffed as she slid by me. "There's nothing ostenta-
tious about a press pot, I guarantee you. It just makes good
coffee."

Moss pulled a chrome and glass pot from the cabinet behind
me. She pointed to the teakettle on the stove as she opened
another cabinet and pulled out a bag of ground beans. "Can you
turn that on? There should be water in the kettle."

I checked to make sure before lighting the stove while
Moss measured out a few scoops of grounds into the pot. Even
from a few feet away, I could smell the rich, earthy scent of the
beans. She set the filled pot next to the stove and nodded
toward her pastel blue refrigerator, one with a chromed handle
and a gleaming Sherman Industries logo across the front. "I
think I have some leftover brew in a mason jar if you're
desperate."

I snorted. "Sorry. I probably looked like I was going to bite
your head off. I'm not much of a morning person."

"So I'd gathered," said Moss with a smile. "Which is why I
offered the reserves."

I held up a hand. "I appreciate the offer, but I'll wait. I like it
hot. And I didn't mean to disparage your coffee pot. Mornings
minus caffeine equals cranky Nell."

"All is forgiven," said Moss. "And I don't blame you for not
knowing what it was. I've been trying to convince the bean-
counters at the precinct to buy one for the break room for ages,
but I'd have more luck convincing a tree to dance. I'd bring one
in and leave it there, but you know nobody's going to clean it,
and that's if some butter-fingered jerk doesn't break it and slink
out without saying anything."

I lifted an eyebrow. "I didn't realize you're so particular about your coffee."

Moss shrugged. "Some things in life aren't worth getting your britches in a bunch about. Other things, I'm particular about."

I looked around the rest of the condo, at the sofas and the dining table that could seat eight and the grandfather clock that looked as if it had been hewn by an elven master-craftsman who might've employed a puppet turned real boy in his workshop. "I can tell."

Given how late we'd arrived from work the evening prior, we hadn't had much of a chance to discuss Moss's living situation. I think she got the gist of my thoughts off my face.

"I'm blessed, I'll admit," she said. "My father set up a trust fund for me when I was a teen. It's how I afford these creature comforts. And I know what you're thinking. If I have enough money to afford a place like this, what am I doing working my ass off as a detective? Well, *Dad*, it's because there's more to life than money. There are things in life that can't be bought and ways to get them without feeling skeezy."

I recalled one of our first meetings, where Moss and I dropped by a rich divorcee's mansion in Brentford. She'd made an offhand comment about rich folks cheating and stealing their way to their fortunes. I'd assumed it was the idle musings of a jaded detective, but I hadn't considered she might be speaking from experience. "You don't have to explain anything to me. I'm just grateful you're willing to let me stay with you until I find a new apartment. Making things work at my old place with my ex-boyfriend would've been awkward to say the least, and I didn't want to impose on my nana again. Not to mention she doesn't live anywhere close to the precinct."

"It's all good." Moss leaned against the counter. "You're welcome to stay as long as you need, even if that ends up being longer than you want it to be."

I smiled. "Thanks. At least tomorrow I won't wake you up banging around the kitchen at the crack of dawn."

Moss shrugged. "You didn't wake me. I couldn't sleep. Couldn't turn my brain off."

I snorted. "You, too, huh?"

Moss nodded. Neither one of us had to go into detail as to what kept us up. The afternoon prior as I'd been getting ready to leave the police station, Detective Alton Dean, for whom we worked, had received a call. The person on the other end of the line had muffled his or her voice to keep their identity secret, but their claim had been enough to chill anyone's blood: they were the Tarot Card Killer, and they intended to strike again overnight. We'd stayed by Dean's side until late in the evening, but without anything to go on other than the call, there was nothing we could do but head home and wait for the inevitable.

Moss shook her head, chewing on her lip as she did so. "I feel for Dean. He's shouldered that case as a personal responsibility, but to get a direct call from TCK? It's going to make it that much worse, especially if TCK followed through on his threat."

I felt a pang in my chest, the sort of hollow emptiness associated with losing a loved one. "I know how he feels. I've only been working with you guys a few weeks, and I already feel responsible for the murders. It's eating at me."

Moss stood a little straighter and gave me a stern glance. "Don't do that, Nell."

"Do what?"

"Blame yourself for a perpetrator's actions," said Ginger. "It serves no purpose. You didn't murder anyone. You're not at fault. Not in any way, shape, or form. I know you might feel a connection to this case because you happen to be the closest thing to a witness we have to any of the murders, but that doesn't mean you're at fault. None of us are, Dean included. He knows that, much as he might still shoulder the responsibility for not catching the killer."

I put up my hands. "Fair enough. Perhaps I used a poor choice of words. I simply meant..." I sighed. "I feel like I should've made more of a contribution. Dean's been working his butt off, investigating TCK even while the rest of us have focused on other cases, and what have I done?"

"You've cracked the only two cases you've assisted us with, is what," said Moss. "One of them you weren't even a member of our team yet."

"But I could be doing more," I said. "I should be doing more, and... I don't know if I'm ready to."

Moss reached out and grasped my upper arm, squeezing the muscle. "Phair, we've been over this. You have all the tools you need to be a good investigator, and you're only starting to learn how to use them. All you need is experience, same as anyone else in your shoes would. There's no need for a crisis of confidence. Trust in yourself for once."

I nodded as Moss took her hand back. "Thanks, but that's not what's bothering me. I actually *do* believe I can do this job. Investigation comes naturally to me, it seems. But TCK? This is a different ordeal. We're not just solving a mystery. We're trying to stop someone. Someone who tortures and murders innocent women. He's proven he'll kill again and again if we don't stop him. This isn't a puzzle to solve. People's lives are on the line."

Moss gave me a sideways look. "Now you know why Dean's

been so invested in this for the last two months."

"So you're saying I'm right and I should deal with it?"

The teakettle started to whistle. Ginger lifted it off the heat and turned off the gas. "You could suck it up and deal with it. That's how some members of the force handle the weight of responsibility. Others self medicate with alcohol, but there's a better option."

"Being?"

Moss poured hot water into the press pot until it reached a line near the top. "To trust in your team. Yes, we've all been pulled in different directions. That's the nature of the job. There's never enough time and always too many cases, but when it matters, we pull together. We support each other, and we work as a team. We've done it before, and it's what we're going to do to find and stop TCK."

Apparently, Moss had a knack for unprompted inspiring speeches, even ones delivered at six in the morning. I gave a halfhearted smile. "You really think so?"

Moss plucked a couple mugs from a shelf and handed me the press pot. "I know so. No case falls on any one of us alone. We shoulder the responsibility together. My shoulders may not be as broad as yours, but trust me. It lightens the load."

I snorted as I followed Ginger into the dining room. I'd seen too much inter-department politics to totally buy into Moss's all-for-one, one-for-all ethos. From what I'd seen, success in the NWPD was more of a free-for-all, but perhaps she was right about our investigative team. About Dean, Justice, her, and me. I *hoped* she was, anyway. Because as much as my confidence in my investigative abilities had grown, I knew there was no way I was going to break the tarot card murders by myself.

We'd be lucky if all of us put together could.

CHAPTER TWO

Ginger drove us to the Fifth Street Precinct in her glossy black Howardson Hornet, the presence of which I would've attributed to her wealthy parents if I wasn't familiar with the cars Detectives Dean and Justice drove. Apparently, while the department's accountants wouldn't pony up for fancy coffee makers, they were willing to spring for decent cars for their detectives.

Ginger parked in the adjoining garage and we walked into the Fifth through the side entrance. As seemed to happen every few days, the lobby was a hive of activity, and it buzzed almost as loudly. I counted at least a dozen punks, all male but of every race, color, and size, split between the chairs in the pit and those in the lobby, all of them handcuffed, sullen-looking, and with officers standing watch over them. None of them had the scarred cheeks, broken noses, and bloodied knuckles of your average street tough, but they shouted curses like sailors. More than one had ink stains upon his shirt and fingers.

Moss waved to the officer at the reception desk, a clean-cut half-elf who seemed to get more than his fair share of the duty. Maybe he had a bum leg. "Morgan! What's all this?"

The young half-elf nodded as we walked up. "Morning, Detective Moss. Officer Phair. As I understand it, this is the better part of the Willow Creek gang. Some of them are still in the wind, but there can't be more than three or four we didn't catch."

I snuck another look at the apprehended lot. "These guys are in a gang?"

"They're forgers and counterfeiters, not gun-runners or drug dealers," said Morgan. "Detective Wallace in financial crimes said they could be responsible for up to five million crowns a year of fake currency. Not only have we brought in most of them, but we seized their presses and their stock. Should be a big win for the department."

Moss bobbed her head, her lower lip jutting out in approval. "Five million? Not too shabby. Captain Ellison'll be pleased."

"About the Willow Creek gang, sure," said Morgan. "But you know how he is. There's more going on than this one bust, if you catch my drift."

I don't think Morgan meant that as a personal attack, but Moss and I both knew exactly what he was talking about.

Moss gave me a nod. "See you upstairs."

I nodded back and headed down the adjoining hall toward the changing room. Admittedly, my jealousy toward Moss extended past her lavish condo. I envied the fact that she wore plainclothes whereas I had to stuff myself into a uniform that wasn't terribly flattering, but it's not as if I hadn't known about the dress code when I joined the academy. Besides, Moss had paid her dues, spending her couple years on the beat before climbing the ladder of advancement onto Dean's team. I'd made the leap faster, even if my advancement hadn't come with a pay raise or the perks of greater sartorial freedom.

Perhaps it was for the best. I didn't have the same eye for fashion everyone else on our team did. Moss dressed predictably but with an aura of cool I could never match, always pairing her well-worn leather jacket with a low cut blouse or a fancy shirt with wide lapels. Dean seemed to understand color theory as well as he did investigation, wearing colorful shirts alongside gray or black slacks and jackets, except for when he reversed the trend and wore a colored suit over a plain white shirt. Honestly, the man could probably wear a tie-dyed suit and still look good in it, what with the way his shirt was fitted to his broad shoulders and slender waist and his slacks fit him snuggly around the rear. Then there was Justice, who I'd never seen in anything other than a three-piece suit. The big fellow didn't even like to take his jacket off unless the heat demanded it, though I knew the look was purposeful. To be taken seriously, he had to look the part, he claimed.

I guess I had to look the part, too, and mine was in uniform. Thankfully, because of the limited gender diversity of the department, I didn't have to share the changing room too often. It was once again empty as I undressed, slipped into my navy blues, and tied my hair behind my head. With my belt tightened and my sidearm secured, I headed up the stairs to the third floor.

Our team owned a cluster of cubicles in the back, about as far as you could get from the stairwell. When I arrived, I found Dean and Justice's desks empty, but Moss sat at hers, sifting through the contents of a file that appeared to have been left there by CSU.

"No Dean?" I took a seat. "I figured he'd be the first one in."

"I was more afraid he'd never head home," said Moss

without looking up from her documents. "He said he'd stay up all night if he had to."

"I'm sure he would, but it's kind of hard to work through the night when you don't know who you're after." I grimaced, thinking of Dean on the streets, driving aimlessly and getting progressively more tired and frustrated and self-destructive. "He probably just overslept, right?"

"I wouldn't call it oversleeping," said Moss. "It's not even eight."

"You know what I mean."

One of Moss's eyebrows inched up. "Are you worried about him?"

"Do I think the Tarot Card Killer strung him up by his toes and is slowly bleeding him dry? Of course not. Am I concerned about his mental state following yesterday's call? I don't know. A little."

Moss folded the papers back into the file. "You want me to ring his apartment?"

I shrugged, but I must not have done it convincingly. Moss picked up her receiver and asked the operator to connect her to Alton Dean, 1037 Swiftmare Avenue. I could hear the phone's tinny ring through the speaker held loosely against Moss's ear, but after the seventh or eight try, she hung up. "Either he's tired enough to sleep through a tsunami, or he's on his way in."

I chewed on my lip in response.

Moss's eyebrows went up in tandem this time. "You really think something bad happened to him?"

"Well... I don't know. I've seen men get that focused before. They can make bad decisions in those moments, even men as smart as Dean. Plus there's something unsettled in my stomach. Call it a woman's intuition."

"I think that's what happens when you eat an apple fritter after sucking down three cups of my stronger-than-normal coffee."

"*Moss...*"

She held up her hands. "I'm joking. But I have a woman's intuition, too, and I've known Dean longer than you have. He has a tendency to hyperfocus. Perhaps he's doing that to a greater degree on this case than any other, but he's not going to let it cause him harm. He's self-aware enough to avoid that."

I shrugged again, not totally believing her. I don't think Moss would've challenged me on the issue further, but Justice arrived at that moment to break up the tension.

To say Detective Ogden Justice was a big man wouldn't be totally accurate. For one thing, he wasn't a man. He was a full-blooded ogre, dark of skin and heavily muscled. For another, he wasn't big. He was *enormous*. If he put on platform shoes, he could probably hit seven feet, and though I didn't think he tilted the scales north of four hundred pounds, it might depend on what he had for breakfast. Despite his size, however, he wasn't particularly intimidating. He had a brilliant white smile that paired well with his broad nose and wide mouth, and when he flashed it he could melt many a lady's heart, although I'd suspected for a while it was the male hearts he was more interested in. I'd never seen him lose his temper, but I imagined if his smile turned to a scowl he could probably make just about anyone rethink their actions. Good thing he was on my side.

"Morning, Justice," I said as he turned the corner.

The big guy bobbed his close-cropped head. "Hey, guys. You ready to head out?"

"Where to?" asked Moss.

"A nightclub, on Eighth near the river," he said. "Don't

know anything for sure yet, but seems like TCK made good on his promise."

I'd expected the news, but my stomach nonetheless churned. I knew investigating violent murders was the greater part of the job, but I nonetheless dreaded what awaited us.

Moss glanced at the empty desk behind her. "Shouldn't we wait for Dean?"

Justice snorted, but there wasn't any mirth to it. "How do you think I found out? He's already there, waiting for us."

CHAPTER THREE

J ustice led the way in his boat-like Howardson Phantom, driving east along 5th before turning north a few blocks shy of the Earl River, while I followed along in Moss's car. The neighborhood was one that had gentrified over the past decade or two, evolving from one filled with pickpockets and entrepreneurs peddling knockoff watches to one where trendy couples in their twenties and thirties strolled between microbreweries at two in the morning without fear of getting assaulted. The decrease in property crime and improved safety were good things, but it came at the cost of skyrocketing rents. As far as I knew, the apartments in the district were nearly as expensive as the riverside ones, but I suppose the rents were too damn high everywhere in New Welwic. The pickpockets and street peddlers hadn't fled the city, though. They'd simply moved to neighborhoods where the landlords didn't bat an eye at twelve people sharing a room and where the local patrol officers were too tired to shoo them off park benches in the dead of night.

Justice hadn't mentioned the name of the club we were

heading to, but based on the cluster of police cars parked outside a place by the name of The Library, I figured that was our target. Justice cruised past the lot of them and parked at the intersection of 9th and Forrest, leaving Moss to pull into the open spot behind him. Good thing she was driving and not me, otherwise the patrol car behind us might've lost a bumper in the inevitable collision.

Once she'd parked, I hopped out, meeting Justice on the sidewalk. Moss came around and the three of us walked back toward the commotion outside the bar. I didn't spot any yellow tape as we passed a white CSU van and approached the front, but a pair of patrol officers whose names I couldn't remember waved us past. I heard a mechanical click and saw the burst of a flash going off in the alley to the side of the club, but that didn't attract my attention. What did was the smell of cigarette smoke wafting from an emerald green Viper parked in front of The Library's closed double doors.

Detective Alton Dean leaned against the hood of his sleek cruiser, one foot on the asphalt and the other propped up on the chromed bumper. Like most dark elves, his skin was more dark gray than true brown, which perhaps explained why he wore more cool-colored suits than warm ones, like the ash gray one which currently hugged him. Then again, perhaps the lifeless color reflected his mood.

I stopped beside the car. "Dean?"

He didn't look up, his eyes cast in the direction of the cruiser parked across from him. His broad shoulders stretched the same portions of his jacket, though he sat without his usual pristine posture. Smoke curled lazily from a cigarette grasped between the fingertips of his right hand. A light breeze blew, tousling the short white hair he parted on the side and styled over the crown of his head. The cigarette burned as the wind blew, the lit end smoldering close to the elf's skin.

I took a step toward him. "Dean? Are you okay?"

Dean brought his cigarette to his mouth and took a long drag, sucking what was left of the paper and tobacco near the filter. He pulled it back and after a pause let out a long stream of smoke which the wind wicked away.

He didn't look my way as he spoke. "I really thought I had a chance, you know."

I felt Justice's presence at my back, like the gravitational pull of a small moon. I assumed Moss must be there, too. The pair of them must've seen the look on Dean's face and figured they'd let me do the talking, since I was the one dumb enough to open my mouth in the first place. "A chance at what?"

"Intervening." Dean waved weakly with the smoldering stub toward the alley.

I cast a glance over my shoulder, hearing another snap of a camera and catching the flash that reflected off the red bricks. "TCK?"

Dean nodded.

"How bad is it?"

Dean shrugged, his shoulders barely moving. "Bad."

I swallowed hard, hoping the image I was building in my head was worse than the real thing. "Bad enough to make you retreat to your Viper?"

Dean looked up for the first time, freezing me in place with his ice blue eyes. "You think I'm here because I couldn't stand it? Because I couldn't stand the stink of blood in my nostrils or the way it made my stomach churn?"

I swallowed again, this time at the cold furor directed toward me. "I didn't mean—"

Detective Dean flicked his cigarette stub to the asphalt, the smoldering end sparking as it hit. "No. You're right. I couldn't take it. I ran, but not from the blood. Not from the stink. I ran from the victim. I ran from the look she gave me. The cold stare frozen onto her face that until recently would've been brightened by a joke or a laugh or a snicker. I ran from her heart, full of love and warmth and humanity just eight hours ago. I ran from the future that was stolen from her because I failed to do my job."

Moss spoke at my back even as I felt myself rooted to the ground in shame. "It's not your fault, Dean. You can't blame yourself for someone else's actions."

Dean stood and pulled a pack of cigarettes from his jacket pocket, his fingers wrapping around it like a python around prey. "I don't blame myself for the murder, if that's what you're implying. I'm not prescient. I don't think I can stop crimes before they're committed. Only a god could've stopped the Tarot Card Killer's first murder. It would've taken a better investigator than me to stop him before he struck again. But by the third? I should've found him, Ginger. I should've found him and stopped him, but I didn't. Now there's a fourth victim. A *fourth*. So no. I don't blame myself for anyone's murder, but I do hold myself accountable for my incompetence. It's killing people."

Throughout Dean's speech, his hand had gradually tightened, the paper of his cigarette case crunching and the thin plastic wrapper crackling. His arms hung at his sides but not loosely. They were coiled with restless energy. If we were inside the bar after a few drinks instead of at work, I might think Dean intended to take a swing at one of us, even if just to give himself a target upon which to focus his frustrations.

Moss stepped up beside me, speaking in a firm tone. "You're right, Alton. I'm not going to argue with you. But if you're at fault for a lack of insight or effort or will, then we all are. I'll tell you the same thing I told Phair earlier this morning. We're a team. We work together. We succeed together or we fail together. You know that. You're the one who ingrained it in me. As much as we might've failed to catch TCK until now, I know for a fact we won't catch him by standing around lamenting our failures. We can't change the past, only the future. You need to pull it together. All of us do. As you said, lives depend on it."

Dean stood there, unflinching in the light breeze. He could've responded with anything from a snort to a curse to a shove, but instead he plucked a cigarette from the crumpled package in his hand and popped it between his lips. The package disappeared into his jacket, replaced in hand with a lighter. A flame licked the end of his cigarette. A thin curl of smoke lifted off its tip, followed by a stream of smoke blown from between Dean's lips.

Finally, he nodded. "You're right, of course."

"I usually am," said Moss.

Dean snorted, and with it the hardened pane of his emotions broke. He waved toward the alley with his smoldering cigarette. "Well? What are we standing around for? We've got work to do."

CHAPTER FOUR

There was a ten foot gap between the side of The Library and the red brick building opposite it, roughly half of which was filled with garbage cans, wooden pallets, and abandoned cardboard lean-tos that might've served as homeless shelters on cold or rainy nights. Surprisingly, there wasn't much of an aroma in the alley, either of urine or composting garbage, but as I followed Dean and Justice past the waste bin blockade toward a metal door in the side of The Library, a metallic tang entered the air, landing more on my tongue than my nostrils.

The scent of blood.

Not far outside the closed metal door, a woman was sprawled across the concrete, her lightly curled chestnut hair lying lifelessly across the ground at her side. She wore a pair of tight jeans and a form-fitting top underneath a stylish brown leather jacket, but as to the color of the blouse I couldn't say. The entire thing was stained dark crimson.

One of the department's crime scene photographers knelt beside her. The large bulb of his camera flashed as he snapped another photo. The shutters snapped, sharp as an alligator's bite, then the camera rattled as the man ratcheted the lever to advance the film.

Dean waved to him as we approached. "Why don't you take a break, Stan? Need to go over a few things with the team."

The man nodded as he stood. "No problem, Detective. I'll come back in fifteen."

He sidled past us toward the street while the rest of us took positions around the body, Justice furthest in back to avoid blocking out the sun.

Moss nodded toward the woman. "Do we know her name?"

Dean took another drag from his cigarette and blew the smoke toward the wall. "Lacy Breen. She had her license on her, so we've got a home address, too. That's about all, though."

Despite the blood that soaked her shirt and stained the ground underneath her, the scene wasn't as horrific as I'd feared. Ms. Breen's face hadn't been pounded into a pulp. Her throat hadn't been savagely cut, and all her limbs were still where they were supposed to be. Her torso, however, was a mess. At least two dozen small holes punctured her shirt and portions of her jacket, around which the garments were slick with blood.

Justice must've noticed the same thing I had. "Looks like she was shot with a shotgun. Probably at close range given the spread."

Dean tapped a few ashes from his cigarette to the ground. "Possibly, but I'm not convinced. I haven't seen any stray shot or casings. CSU hasn't picked any up either, not to mention I didn't smell any cordite on arrival. She could've been stabbed."

"Not with a knife," said Moss. "Not with those entry wounds."

"I was thinking an ice pick," said Dean, "but we'll know soon enough. I requested a coroner. They'll be here soon."

I knelt next to the deceased, trying to avoid staring into her glassy eyes. She was an attractive young woman, probably in her twenties, with smooth olive skin, high cheekbones, and carefully plucked eyebrows. More importantly, though, her face hadn't received the same treatment as her torso.

"Doesn't look like she fought against her attacker," I said. "I don't see a single scratch or bruise anywhere, and her clothes are only torn at the incision points."

"Which is what you'd expect if she was shot," said Justice.

Dean gave a small shrug, the glowing tip of his cigarette creeping toward his fingers. "We'll see what the coroner says. Being shot wouldn't fit the Tarot Card Killer's MO."

"Are we even sure it was him?" said Moss. "This woman could've been the unfortunate victim of some other violent crime."

Dean snuck his free hand into his jacket and produced a clear plastic baggie. I couldn't tell what was inside, but it looked like a scrap of card stock smeared with blood. "Corner of a tarot card. Found it in her jacket pocket, all the way at the bottom, tacked to the liner."

"Could've been a copycat," rumbled Justice. "Especially if she was shot. I mean—"

"He called me last night, Ogden," said Dean, his voice as icy as his eyes. "He said he'd kill, and he did. It was him."

Justice held up his hands, showing he didn't want a fight.

I eyed the baggie in Dean's hand. "He only left a piece of a card? That's a shift from his MO, too, isn't it?"

Dean shook his head. "The papers always misreported it.

Made it seem as if he left a whole card. It's always been a corner, tacked to the clothing with a quick, simple stitch. Easy to get on, easy to miss if you're not looking for it."

"But the pieces have been tacked on after the victims are murdered, right?"

Dean shook another few embers off his cigarette as he brought the thing to his mouth. "Not necessarily. That's one of the many things we're not a hundred percent sure about." He took a quick puff of his tobacco.

Moss sighed, her focus firmly on the woman. "Okay. Let's walk through this. This is Lacy Breen. Given her proximity to this door, I think it's safe to assume she'd been hanging out inside. She's dressed for a night on the town, at least." Moss pointed to a cigarette butt on the ground near her. "Chances are she came out for a smoke—unless that one's yours, Dean?"

Dean didn't scowl, but his gaze could've frozen a lake in August. "I'm frustrated, Ginger, not sloppy. Don't mistake the two."

Despite her diminutive size, she wasn't as easily cowed as Justice. "Just making sure. So Lacy comes out for a smoke. Probably toward the end of the night, maybe even after hours. That would explain why she wasn't found until morning. While she's smoking, TCK approaches her. Maybe he'd been in the club, watching her. Following her. Perhaps he picked her because he was attracted to her."

Justice lifted a meaty finger. "Attraction is subjective, so I won't go that route, but not all the victims have been of a particular physical type. Age has been the common factor, not looks."

"Fair enough," said Moss. "Regardless, she catches TCK's eye. He'd probably been trailing her for a while. Knew she'd be here. She might be a regular at the bar. We should try to round up last night's guests and staff. They might be able to tell us more."

Dean blew out another stream of smoke, the cigarette now reduced to little more than a stub. "Already ahead of you. As soon as she was found, I had the station contact the owner. Whoever was working the bar last night should be on their way to answer our questions."

"Like why no one responded to the sound of a shotgun going off." Justice shrugged as we all looked at him. "What? I still think it's the most likely scenario. Though it is the sort of thing that would've been reported if anyone heard it in the wee hours last night. Then again, you'd think someone would've reported this woman's screams, too."

"Whatever tool she was stabbed with could've punctured a lung," said Dean. "Lungs filling with blood combined with the paralyzing fear of your impending death might make it hard to make yourself heard."

Moss kept going, seemingly oblivious to the exchange. "If she'd been at the bar, she'd probably been drinking. The tox report will let us know. That might've dulled her wits. Helped TCK get the drop on her. Did she have anything on her when you searched her, Dean? Any narcotics?"

Dean ground his cigarette butt against the red bricks at his side and palmed the dead stub. "No narcotics, and nothing else of consequence. Keys. Some cash. The things you'd expect. Nothing appeared to have been taken, as we've come to expect."

"Ah... excuse me? Detectives?"

We turned toward the mouth of the alley. One of the patrol officers who'd waved us through the perimeter stood beside the garbage cans, thumbs hooked in his belt. "Sorry to interrupt, but we've got someone here from the club. Says his boss called him and told him to show up. Name of Nance, I think."

"That'll be the staff," said Dean. "Come on. Let's have a chat with him."

CHAPTER FIVE

W e found the aforementioned employee fumbling with his keys and fighting off a yawn as we rounded the corner.

Dean led the way. "Excuse me? Mr. Nance?"

The guy doubled over as another yawn overtook him. He was pretty average looking, with light brown skin and dark curly hair that flopped over the top of his head with as much grace as a used mop. His plaid shirt was rumpled. One of the buttons had been skipped in favor of the one underneath, creating a fold no amount of smoothing could cure, and the fuzz on his cheeks suggested he hadn't shaved in at least a day or two.

The guy found his voice at the same time he found the key he was looking for. "That's me. Call me Mike."

"I'm Detective Dean. These are Detectives Moss and Justice, and that's Officer Phair assisting us. We have a few questions for you."

He plugged the key into the lock. "I kind of figured you would after my boss called at the crack of dawn and told me to get my ass down here." The latch clacked as he twisted the key to the side. "Gods, I need a cup of joe."

Nance pushed into the bar. Dean followed him while Justice held the door for Moss and me. I'm not entirely sure what I expected out of a club by the name of The Library, but I figured there would be more to the motif than a single bookshelf above the bar filled with tomes that had been sorted based on the colors of their spines rather than their titles, authors, or any of the knowledge held between their covers. The rest of the place was utterly unremarkable, with green walls, natural wood accents, and worn stools oriented around tall round tables in groups of three. If I was in charge of décor, I would've invested in a few signs with scantily-clad pinups telling the patrons to be quiet, but apparently the bar's owners were content enough with their business to stick to the bare essentials.

My shoes stuck to the floor as I walked around, squelching as I ripped them free. Meanwhile, Mike ducked behind the bar and started to manhandle the percolator. He tossed the lid and the spreader plate to the side as he pulled a bag of ground coffee from under the counter. "Well. Go on. You can ask whatever you want to ask. I'm used to multitasking while I make drinks."

Dean approached the bar, but he didn't sit. "You were working last night?"

"Sure was," the barkeep said. "Me and Lacy, all the way until closing. Which was only about six hours ago, I might add."

"Lacy?" said Justice. *"Lacy Breen?"*

Mike nodded as he dumped ground coffee into the top of the percolator. "She's the one. My boss said he called her, too, but apparently she wasn't answering her phone at seven in the morning after four hours of sleep. I always knew she was smarter than me. Now I have definitive proof."

Dean laid both of his hands against the worn wood of the bar and gave a heavy sigh. "Mr. Nance, you might want to take a seat."

"I'm a little busy at the moment," he said as he poured water into the percolator. "You ever try to make coffee sitting down? Not a lot of stools back here for bartenders."

Moss sidled up next to Dean, her face wracked with the anxiety of what she knew awaited us. "Mr. Nance, he means *you should sit down for this.*"

Nance gave them a weird look as he planted the percolator on the stove and turned on the heat. "I told you guys, call me Mike. And what are you talking about? What the heck is going on here?"

Dean slid his hand into his jacket, and I heard the crinkle of his cigarette wrapper. He seemed to think twice, though, as he brought his hand out empty. "There's no easy way to say this, Mr. Nance, but your co-worker Lacy Breen was murdered last night."

The electric stove hummed as electricity coursed into the coil. Nance turned slowly, his eyebrows rising. *"What?"*

"We've started a preliminary investigation," said Dean. "We're trying to confirm the exact cause of death, but we're confident it was murder. You have my condolences."

Mike snorted, and his forehead wrinkled in annoyance. "You're kidding. This has to be some kind of prank. I saw her a few hours ago."

"If that's true, you might've been the last person to see her alive apart from her killer," said Moss. "We found her in the alley behind the bar. I'm sorry you had to learn about it this way. Were the two of you close?"

"No. No, no." Mike waved us off. "There's got to be some

mistake. You've got the wrong woman. Let me see her. I'll show you."

"That might not be a great idea," said Moss. "Seeing someone you're close to dead can be shocking, especially someone in the condition Ms. Breen is in. We should wait."

I could see the moment at which Mike started to doubt that we'd come to his bar in error. His jaw clenched, and his shoulders stiffened. His eyes widened, and he sucked air in more greedily than he otherwise might've, as if preparing for a fight. He darted around the edge of the bar, rushing toward the side exit. "Just show her to me. I need to see her. Please."

Justice planted a meaty paw to his chest, stopping him in his tracks, but Dean gave the ogre a nod. "Might as well let him. We'll need someone to corroborate the license we found."

Moss sighed and moved to intercept him. "Alright. Come with us. The back door is too close to the scene. We'll go around."

She headed out the front doors, and Mike followed closely. I glanced at Dean to see if he was going to come with, but he'd sat at the bar and started to play with a coaster left there from the night before.

Justice caught my eye, nodded, and we headed out. Moss and Nance had enough of a head start that I didn't see the bartender's initial reaction, but I caught the gist of it. As I entered the alley, I heard Nance cry out. "Oh, no. No, no. Lacy! Oh, gods..."

I was just reaching the choke point with the garbage cans when I spotted Nance. His cheeks had taken a decidedly greenish turn. I pressed myself against the wall, calling for Justice to back up as Nance turned and fled toward us. He only made it about ten feet from the crime scene before he bent over and erupted, shooting bile across the concrete.

I hid behind the trash cans, thankful to have stayed out of the splash zone as Moss came up behind.

She patted Nance on the back as he held himself against the red bricks with an outstretched arm. "And that's why we wait. Come on. I bet the coffee's almost ready."

CHAPTER SIX

We'd pulled up a few extra stools, but we didn't all fit around the small tables inside. As a result, Justice sat further outside our circle while Nance hung over the table, his head in his hands. Wisps of steam curled off a cup of coffee beside him, while the rest of us nursed ours.

Nance ran a hand through his tangled locks. "She was a good girl, you know. Genuinely nice. Girls who work the bar are usually attractive. Cute girls get more tips, and most of them know how to work the barflies to get more change in the jar. But it's an act. They smile and nod and say pleasant things, and the lonely guys at the bar reach for their wallets. It wasn't an act with Lacy, though. She'd engage the patrons. More importantly, she'd listen. When they bitched about their problems, when they talked about their sick mom or their estranged kid or their angry cat. Whatever. She earned more tips on the nights we weren't busy, and that was why. When she was bustling back and forth trying to pour as many pints as she could, she didn't have the spark some of the other girls do, but when she could talk to you? She made you feel like you were special. Like you meant something to her. Maybe we did."

Nance stared through the worn wood of the table, unshed tears in his eyes. Perhaps he spoke the truth. Perhaps Lacy had been kind and gentle and honest with everyone, or perhaps she'd played Mike the same way she played everyone else. He wouldn't have been the first guy to see the spark of a relationship where none existed.

Dean stared quietly at the table, but Moss gave me a sideways glace that suggested she thought the same about Mike's pining as I did. "Did you have feelings for Lacy, Mr. Nance?"

Mike looked up, wiping tears from the corners of his eyes. "What? No. I mean... maybe. I don't know. We got along. She was nice, but I didn't want to let anything get in the way of our work. She probably didn't either."

Or Mike had never worked up the courage to talk to her about his feelings, and now that she was dead it was easier for him to tell himself there was nothing there to mourn.

"What can you tell us about her personal life?" asked Moss.

Nance shrugged. "I don't know. Like I told you, we were coworkers. Friends, maybe, but that was it."

"Do you know if she had a boyfriend or a husband?" asked Moss. "Does she have any family in town?"

Nance shook his head. "She was single, or at least that was the impression I got. She never mentioned a significant other, and she was, well... flirtatious at times. As for family, I don't really know. That didn't come up often. Though now that you mention it, she did mention something about lunch with her mom months ago."

Justice cleared his throat. "Can you go through her work

routine for us? What time she'd arrive, what time she'd leave, and everything in between."

Mike nodded. "Sure. Looked a lot like my days. We're technically bartenders, but we do everything here. Opening, prep work, serving, cleaning, closing. All falls under the same umbrella. On nights she was working she'd arrive around seven, maybe six-thirty if there was a lot to do. Place opens at eight, but it doesn't get busy until at least nine. The rush lasts from nine, nine-thirty to about midnight. Those three hours are spent mixing and pouring drinks and maybe wiping down the bar. The place doesn't close until two, though. At that point, we kick out anyone who's still around, wipe off the tables, take out the trash, and head home, though Lacy would usually take a smoke break out back before leaving."

"She do that last night?" asked Justice.

Nance nodded, and his eyes sparkled with tears again. "Yeah. Shit."

"Walk us through that last part," said Justice. "The more specifics the better. With time stamps, if possible."

Nance took a deep breath, focusing on his cup of coffee. "There's not much to it, really. We tried to close at two, like normal, but there were a couple stragglers. Probably didn't get them out the door until fifteen after. I cleaned and organized the bar while Lacy handled the tables. When we finished, Lacy gathered her things, said goodnight, and went out back for her smoke. I went out the front a few minutes later and locked up before heading home."

"When did Miss Breen head out for her smoke?" asked Justice.

Nance shrugged. "Two thirty? Two thirty-five maybe?"

"Did you hear anything from the back alley in those few

minutes between when she left and you did?" asked Moss. "Any voices?"

"No. Nothing." The tears in Nance's eyes lingered, as if the man regretted not going out to check on his co-worker despite not having a reason to. Meanwhile, Dean continued to stare at the table. I assumed he was paying attention, but I'd never seen him so disengaged.

"Let's back up an hour or two," said Justice. "Were any of the patrons lavishing extra attention on Miss Breen last night? Anyone giving her a hard time?"

Nance surreptitiously wiped his face again, as if none of us had noticed the tears. "No more than normal. There was always someone leaving generous tips in hopes of getting her attention, or at least what they *think* is a generous tip. There might've been a couple of those last night, but no one harassed her or said anything offensive, not that I overheard."

Moss shot a raised eyebrow toward Justice. "You really think he was here? As a patron?"

"Not especially," said Justice. "But it's a possibility we can't ignore. He must've cased this place at some point and followed Breen enough to get an idea of her schedule."

Nance's forehead creased at the turn in the conversation, but Justice didn't give him a chance to ask any questions. "We're going to need you to provide us with a list of the bar's regulars. Not just the ones who were here last night. All of them."

Nance let out a heavy puff of air. "That's a tall order. I know a lot of them, to be fair. There's Jim Pearson and Rick Moffett. They were both here last night. Bill Turing. He's practically an institution. Guy must be pushing eighty. Then there's Estevan Fortanblue. Hard to miss. He's like a flag pole, tall and skinny and with a long mustache that waves in the breeze. He's—"

"We don't need the specifics," said Moss as she hopped to her feet. "But we will need those names written down. Why don't we go in back and you can grab a pen and paper?"

Nance nodded. He pushed himself off the table and headed past the end of the bar. Moss followed. As she walked, she looked back and gave Justice a significant glance, followed by a tip of her head in Dean's direction. I didn't really know what that meant, but Justice got the gist of it.

Justice sat in the newly formed gap at the table. He spoke in a low voice, more to Dean than me. "Think he did it?"

Dean didn't look up, but he did answer. "Highly doubtful. Nance's reaction seems legitimate. I don't think he knew about Miss Breen's death much less had anything to do with it. Besides, if the Tarot Card Killer is responsible for her death, there's no reason to think he would have any connection to her at all. It would be a complete departure from his modus operandi, not to mention a critical error on his part."

So Dean *had* been paying attention. Justice looked as relieved as I felt. "My thoughts exactly. Still worth looking into the regulars, though. TCK must've come through here while picking Breen as his next victim. If he so much as set foot in this place, we'll find him."

Dean looked up. His face was impassive, his icy blue eyes hollow. "That's what we thought at the bowling alley, too. How did that turn out?"

Justice frowned and chewed on his lip. Meanwhile, Dean stood. He pulled his pack of cigarettes from his jacket pocket and tapped it idly onto the palm of his hand. "I'm going out for another smoke. Be back in five."

Justice sighed and shook his head as Dean left.

I watched him as he pushed his way through the front door. "I'm guessing he wasn't this bad after the first three murders."

Justice followed my glance. "I'm not sure I've *ever* seen him like this. But he'll bounce back. He just needs time."

"How can you be sure if you've never seen him in this state before?"

Justice took a deep breath and let it out slowly, but he didn't say anything. Maybe he didn't know what to say.

It's possible Justice stayed in his seat because he knew to give Dean space, or perhaps that was just his style. He was compassionate at heart, but he didn't always show it on the clock. I couldn't sit on my hands while someone I cared about hurt, though.

I stood and adjusted my shirt. "Guess I'm taking five, too."

Justice still didn't say anything, but he gave me a curt nod.

I found Dean on the front steps of The Library, a light smoke curling from the tip of the cigarette between his fingers. He leaned against the building's weather-worn facade, the smell of his Slowburn Lights hanging over him like a shroud.

I'd tried a direct approach when I'd found him sitting on the hood of his Viper and hadn't fared particularly well. Perhaps a bit of idle chatter would pull him from his thoughts into the here and now.

I nodded toward the van that had pulled in among the police cruisers. "Looks like the coroner arrived."

Dean grunted and took a drag from his cigarette.

Swing and a miss. Strike one. "What was that about a bowling alley?"

"Hmm?" Dean glanced at me as he blew smoke to the side.

At least I connected on the second pitch. "You mentioned

things not working out at the bowling alley. What was that about?"

Dean's brow creased, and he let his cigarette hand dangle at his side. "The site of TCK's first murder."

"Ah."

One of his eyebrows inched up. "Did you forget?"

"Actually, we've never discussed the TCK murders. You said I was too close to them, given I was near the site of the third murder when it was committed. I don't know many details of the case."

Dean sighed. "So *I* forgot. Great."

"There's nothing to be ashamed of," I said. "It's early, and you've been at this most of the night. I just got here, and my wits are already addled from seeing Miss Breen's corpse." I shivered as I brought her still form to mind. "It... takes you to a different place."

"That is does." Dean sucked on his cigarette. He waved with it as he pulled it from his lips. "You could check in with the coroner. See if they have anything to add. When I'm done with this I'll find you, and then... I'll bring you up to speed."

CHAPTER SEVEN

A lump crept into my throat as I rounded the pallets and garbage cans to the scene of Miss Breen's murder, but my apprehension at seeing her again lessened at the sight of the coroner hunched beside her.

Emmett Jowynn was an elf like Dean was, but of the pale-skinned kind, not a drow. He was tall, which wasn't unusual given his race, but unlike most of his brethren, he lacked an air of elegance and sophistication. His brown hair was perpetually mussed, looking as if it had never been introduced to a comb, and his rectangular glasses never sat evenly upon the bridge of his nose. The collar of his shirt poked up underneath his white jacket, folded over and irreparably rumpled, but for all his unkemptness, he wasn't unattractive.

As if to confirm that fact, Emmett looked up as I arrived, affixing me with a bright white smile as his dark eyes crinkled. "Officer Phair. Wasn't sure I'd see you here."

He rose to his feet even as I waved for him not to. "I may not have been working the TCK murders so far, but things have changed. I get the impression it's all hands on deck now." I left off that Dean might need all the help he could get, given his state of mind.

"Well, ah… it's good to see you regardless, even under the circumstances." Jowynn's smile wavered as he glanced from me to Miss Breen and back.

It hadn't taken me long to realize Emmett liked me. As clueless as I was about many things in life, I'd always been well attuned to the romantic intentions of the men around me. While I didn't currently reciprocate Emmett's feelings, they didn't bother me either. Emmett was cute in a nerdy, shy sort of way, and he'd been nothing but professional in our interactions, even if he couldn't hide his occasional nervous stammer. That said, I seemed to have made an impression on him, which I still hadn't totally figured out. Not that I thought myself unattractive, but the department uniforms weren't the most flattering of outfits. Then again, it hadn't taken me long to rope in my ex-boyfriend Cliff when I'd started police academy a few months ago, and the outfits we'd worn there were similarly bland. Maybe I wasn't giving myself enough credit. Clearly something about me attracted men like moths to a flame.

I cleared my throat as I waved to Miss Breen. Seeing her the second time wasn't as unnerving as the first. "So what's the word? Have you gleaned anything the detectives might've missed?"

Emmett shuffled his feet, refusing to meet my eye. "Well, I wouldn't go so far as that. The detectives are excellent at what they do. I'm simply a coroner. I wouldn't pretend to be able to do their jobs, let alone to do it better. I mean, in some ways, our jobs are similar. We both study the evidence in front of us, make inferences and draw conclusions based upon facts, but my job is scientific in nature. I don't have to make many deductive leaps, just find the question that leads to the answer in front of me, if you will. Not to mention I have no idea what insights the detectives already came away with."

I sighed, regretting my choice of words. "I was simply looking for your take on the murder, Emmett."

Emmett blinked, and the sheepish smile returned. "Right. Well, in that case..." He knelt next to Miss Breen, careful to avoid stepping on her chestnut hair. He pointed at her with a gloved hand. "First things first, the deceased was clearly attacked from the front. You can tell based on the way the fabric has torn at each of the wounds, though it's also obvious from looking at her from the back. Not all of the attacks went through her, which isn't surprising given the sheer number of times she was stabbed."

"So she *was* stabbed, then? This isn't a shotgun wound?"

Jowynn blinked, his eyes large behind his glasses. "Most definitely not. Was that a point of contention?"

I didn't want to throw anyone under the bus—not that I could throw Justice much of anywhere. "How do you know for sure? The lack of lead shot?"

Emmett shook his head. "Birdshot can be tricky to find. Even if the deceased had been shot, I wouldn't necessarily find the pellets until I performed a full autopsy. That's not the giveaway. The blood splatter pattern is."

I forced myself to look carefully at Lacy. Her shirt and portions of her jacket were torn halfway to shreds, with blood soaking any cloth that would wick it up. "You can tell she was stabbed based on *that?*"

"Based on the *splatter*, yes," said Emmett. "When you shoot someone, whether it's with a bullet or lead shot, there will be an entrance wound and an exit wound, but the projectile only goes in one direction. An implement that is used to stab first goes into the body, then back out." Emmett mimed a stabbing motion. "When that implement is pulled from the body, it doesn't come out clean. Small particulates come along for the ride. You can see some of those blood splatters on her pants, the edges of her jacket, the pavement. There's even some on the door. See?"

I'd noticed the blood spray, but how Emmett could determine it came from a backwards stabbing motion was beyond me. "I'll take your word for it. Dean thought the same thing, anyway. He suspected Miss Breen had been stabbed with an ice pick."

Emmett nodded. "Whatever implement was used wasn't serrated, and it was also quite thin. An ice pick could be responsible for the wounds, though it's not the only option. A knitting needle could've done the job, for example."

I lifted an eyebrow. "A needle?"

Jowynn shrugged. "An ice pick is probably more likely, simply because it has a handle. Hard to put a lot of oomph behind a needle."

As I stared at Lacy's mangled chest, I suffered a vision of what her attack must've been like. Her attacker, closing in on her, ice pick in hand. How close he must've been. The heat of his body, the stink of his breath, the spray of her blood as he struck over and over and over again.

I turned away, trying to blink away the nightmare. "Makes sense, Emmett. Anything else?"

The coroner's face tightened in concern at my reaction. "Nothing I'd wager money on right now. I don't see any additional wounds or bruising. That usually suggests the victim didn't put up a fight, but that sort of trauma can be tricky to spot in poor lighting. I'll know more once I get her in my lab. Then I can do a thorough exam, scrape under her fingernails, check for skin cells. That sort of thing."

I heard footsteps behind me as Emmett spoke. Once he finished, a female voice filled the void. "Excuse me, Officer? Are the detectives around?"

I turned to find one of the CSU technicians standing in the alley. She was short and bookish, with her hair tied in a ponytail behind her head. She wore a white jacket that was shorter than Emmett's and had more of a utilitarian feel to it.

I shot a thumb over my shoulder. "They're either in front or in The Library. What do you need?"

The tech lifted a clipboard. "I finished cataloging the items in the alley. Figured I'd hand over the list. Also, I was wondering what you wanted me to do about the rat."

I blinked. "Uh... rat?"

The tech nodded. "There's a dead rat by that dumpster. I marked it with a placard and listed it in the catalog, same as everything else, but since I've already gloved up, I figured I could bag it and throw it away before the smell gets any worse. Not really something you want to leave lying around, you know?"

"Yeah, sure. Makes..." I started to nod, but halfway through the motion, I paused. My mind drifted to Miller's Creek Park, where I'd sat on a bench beside Detective Justice, him trying to soothe me after the shock of finding out I'd narrowly avoided the Tarot Card Killer as he struck his third victim. He'd been curious at my account of my walk home the night before, asking about a squirrel that had crossed my path as I'd been stricken with a sudden sense of unease. That same squirrel, or perhaps one of the same color and kind, had been found dead near the victim the next morning.

I closed my mouth, realizing I'd let it hang open. "This rat. How did it die?"

The technician's face screwed up. "Umm... what?"

"I mean, did it have any obvious wounds? Had it been stabbed? You know what? Just show me the animal. Emmett? You mind?" I crooked my finger at him.

I don't think the poor coroner had any idea what was going through my head, but he was eager to please nonetheless. He hopped to his feet. "Sure. What's going on?"

I gestured for the tech to lead the way, and she ushered us twenty feet down the alley to the aforementioned dumpster. There, near one of the corners, was a fat city rat, lying on its side, motionless, with a white placard with the number twenty-three placed beside it. A fly buzzed around the dead animal, but it seemed to be the only one.

I knelt next to the rodent. There was an unpleasant aroma in the air, but I wasn't sure how much of it was the rat and how much was the giant trash bin next to it. For its part, the rat seemed to be in pretty good shape. It hadn't been savaged or bitten, nor was it covered with maggots. Frankly, it looked like it had keeled over on the spot.

Emmett knelt next to me. He tried but failed to keep the curiosity off his face. "What are we looking for, Phair?"

"Any signs of trauma," I said. "Any signs this rat might've been murdered."

To his credit, Emmett didn't laugh, nor did he look at me like I'd lost it. He reached out with his gloved hands and turned the animal over, peering at it intently.

After a moment or two, he turned it back. "Doesn't seem to have any external wounds. Might've been poisoned, or it could've just died. Small animals aren't immune to cancer or heart attacks, same as us." Emmett chewed on his lip. "Can I ask why you're interested in this?"

"There was a dead squirrel found near the Tarot Card Killer's third victim," I said. "It could be coincidence, but it might not be. This rat is evidence."

I heard the tech shuffle her feet behind me. "Even if that's the case, I can't tag and bag this. It's a dead animal. The decomposition process has started. It could contaminate everything in evidence lockup."

I held up my hands. "Look, I know it sounds crazy. All I'm saying is, this animal is near the victim, and there might be a connection between it and the previous slayings. We can't ignore it, we can't leave it here, and we certainly can't throw it away."

Jowynn pursed his lips. "I could leave it at the morgue for now. Put it into cold storage with the rest of the corpses. It won't stink up anything while we figure out what the proper course of action is."

From the mouth of the alley, I heard Dean calling. "Phair? You ready to go?"

I wasn't sure where Dean intended to take me, but I didn't want to keep him waiting. "Sounds great, Emmett. We'll follow up on this later, okay? Gotta go."

CHAPTER EIGHT

I found Dean at the mouth of the alley, stinking of cigarette smoke but without a stub between his fingers. He eyed the clipboard in my hands. "What's that?"

"Catalogue of items found in the alleyway. CSU thought you might want to see it."

Dean grunted. "Hmm. Hand it to Justice and meet me at my car."

"Sure," I said. "Where are we heading?"

"Miss Breen's apartment," said Dean. "Nance confirmed her address. I don't expect to find much, but you never know. I can bring you up to speed during the drive while Justice and Moss work Nance and organize a canvass."

I nodded and hopped to it, heading inside and leaving the clipboard with Justice before ducking back out and climbing into the passenger seat of Dean's Howardson Viper. I buckled my seatbelt and waited, but Dean just sat there in the driver's seat, his eyes unfocused and distant.

I waited what to me seemed like a respectful pause before speaking. "Dean?"

I'd thought perhaps he'd drifted off again, but he surprised me. He lifted his head and fixed me with a gaze that was equal parts frustrated and apologetic. "Sorry for my behavior out there. I'm not used to being made feel inadequate by a case, and I've responded poorly. I'm going to get my head in the game, starting now."

I felt like we'd already been through this, but I played along. "You don't have anything to apologize for. We're in this together."

Dean's shoulders inched upward in the barest approxima-tion of a shrug. "Perhaps. But I need to be honest. You need to know when I'm not at my peak so you can step in as need be. I'm going to focus and apply myself to the best of my abilities, but I frankly don't know what my best is right now."

Was Dean talking about our team, about Moss and Justice and the department as a whole, or was he saying *I* needed to step up? Because as much as I fancied myself a detective in training, I was still an inexperienced junior officer weeks removed from police academy graduation. If Dean was crum-bling under the weight of expectations, what chance did I have?

I took a deep breath. "I'll do my best, too. Whatever you need, I'm here for you."

Dean met my eyes, and a hint of a smile pulled on his lips. He nodded and turned the key in the ignition. The engine purred as we pulled onto the boulevard, and a police cruiser jerked out of its spot and settled in behind us. Apparently, Dean had asked for backup. Either that, or someone else had asked on his behalf. Maybe Moss?

Dean kept his eyes on the road as he drove. "How much do you know about the TCK murders?"

"Not nearly enough," I said. "I never got the full blow-by-blow of the murder in Miller's Creek Park, and the only details I know about the first two victims are what was released in the papers."

"Not all of which is accurate," said Dean. "I'll start at the beginning then. That's the easiest way to do it. The first victim was a young woman by the name of Sherryl Towns. She was a hairdresser, twenty-six years of age. Her body was discovered outside a bowling alley. It was reported she was in a parking lot, but that's not entirely true. She was found to the side of the bowling alley in a shaded area next to some bushes. She hadn't driven to the facility. It's presumed she was walking home when she was attacked. It's not a big point, but that's the first thing the papers got wrong.

"She was discovered dead early morning, about six-thirty. This was on the fourteenth of August, but the medical examiner put her death about seven or eight hours earlier, late evening of the thirteenth. Based on interviews with other folks at the bowling alley, we know she left the establishment at about eleven o'clock, so we suspect she was attacked right after. How nobody heard or saw the attack take place is still a mystery. We suspect the Tarot Card Killer struck as she passed into the shadows next to the building, outside the light provided by the lampposts over the parking lot. That nobody noticed her until the next morning is surprising, but I guess people can miss what they're not looking for.

"Regardless, there weren't any witnesses to the attack, or at least none who admitted to it, though based on the attacks since, I have to believe everyone we spoke to inside the bowling alley was telling the truth. As to Miss Towns herself, the papers did get the method of her death more or less right. Her neck had been snapped. Not twisted around a full hundred and eighty degrees as reported, but the trauma was violent enough to not make a real difference. The autopsy found that not only was her spinal cord severed, but several of her cervical vertebrae were shattered and the muscle tissue throughout her neck was torn. That said, despite the internal trauma she suffered, there weren't many external signs of distress. There wasn't any bruising to the soft tissues of her upper arms or shoulders where you might've expected her attacker to grab her before twisting and snapping her neck, nor did she exhibit any bruising upon her head."

"And the tarot card?" I asked.

Dean shook his head as he slowed for a red light. "I still don't know how that particular piece of information leaked to the press. I wish it hadn't, but there's no use getting upset about it all over again. As with Miss Breen, there was a portion of a tarot card found on Miss Towns. Just a piece, sewn onto the hem of her dress via a simple tack stitch and positioned where it wasn't immediately obvious to anyone not looking for it.

"The second victim, Ellowyn Farview, also had a corner of a tarot card tacked onto her clothing, but in many ways, her murder hasn't fit with the others. Though she was a similar age as everyone else, she's the only elven victim thus far. She's also the only victim who hasn't had a job. She was a wealthy socialite, and she was on her way to a party the night of her murder. More importantly, the timing and method of her death aren't what we've seen with any of the other victims."

I nodded. "I remember reading in the papers she'd died in a car crash, but when emergency workers pulled her from the wreckage, they found the tarot card on her."

Dean kept his focus on the road, but he did a decent approximation of rolling his eyes with his eyebrows. "Another liberty taken in reporting. Technically, it's true. According to the medical examiner's report, the trauma from the car crash killed her, but she would've died sooner or later even if she hadn't crashed. She was being strangled."

I blinked, suddenly confused. "She was strangled *while driving?*"

The light turned green. Dean nodded as he gave the Viper some gas. "It's odd, to be sure. I've seen people strangled in their cars before, often in mob hits. The killer waits in the backseat until the victim gets in, and then they strike. It's effective, given the seat prevents the victim from taking some of the few actions that might otherwise save their life, but in those instances, the killer strikes before the victim starts the car. I can't imagine why the Tarot Card Killer might've waited until Miss Farview had already started driving to attack. It wasn't even an attack right after she pulled out of her spot, either. We pieced together her movements. By our best guess, she crashed two-thirds of the way through her drive from her apartment to the party. She'd been driving for over ten minutes when she crashed."

"So what happened to the Tarot Card Killer?" I asked. "He clearly wasn't pulled from the wreckage alongside her."

This time, Dean snuck a quick glance at me. *"That* is the question, more than any other, that's kept me up at night for weeks. The crash occurred at a quarter after ten. Eyewitnesses report seeing the car veer off the side of the road and plunge into a drainage ditch along the side of 34th, near the intersection with Westlake Boulevard. A young man by the name of Lithos Loukas was the first on the scene. By his testimony, he climbed into the ditch, saw the bloodied Miss Farview slumped over the steering wheel, and tried to open the car to pull her out, but the entire front of the vehicle was crushed. The door wouldn't budge. That's when he climbed back to street level to call for help."

"I'm guessing he didn't see anyone else in the car with her?"

Dean shook his head as he slowed to turn a corner. "Nope. Neither did any of the other witnesses who came to the side of the ditch and gawked until police and paramedics arrived. My best guess is the killer climbed from the wreckage through one of the broken windows in the minute and a half or so between the moment of impact and the arrival of Mr. Loukas. I still think he escaped the scene via the drainage system. I'm not sure how familiar you are with the city's drainage architecture, but there are tons of ditches and holding ponds that all feed into a massive underground cistern that connects most of New Welwic. Not thirty feet from where Miss Farview crashed, the ditch dips underground, feeding into the cistern. Once TCK made it there, there was no way to track him."

"Not even with bloodhounds?" I asked.

"Water makes it harder for hounds to track," said Dean. "But we tried. We brought the canine unit out, but the poor dogs couldn't even track him to the cistern entrance. They didn't have a scent off of which to work."

My face scrunched up. "What do you mean?"

Dean sighed. "I mean, it's as if the killer was never there. The dogs could only catch Miss Farview's and Mr. Loukas's scents. Later, when CSU did a thorough sweep of the vehicle, they never found a single piece of physical evidence to suggest anyone had been waiting in the backseat to murder Miss Farview. No stray hairs, no clothing fibers, no blood splatters that couldn't be attributed to Ellowyn herself. The team did pry some partial prints off the dashboard we later matched to Ellowyn's on-again, off-again boyfriend, Zachary Wainwright, but the man was at the party Ellowyn was en route to. He alibied out. Trust me, it wasn't him. We've turned that stone over so many times, it's now smooth."

My face still hadn't unscrunched itself. "That's impossible. Not the boyfriend angle, I believe you on that, but TCK not leaving a shred of evidence? After suffering the same car crash Miss Farview did? How did he even get out alive, much less without leaving a trace?"

Dean shrugged. "I wish I could tell you, but I frankly don't know. There's a reason we haven't been able to crack this case, Phair. For all the media sensationalism about it, the facts of the murders are far stranger than most people know."

I still couldn't wrap my head around what I was hearing. "What about this Loukas character? Could he have been behind it?"

"That's another stone now smooth from wear," said Dean. "Other eyewitnesses confirm seeing him respond to the accident first. He wasn't in the car. He was a bystander, nothing more."

"And we're sure someone was with Ellowyn in the car at the time of the crash? She wasn't just... I don't know—half-strangled earlier?"

Dean didn't laugh, as I thought he might. "We considered that angle, too, but ultimately we have to trust in the experience of our coroners. Three different professionals from our department worked together to confirm the diagnosis, Jowynn among them. They all agreed. She was being strangled at the time of her death."

I thought for a moment. "Could she have strangled herself?"

Dean shot me another quick look. "Interesting question, but no. She would've needed a complex rig to achieve that, none of which was present in the wreckage. Neither was the rope that had been used on her."

"It was a rope, then?"

"Ligature marks on her neck confirm it."

I was silent for a while as I let the facts bounce around my head. Dean must've assumed it was safe to move on.

"The third murder you're more familiar with," he said, "but I don't know how many of the details we shared with you, as you weren't a part of the team yet. The victim's name was Maggie Richards. As you know, she was found off the beaten path in Miller's Creek Park. Autopsy suggests her time of death was somewhere between ten and midnight, so it could've been either before or after you walked through the park on your way home —or during, though let's not dwell on that.

"Regardless, Miss Richards was beaten to death. The coroners found over thirty broken bones upon examination of her remains, including fractures of her skull, right tibia, hip, and half a dozen ribs, not to mention extensive internal trauma. With such severe injuries, you'd expect she might've been beaten with a blunt object such as a bat or a pipe, but that doesn't seem to be the case. The injuries weren't acute enough for that, according to the official report. Coroner Jowynn compared her injuries to those of a man he'd once examined who'd fallen out of a seven story window onto hard pavement."

I flinched at the thought. "There aren't any seven story buildings in the middle of the park, of course."

"Nor trees," said Dean. "Some approach five stories, but

after considering the possibility that Miss Richards either will-
ingly climbed to the top of one of the nearby oaks and jumped to
her death or had somehow been coerced into doing so, we
dismissed it. The forest in that part of the park is fairly thick.
Any climb and subsequent jump would've left a trail of scuffed
bark and broken branches even an inexperienced woodsman
would've instantly spotted, not to mention the indentation it
would've left where Miss Richards landed. Needless to say, we
found none of that."

Dean waved his hand. "And that brings us to this morning
and Miss Breen. It's not exactly a full report, but it should be
enough to get you more or less caught up. Do you have any
questions?"

I shook my head. "Probably more than you can answer."

The radio in Dean's console crackled and the operator's
voice filled the air, calling units to respond to a robbery in the
dock district. Dean turned down the volume. "Probably, but
there are no silly questions. Sometimes asking the right question
can push the mind into a new, creative line of thought. Ask
away."

I didn't know where to start, so I asked the first thing that
came to mind. "What did the third woman do for a living?"

"Miss Richards? She was a paralegal."

"I'm guessing she was young."

Dean nodded. "All the victims have been between twenty
and thirty years of age, assuming Miss Breen fits the bill, which I
suspect she does."

I chewed on my lip. "Was she pretty?"

Dean shrugged. "As Detective Justice mentioned, that a
subjective question, but all of the victims have been reasonably

attractive in the classical fashion established by men and elves. It's one of many common threads between the victims."

"Common threads?" I asked. "I was under the impression the murders were all disparate in nature."

"In some ways. There's no particular modus operandi in regards to the means of death, for instance, and to the best of our knowledge, none of the victims had any connection to one another, but there are multiple ways in which the murders and the victims mimic each other." Dean lifted a hand off the wheel and began ticking items off on his fingers. "The victims' age and general appearance we've already discussed. None of them were in committed relationships, and all lived alone, Miss Breen pending. Then there's a number of common threads between the murders themselves. No physical evidence from the killer has been found at any of the crime scenes, whether it be blood, hair, fingerprints, clothing fibers, or footprints. None of the murder weapons have been recovered, though we're not entirely sure if any weapon was employed in the slayings of Miss Towns or Miss Richards. The deaths have been violent but not sexual in nature, and we don't have any witnesses to any of the murders. You and Mr. Loukas are the closest we have in that respect. And of course, there are the tarot cards. Each victim had a portion of a card affixed to their clothing with a simple stitch. If not for that, there'd be precious little that definitively ties the murders together."

Dean slowed and pulled over in front of a five story brick apartment building. The squad car that had been following us pulled into a free spot behind us.

"So all the victims were murdered at night?" I asked. "And all were attacked outdoors with the exception of Ellowyn Farview?"

Dean put the car in park and killed the engine. "Correct."

I turned toward Dean. "I know strangulation is violent, but it's not quite as visceral as snapping someone's neck, beating them bloody, or stabbing them repeatedly. Given the differences in how it occurred, are you sure TCK is behind that murder?"

Dean shook his head glumly. "I'm sure of very little in this case, but given the lack of physical evidence at the scene? The way the perpetrator disappeared afterwards? It points to TCK. And, of course, there was the tarot card piece left behind."

I chewed on my lip. "Right. About that. How in the world was he able to stitch a piece of a tarot card onto her clothing and still make his escape in less than two minutes?"

"That's why I was coy when you asked if the cards were being attached to the victims post-mortem," said Dean. "Fact of the matter is, we don't know. In all cases except Miss Farview's that would make the most sense, but in her murder? Either the killer incapacitated her before her murder and attached the card then, or he attached it before she ever left home to go to the party."

I glanced at the building beside us. "That's why you want to search Lacy's apartment? To see if the killer might've been at her home, as you suspect he might've with Ellowyn."

"More or less," said Dean. "Not that a search of Farview's place revealed anything."

"Perhaps the Tarot Card Killer never went into Ellowyn's apartment," I offered. "Maybe he accosted her in her car. He could've held her at gun or knifepoint, forced her to attach the card to her own clothing. Perhaps he told her to drive once she was done, giving her hope she might escape, only to strangle her midway through the ride. It could explain why he didn't strangle her right away."

"It's a possibility," said Dean. "But the biggest question is how he managed to murder Miss Farview and get away so quickly without leaving evidence. Then again, not leaving evidence seems to be our murderer's specialty." Dean unbuckled and nodded toward the building. "Come on. Let's take a look at Miss Breen's place."

CHAPTER NINE

I headed up the stairs of Lacy's apartment building alongside Dean with Officers Taggert and Mills from the squad car following us. We exited on the third floor and headed down the hall in search of apartment three-fifteen. For all the neighborhood's gentrification, the interior of the building didn't look as if it had been remodeled since the push for electrification some eighty years ago. The wooden floors had been worn so thin as to be almost transparent, and the wallpaper had faded into a uniform cream. I would've mistaken it for paint if not for the occasional sections that were peeling. For all the wear, the place wasn't dirty or decrepit though. The corners had been swept clean. There weren't any discarded bottles of malt liquor hiding inside crumpled paper bags, and the hallways smelled slightly musty rather than stinking of stale urine.

Dean paused as he reached Lacy's door. He removed a pair of latex gloves from his coat pocket and affixed Officers Taggert and Mills with a stern gaze. "Glove up. Everything within this apartment should be considered of critical importance. Since we don't have a photographer on scene yet, we need to be extra careful. If you have to pick something up to investigate it, put it back down *precisely* where you found it. It's better to touch than to handle an object and better yet not to touch at all. If you feel the need to sneeze, leave the apartment, and if you so much as think about taking your gloves off to scratch yourself, let's hope you're the praying sort. Do I make myself clear?"

I think Dean intended the warning for our escorts, but it was a good reminder for me, too. I slipped my gloves on as Dean produced a key from his pocket—the one he'd found on Lacy's person if the enameled cat keychain was any indication—and used it to open the door.

Dean pushed through first, and I followed. Lacy's apartment wasn't much. It appeared to be a one bedroom, though it had a private bathroom, which wasn't anything to sneeze at given the age of the building. The kitchen was more of a nook than a true room, but an oven and a half-size fridge had somehow been crammed into it. A small table and a couple chairs occupied much of the remaining living space, but a comfortable-looking chaise longue had been pushed against the window through which the morning sun now beamed. An aroma of old cigarette smoke hung over everything, and despite the chill in the air outside, the apartment was toasty warm. Must've been the east-facing windows.

One of the officers cleared his throat. As Dean and I turned, neither of them had crossed the threshold into the apartment.

Mills spoke. "If it's all the same to you, Detective, I'll watch the door while Taggert heads to the car to man the radio."

Apparently, Dean's speech had struck fear into the officers' hearts. Either that or they knew there was no benefit to them helping search the place, only potential consequences.

Dean nodded. "That's probably for the best."

The patrol officers retreated and Dean ventured further into the apartment. He hovered over the dining table, his eyes flicking from curio to curio, each getting no more than a few seconds of attention.

I followed Dean into the living space, keeping my hands to myself. Despite the gloves, I didn't trust myself enough to touch anything. "What should we be looking for?"

"Signs of forced entry, first and foremost," said Dean. "Broken windows, damaged frames, scratches on the lock plate on the front door. I already checked for those. Beyond that, any evidence someone who shouldn't have been here was. Shoe scuffs. Cigarette butts, preferably of a different brand than Miss Breen smoked. The remainder of a torn tarot card would be nice."

Dean's joke meant he was starting to get his head screwed on straight. A half-height bookshelf filled with dog-eared paperbacks stood against the wall near the sofa chair, giving a hint as to what the chaise was most often used for, but Dean's instructions drew my attention to a side table instead. There was an ashtray atop it, brimming with butts. "What brand of cigarettes did Lacy smoke?"

"Golden Shoes," said Dean, "or at least that's what we found on her. Those appear to be hers, but we'll have CSU go through them to be sure."

I knew nothing of cigarettes other than that I didn't care for the smell, so I took his word. "I hesitate to ask, but did you find any evidence of intrusion at *any* of the apartments of the other victims?"

"Nothing definitive," said Dean. "But that doesn't mean we didn't glean useful information from the homes. As I mentioned, we're not just trying to establish a pattern among the murders but between the victims, as well. Something has to tie these women together beyond their age. There *has* to be a common thread."

I wasn't sure if Dean was right, but I understood what he meant. There needed to be a common thread between the victims if we had any hope of finding the killer.

Dean swept his eyes across the living room once more before heading into Lacy's bedroom. I followed, watching as he pulled open her closet and began sifting through the jackets and pants and dresses within, checking the collars and cuffs and hems, I assumed for any signs of errant stitching. There were dozens upon dozens of items, from off-the-shoulder gowns with plenty of ruffles to stylish blazers in bold colors and prints. Dean moved efficiently through them, making sure not to move each piece from its spot on the bar.

With Dean occupied by the closet, I turned to the dresser in front of Lacy's bed. It was an old, worn thing, stained burnt umber but criss-crossed with scratches that showed some of the original wood underneath. A half-dozen framed photographs populated the top, showing Lacy in her more joyous moments, smiling for the camera with friends and family. In all of the photos, she held herself with an aura of confidence. Despite their static nature, I got the impression she must've carried herself with a free-spiritedness and glee that, if Nance's testimony was accurate, must've been infectious.

In addition to the photographs, there were about twenty different lighters organized on top of dresser, some solid colors and others with animals or vistas engraved into the metal. I didn't pick any of them up, but I leaned down to get a closer look. "Looks like Miss Breen was a budding collector. Did you see these lighters?"

"I noticed them," said Dean. "Our second victim, Miss Farview, smoked socially, but it didn't appear as if either of the others did."

"Did any of them collect other items?"

Dean moved from a pair of pleated pants to a white collared shirt. "Not in the sense you're thinking. None of the other victims collected curios."

I switched my attention back to the photos, stopping myself as I instinctively reached for one. *Better not to touch at all,* Dean said. In this photo, Lacy wore a jaunty summer dress and stood beside a young man, dark of hair and clean-shaven.

"Do you think it's worth identifying the individuals in these photographs? Not that I imagine TCK has any personal ties to Lacy or the other victims, but still."

"We'll do it," said Dean, "but you're correct. It's been an exercise in futility thus far."

I stared at Lacy, at her bright smile, at the crinkles around her mouth, at the flow of her dress in the breeze. I felt an ache. It started low in my stomach, but it rose the longer I stared, climbing into my throat. I swallowed, but the lump wouldn't recede. In that moment, I felt more than sadness at her loss. I felt anger that anyone would've murdered her, revulsion at the way she spent her final minutes, and despondency that we might never find who'd done it to her.

I snorted in disgust as I turned away from the photographs. "This job sucks sometimes, you know that?"

Dean stopped what he was doing. He met my gaze, his eyes somber. "It can be the worst job in the world at times, yet I couldn't see myself doing anything else. I wish I could say it gets easier over time, but you've seen me. If anything, it gets harder." He pointed to the photos. "A piece of advice I can give you is don't let yourself get too close to the victim. You have to approach everything objectively. Rationally. Emotions only get between you and the job."

"And how well has that worked for you today?" I snapped.

I knew it was a cruel thing to say as soon as the words left my lips, but I'd never been great at controlling my emotions.

Dean didn't bite back, though. "The reason I've been upset is *because* I'm approaching the case objectively. I haven't gotten the job done. I hold myself to a higher standard, Phair. I need to do better."

Despite the lack of emotion in his voice, I still felt as if I should apologize, but I didn't get the chance. I heard clomping footsteps, and Taggert appeared in the door.

"S'cuse me, Detective," he said. "Call came through the radio. The captain wants to see you. Dispatch made it sound urgent."

Dean's expression didn't change, but I'm sure I lost a little color. I may not have been on the force that long, but even I knew that sort of summons didn't portend good news.

CHAPTER TEN

Officer Taggert had told Dean the captain wanted to see him, not me, but Dean insisted I accompany him to the precinct anyway. For one thing, he hadn't seen anything during our initial pass of Lacy's apartment to suggest the killer had been there. More importantly, he thought it would serve me well to delve into the case files for the first three victims. For as much as he'd shared on our car ride, there was loads more to learn, and more eyes on the evidence collected thus far couldn't hurt.

We parked in the garage next to the station and walked in through the side door, as I had earlier in the morning. This time, there wasn't any buzz inside. A quiet futility hung in the air, thick enough to chew. Cops sat at their desks in the pit, backs hunched and heads hanging low as if they were mourners at a funeral. It was a poor omen given the urgency with which we'd been called back to the precinct, but I didn't think the atmosphere was related to what awaited Dean and me. Rather, I suspected news of TCK's latest strike had finally spread.

Dean led us to the captain's office, which sat to the side of the main cluster of desks on the first floor. Usually, the captain had the blinds drawn on the windows looking onto the floor, but not today. Every single one had been pulled up and secured, so nothing—or no one—could escape the captain's watchful eye.

Dean stepped to the captain's open door. "You wanted to see me, sir?"

Captain Henry Herbert Ellison looked up from his desk. He was a man of late middle years with thick wavy hair that despite going gray showed no signs of thinning. His skin had a healthy glow to it reminiscent of men ten years his junior. His forehead featured more creases than I remembered, though, and his normally crisply pressed shirt sported a battalion of wrinkles made even more evident by his crooked black tie.

Captain Ellison pursed his lips and beckoned with a couple fingers. "Come in and close the door, Detective. You too, Officer."

I'd assumed I'd be dismissed while the captain spoke to Dean in private, so his summons caught me off guard. Then again, perhaps it shouldn't have. As much as I disliked it, I'd been thrust head-first into interoffice politics the moment I joined Dean's investigative team. While the decision to bring me on board had been Dean's, the decision to give Dean the funding to add me had belonged entirely to the captain, and the decision hadn't been one born out of love and admiration for his star detective. As it turned out, Captain Ellison didn't care for Dean much. While he admired the dark elf's intellect and deductive sense, Dean's independent streak irked him to no end. While the Captain expected subservience, Dean had a history of ignoring the chain of command if it meant solving a case that otherwise might be mothballed. While Dean saw my hire as one based on merit and potential, the Captain had been blunt in telling me I was there to rein in and report on Dean's order-breaking impulses.

Unfortunately for me, I'd already decided I'd rather side with Dean. While I put on a good face in front of the captain, the fact of the matter was I'd already ignored his commands. I'd helped Dean continue an investigation after the captain told us to close it. I didn't think the captain knew, but I was walking a thin, dangerous line.

I closed the door as I took a seat in one of the two plush blue chairs in front of his desk. Dean sat in the other, but his back remained as rigid as if he'd been sitting in a chair of unrelenting hardwood. "Captain?"

Ellison intertwined his fingers, his brown eyes dark and unreadable. "I just got off the phone with the chief. It seems news of the Tarot Card Killer's fourth victim has spread."

Dean spoke evenly, without emotion. "We're doing everything we can, Captain. Detectives Moss and Justice are on the scene alongside CSU, the mortuary team, and patrol. Officer Phair and I already visited the victim's apartment, and CSU is on their way as we speak."

"Do you have any definitive leads yet?" asked the Captain.

Dean hesitated a second before answering. "We're working on it."

The captain's lips bent into a frown. "Detective, I've stood by you throughout this investigation. When we assigned you the case after the first victim was discovered, I had no doubt you were the right man for the job. After the second victim was discovered and weeks came and went, I still maintained you would solve this, but that's become a harder pitch to sell these past few weeks. We've now had two more slayings in quick succession, and you haven't made any meaningful progress."

Dean's jaw tensed. "You're taking the case away from me?"

Ellison gave his head a taut shake. "I'm not. Chief Cole is. He's handing lead investigative duties to MCD."

I thought Dean might snarl or snap, but he just bobbed his head in acknowledgement.

Meanwhile, I sat there confused. "I'm sorry, sir. MCD?"

"Major crimes division," said Dean. "You know the tall building on the corner of Third and Riverside? The department offices? MCD has the sixth floor. They're the city's bureaucratic detective squad. They handle all the big cases—or at least those they choose to swipe from the individual precincts."

"It's more requisitioning than swiping," said the captain, "and they've earned that right by virtue of their track record and seniority. Even though you have a hard time hiding your contempt for the detectives of the MCD, even you'd have a hard time arguing they aren't justified in taking the lead on this one given your lack of results."

Dean swallowed hard, but he didn't flush. "Who's taking the case?"

"Glenwell and Hawkins," said the captain.

By this point, I was so used to Dean's emotionless mask that his sudden snarl made me jump. "*Hawkins?* You've got to be kidding me."

Ellison's eyes narrowed into a squint. "Hawkins comes with Glenwell, Detective. They're partners, two to a pair. You'll recall your arrangement with Moss and Justice and Officer Phair is the exception rather than the rule. It's not as if I had a say as to who was taking over. The chief informed me of his decision. He didn't ask for my input. I had to put my ass on the line to make sure you weren't kicked off the case entirely."

I probably shouldn't have said anything, but I'd never been

great at keeping my mouth shut. "Pardon me, sir... so we're *not* being removed from the investigation?"

The captain's glower didn't fade, but he kept his eyes on Dean rather than me. "I said the chief was handing *lead* investigative duties to MCD. Thanks to my silver tongue, I was able to keep you on in a parallel investigation, but the chief didn't mince words. Not only will you report to Glenwell and Hawkins, but you'll follow their orders as if they were coming from me. Are we clear, Detective?"

Dean nodded, but I wondered if the captain hadn't phrased things poorly. Dean didn't exactly treat all of the captain's orders with the weight they deserved.

"The chief also said there would be additional changes made to your efforts, but he didn't elaborate. For now, you need to get to the MCD offices. Get Glenwell and Hawkins up to speed—preferably without making your contempt of Hawkins quite so obvious lest the chief change his mind."

"Yes, sir. On our way." Dean stood and gave me a nod. Together we exited the captain's office.

Dean led us back through the pit toward the parking garage. His spine was straight, but he didn't stomp his feet as he walked and his face wasn't scrunched up in anger. Given what had transpired, I'd assumed I'd be able to see smoke leaking from his pointed ears.

"Well, that didn't go great," I offered.

Dean cast me a quick glance. "It could've gone worse. We didn't get pulled from the case. That's all that matters."

I'd already been exposed to more of Dean's thoughts and emotions today than in my entire time as part of his team. I figured if we were on a roll, why stop now? "You'll pardon my saying so, but you're taking this really well. Not that you're on an uneven keel most of the time, but given how big a case this is, I'm surprised you're not more upset about losing control of the investigation."

Dean shrugged as we pushed into the garage, where the street noise and honking horns crashed into us with the force of a wave. "I'd prefer to be the lead, don't get me wrong, but it's not as big a change as you might think. MCD has been running a parallel investigation for a while now. Capturing TCK is too important a task to lay at our feet alone. All that's changed is who's in charge. And quite frankly, I don't care who gets the glory. All I care about is bringing the killer to task and getting justice for the families of the dead."

We rounded on Dean's Viper, climbing into our seats and clanking the doors shut behind us. The engine roared as Dean turned the key in the ignition, and we backed into the aisle between the cars.

I shook my head as we headed toward the exit. "There's still one thing I don't get. I thought the captain didn't like you very much."

Dean snorted. "That's putting it mildly. He'd love to get rid of me, if he could."

"That's just it," I said. "If he'd rather ship you out, then why in the world did he go to bat for you with the chief? Why fight to keep you on the investigation?"

"Because keeping me involved achieves all his goals," said Dean. "You have to understand, if MCD takes over the case and solves it while we sit on the sidelines, that makes our entire department look bad, not just me. It's a black eye the captain would be hard pressed to hide, and he has aspirations of his own. If we find TCK, that goes on his resume, too. If we all fail with MCD leading the way, then it no longer reflects negatively on him. But you can be sure it'll look bad for Glenwell and Hawkins—and for us, now that we're still on the case."

I gulped. "The scheming never stops, does it? So this case could make our break your entire career? All of ours?"

Dean pulled onto Fifth and hit the gas. "It was always going to. But it'll make or break more than our careers. If we don't catch TCK, I guarantee you this case will break *me*."

CHAPTER ELEVEN

I'd seen the police department headquarters from street level before, but I'd never given it a passing thought. It was an unimaginably bland building, tall and boxy and made from flat gray concrete upon which light died without casting a single shadow. It was probably constructed right when architects and engineers first accessed steel-reinforced concrete, before they had any idea how to make skyscrapers that were both structurally sound and aesthetically pleasing. Never mind ancient builders had navigated the two just fine using masonry arches and flying buttresses.

Still, it seemed fitting that a police building should be ugly but functional.

Dean parked in the garage across the street and we headed inside. There weren't any beat cops wrestling with captives as there might be in a precinct lobby, just uniformed officers manning a reception desk and plainclothes officers walking between offices. There was a quiet authority in the air that made clear the sort of building you'd walked into, though.

We took the elevators to the sixth floor. There, Dean asked a few questions of the watch commander before leading us to a conference room on the northeast side.

We weren't the first ones to arrive. Two detectives already sat at the long oval table in the middle of the room. One was an old dude, a police lifer who'd probably cut his teeth when officers carried cudgels and when the best option for calling for backup was literally to shout. He was squat and rotund with short spiky hair that stood straight up in the few spots in which it still grew. He was wrinkly as a prune, but at least a prune has some form to it. This guy oozed. His sagging neck hung over his collar, and his gut pressed against his front buttons, as if they were the only thing keeping his stomach from spilling out. His chins lifted in an approximation of a smirk at the sight of us.

The other detective stood as we entered. She wasn't exactly the polar opposite of the living blob, but she was as close as detectives came. She was an elven woman, tall and svelte and sophisticated, with dark brown hair that fell over her shoulder to chest level. Her overly large hazel eyes practically glowed, accentuated by the warm mocha of her suit jacket and slacks, both tailored so they showed her figure while remaining professional.

Quite simply, she was stunning—not to mention intimidating.

The elven woman extended a hand. "Alton." Her voice was firm without being stern, friendly yet distant.

Dean shook her offering. "Lynne. This is Officer Penelope Phair. She's part of my team now. Still learning the ropes."

The woman extended her hand. "Pleasure to meet you, Officer. I'm Detective Glenwell."

I shook her hand by rote. "Uh... likewise." Somehow I'd assumed the elegant, worldly elf in front of me would be Dean's foil, but I quickly realized that made no sense. Dean was young. Progressive. Moss was a part of his team, and so was I. There was no reason he'd feel emasculated working under the supervision of a strong, confident woman. All of which meant the hated Hawkins was…

The old lump groaned as he pushed himself out of his chair, his arms jiggling under the exertion. "Well, if it isn't the golden child himself." His voice sounded as if it had been passed through a meat grinder, all rough and raspy and strained from decades of heavy smoking. "How's that rarified air up in your tower, Dean?"

"I work on the third floor of my building, Detective Hawkins," said Dean coolly. "You're on the sixth. If anyone's breathing rarified air, it should be you. Though you might want to breathe more of it. You sound terrible."

Hawkins snorted, though it came out as a wheeze. "You're only literal when it suits you, but you're full of yourself twenty-four seven." He cast me a dismissive glance. "So, you're growing your team? Seems like the belt's not cinched as tight at the Fifth as in most stations. Seems like something else the chief should be made aware of in addition to your failings on the tarot card murders."

I had a barb about Hawkins' own belt being cinched too tight on the tip of tongue, but Glenwell beat me to the punch. "You don't have to like the detective, Elmer, but you have to be civil. *All* of us do." She shot a glance at Dean to make sure he understood as well. "I refuse to work in an environment where anyone puts their ego above the case. We won't have any issues, will we?"

Glenwell lifted an eyebrow, and Dean nodded in agreement. He didn't seem upset by her commanding nature.

Hawkins grunted as he flopped into his chair. "Don't you worry, Glenwell. Ego is the one thing I don't carry too much of. You can be sure *I* won't be a problem."

The elven woman pursed her lips, looking as if she didn't believe him. "I'll hold you to that."

There was a moment of quiet apprehension as Dean eyed Hawkins and Hawkins pointedly ignored Dean and Glenwell took stock of everyone to make sure the promises made would hold firm.

Dean took a steady breath and gave Glenwell a nod. "How is this going to work?"

"The departmental cooperation?" she asked. "Simple. You share all your information on the case, and when you gain more, you forward that, too. We'll need you to give us a verbal report on the state of affairs. More importantly, we'll need copies of your files."

Dean cocked his head to the side. "There's got to be more to it than that."

"Not if you do as I say, when I say it," said Glenwell.

"That's something else you could've touched on, then," said Dean.

Glenwell placed her hands on her hips. "Fine. If I call a shot, you take it, and if I tell you to steer clear of a lane, you'll do that, too. I'm in charge, and you'll do as I ask. That doesn't mean I want you to turn into a brain-addled yes man. For the most part, you work best when your leash is as slack as possible."

"When I don't have a leash, you mean."

"Not my call," said Glenwell. "The chief made that clear. So are you going to play along?"

Dean gave a curt nod. "I don't have a choice, but even if I

did, I would. I just want to get to the bottom of this, Lynne. It's not about being in the limelight."

The elven woman's face softened as she nodded back. "I know. It's what we all want, Alton."

Hawkins grunted from his chair. "Yeah, it's what we all want, 'cause we're all so damn altruistic. Maybe we can roast some marshmallows, hold hands, and sing songs around a fire while we're at it."

Glenwell glared at him. The old codger screwed up his lips and held up his hands as if he hadn't just been caught instigating after promising he wouldn't.

To his credit, Dean didn't take the sack of suet's bait. He waved to the chairs. "Should we get started? It's going to take some time to bring you up to speed."

"Have a seat if you'd like," said Glenwell as she settled into her chair. "But I wouldn't start yet. We're waiting on one more."

"Are we?" said Dean. "How many teams are getting placed on this case?"

A voice like a whip cracked through the air. "As many as it takes, Detective, though they're not the ones you're waiting for."

Dean and I both turned. In the doorframe stood a tall man, bald as an egg and with mottled tan skin that showed his age. Despite his obvious years, his back was ramrod straight, and his broad shoulders and barrel chest suggested he still carried a fair amount of muscle on his frame. He strode into the room with a sense of purpose and determination that would've made it obvious he was someone who demanded respect even if the uniform he wore hadn't already done the job.

Dean stood a little straighter, as did I. "Chief Cole," he said. "I didn't realize you were taking a personal interest in the Tarot Card Killer case."

"I take an interest in any case that impacts the safety and wellbeing of the people of New Welwic." The chief brushed past us and took a seat at what served as the head of the oblong table. "I've been keeping tabs on progress to find the killer since the moment the media decided to turn a serious investigation into a circus, but that was mostly for PR reasons. It was also three murders ago. I don't have the luxury to take a hands off approach anymore. Have a seat, Detective. Officer? Dismissed."

The title would've made it clear Chief Cole was referring to me, even if he hadn't affixed me with a stern glare as he spoke. I hesitated, simply because I knew I needed to get up to speed on the case as well.

This, however, was clearly not the time. I snapped my heels, said "Yes, sir," and headed out the door, closing it behind me.

CHAPTER TWELVE

I sat on a bench in the hall outside the conference room, biding my time. I'd been there a while, long enough for my butt to feel like a lead cushion but not so long that I'd started pining for lunch. At first, I'd hoped I might be able to hear what was going on inside, but either the walls were properly insulated or none of the participants felt the need to start shouting uncontrollably. It was probably good I hadn't heard anything. That suggested the chief was letting Dean do the talking rather than lambasting him for failing to wrap the case several murders ago. I didn't know enough about the chief to know if that was his style. On the one hand, he looked as ornery and tough as anyone his age could get, but someone wouldn't have risen to his rank without being a diplomat. Besides, he hadn't mentioned anything about Dean being punished, just that he was losing the lead on the case. He'd be fine. At least, I hoped so.

The bench shifted and creaked as someone else settled onto the wood. I looked up from the patch of wall I'd been staring at to find a middle-aged man in a brown suit next to me. His hair was shorn short on the sides and left slightly longer on top in the traditional police officer style. His cheeks were shaven smooth, though he was already developing a hint of an 11 AM shadow. As I straightened, I realized I was probably taller than him, but the guy had a solid build. He gave me a perfunctory nod, the light glinting off eyes the color of slate.

I nodded back before returning my attention to the conference room. I tried to stare through the drywall, envisioning Dean's speech to Glenwell and Hawkins and the chief, but my reverie had been interrupted. It was hard to keep an imagination going when there was a new curiosity afoot, after all.

I waited a good couple minutes, but I was nonetheless the first cookie to crack. "Waiting for someone?"

If the man was surprised it had taken me so long to say anything, he didn't show it. He had a cool, collected air to him as he nodded, and I rather got the impression he'd been waiting to see how long it would take me to introduce myself. "I'm here for Detective Dean. He's in a meeting." His forefinger flicked toward the conference room.

"Here for him how? Is he in some sort of trouble?"

The man's eyes crinkled. "Not to my knowledge. I'm just here to offer my assistance on the case he's working."

"Ah." I felt the tension in my shoulders ease. "In that case, I'm Officer Penelope Phair. I'm part of his team." I eyed his off-the-rack suit. "You're a detective?"

"Not for a while, no." He eyed me with as much curiosity as I did him. "I'm a criminal profiler. Name's Mason. Virgil Mason."

Virgil didn't extend a hand for me to shake, but then again, neither had I. "I don't think I've ever met a criminal profiler. How does that differ from a detective?"

"A detective's job is to solve the crime put in front of them, by hook or by crook," said Mason. "I did that for a while, but it became clear early on that my real talent was in profiling. It's the process of identifying suspects based on mental, emotional, and personality characteristics that can be inferred from clues left at a crime scene or by actions taken by the perpetrator."

I pursed my lips. "No offense, but does that really work? I was under the impression racial profiling was... how should I put this? Morally wrong?"

Mason tipped his head, as if he anticipated the question. "Generally speaking, I'd agree that does more harm than good. Racial profiling is an offshoot of homology, which is the idea that similar crimes are committed by similar people, but that's not all there is to criminal profiling. The bigger piece, arguably, is behavioral consistency. That's the theory that a specific offender's crimes will be similar to one another. It has limited applications depending on the type of crime the theory is applied to. Burglaries, for example, tend to depend more upon the target than the burglar. But for other crimes, such as sexual assaults or serial murders...?"

I saw where he was going. "So basically you get in criminals' heads? Put yourself in their shoes to try and figure out how they think and act?"

Mason regarded me without emotion. "That's an oversimplification, but it's reasonably accurate."

Even the idea of thinking like the Tarot Card Killer sent a shiver down my spine. "I don't think I could do that. I'd rather be on the investigative side, though even that can get creepy at times."

"It's not a career for everyone." Mason eyed my uniform. "You're already working with Dean?"

"You wouldn't think it from looking at me," I said. "You'd think it even less if you knew how long I'd been on the force, but I guess he saw something in me. A combination of ability and desire. Maybe some of my personality traits, too. He's a good detective after all."

"That he is," said Mason.

I lifted an eyebrow. "You know him?"

"Mostly by reputation, though we've crossed paths once or twice. Hard to miss a talent like him. He'll do well so long as this tarot card case doesn't derail him."

I wasn't sure if he meant it in terms of career advancement or if he'd already guessed the case was eating Dean from the inside out. If it was the latter, then he really *was* good at getting in other people's heads.

"So Dean called you to come help us?"

Mason had shifted his focus to the conference room door. "Try someone higher up the ladder."

Captain Ellison's words drifted to me. "The chief. Our captain said he'd ordered some changes."

Mason shrugged. "I'm just here to do my job while leaving the detective work to the detectives. Not just Dean but Glenwell and Hawkins, too. If the chief wants to throw the kitchen sink at this case, that's his prerogative. I don't play politics. I want the case solved, same as everyone else."

I snorted. "You sound like Dean."

Mason met my eyes. "If I do, it's because Detective Dean is a smart man."

The yellow light of the hallway died as it hit Mason's flat gray eyes. I wanted to turn away, but the intensity of his gaze held me in place. I'd met some strong willed people before, people with a strength of purpose and a fire burning in their belly—heck, I might've been one—but there was something about Mason that suggested his dial had been turned to eleven. I wondered if all criminal profilers were as intense as him.

A door clacked, and we both turned toward the conference room. The chief strode out in the direction of the elevators, and a moment later, Dean emerged. He spotted me on the bench and came over.

I stood, and so did Virgil. He stuck out his hand as Alton approached. "Detective Dean? Virgil Mason, criminal profiling."

Apparently Mason did shake hands, just not mine. Either I hadn't warranted it as an officer, or the awkward nature of going through the motion while sitting on a bench had made him skip it.

Either way, Dean shook his outstretched mitt. "Mason. The chief mentioned you'd be working with us. Clearly you've met Officer Phair."

"Indeed," he said. "She's been picking my brain almost since I sat. Must be good to have such an inquisitive mind join your team."

I blinked. I'd assumed Mason hadn't thought much of me given the answers he'd provided. Perhaps he was just being nice.

"She's working on making herself invaluable," said Dean with a smile. "So far, she's well on her way. I'm assuming you're here because you want to dive into the investigation?"

"More because the chief demanded it," said Mason, "but the end result is the same."

Dean gave a small sigh. "Guess it wouldn't hurt for me to give a *third* summary of the Tarot Card Killer case before lunch. Mind if we do it at the Fifth? Officer Phair needs to do a deep dive into the case files, and I'd rather kill two birds with one stone."

"I was going to suggest the same," said Mason. "Meet you there, Detective. Officer?" He gave me a polite nod before heading toward the elevators.

Dean's shoulders slumped as the man left. Not much, but enough for me to tell. To be fair, I probably spent too much effort watching his shoulders, not to mention a few other choice parts of him. "Everything okay, Dean?"

The detective nodded. "As okay as it can get given the circumstances. I'm just tired. I didn't get much rest last night, and today's shaping up to be long."

"I can drive us to the precinct, if you like." While I'd never chauffeured Dean, he had entrusted me with the keys to his Viper before.

A small smile crossed Dean's lips. "I wouldn't say no to that."

My stomach grumbled as we headed toward the elevators. "Does that mean I get to choose where to stop for lunch, too?"

"Choose? Yes," said Dean. "Stop? No. We'll pick something up and bring it to the station. Mason'll be waiting."

CHAPTER THIRTEEN

U pon returning to the station, the first thing Dean did was requisition a space we could take over until the resolution of the case. The captain didn't fight him, so with a conference room on the third floor secured, he moved on to the recruitment of able-bodied officers who could drag everything from the records room and evidence lockup to the newly named war room. I wasn't excluded from the task, and I spent a good half hour alongside Officers Trask, Coldwell, and Wormwood getting everything moved. By that point, the burger and fries I'd picked up from Johnnie Dogs were stone cold. Dean had eaten in the car while I drove, but being the responsible driver I was (at least while piloting Dean's Viper), I'd waited.

As much as I regretted the decision, there wasn't much I could do about it until the moving was done. There's no good way to stuff fries into your mouth while your hands are occupied by cardboard boxes. Meanwhile, Dean talked to Mason, filling him in on the same details he'd told me, the chief, and the MCD detectives. There was enough to tell that he wasn't done by the time the last box had been stacked in the corner. I settled it into place, took my seat, ate cold hamburger meat, and listened while Dean finished the second half of his recap.

I trailed one last salty fry though a pile of ketchup on the paper burger wrapper as Dean filled in the final details about Lacy Breen's murder. While I hadn't been there for the first half of the talk, I imagine Mason sat through it the same way he had the second: stoically, with furrowed eyebrows, a crease in his brow, and eyes lost in thought.

As Dean finished, the room fell silent, broken only by the sound of me scrubbing my oily fingers on the too-thin napkins provided by Johnnie's minimum wage employees. The salt stuck in my throat, making me thirsty, but I didn't dare pick up my paperboard cup and slurp on the sugary drink within for fear of breaking Mason out of his reverie.

Eventually, thirst won over fear. With my throat becoming ever more parched and Mason looking as if he might've truly gotten lost in his thoughts, I grabbed my drink and took a sip. "So, given what Dean's told you, what kind of profile can you piece together for the Tarot Card Killer?"

Mason didn't blink. Didn't act as if he'd been jostled out of a daydream. He gave me a pointed glance, as if he'd been keeping tabs on Dean and me while simultaneously sifting through the information he'd absorbed. "I'm afraid it's not that simple. Crafting a profile is laborious work, and the devil is in the details. Without poring over the clues in these boxes you lugged up, I'm afraid any profile I come up with would come across as... pedestrian."

Dean had paced as he spoke. He finally settled into a chair of his own. "I'm often beset by perfectionism, too, but I've found it pays to start broad and narrow things as you go.

There's no shame in refining an idea as you gain more information."

Mason took a deep breath and let it out through his nostrils. "Fair enough. I suppose there's no harm in giving my initial thoughts. Though each murder has been committed in a different manner, each one has been barbarous, visceral, and very much a hands on sort of affair. At the risk of belaboring the obvious, that tells me we're looking for someone violent. Not just someone who's quick to anger. There are people who are prone to violence when triggered, but TCK is pathologically violent. They need violence, crave it as sustenance as you or I would crave a drink when we're parched or a meal when hungry. Something within this individual has created a driving need for violence, which would suggest to me two things.

"First of all, it suggests we'll find this person involved in an occupation that allows them to sate that hunger. A profession that demands violence. Maybe they're enrolled in the military. They might be a bouncer at a club or a private bodyguard. Perhaps they're part of a gang. One way or another, the individual involved is close to violence on a regular basis, or at the very least they were until recently. It's possible a move away from violence in their career was the impetus for the start of the murders, though that's uncertain.

"The second thing the desire for violence suggests to me is about our killer's upbringing. Needless to say, normal people don't engage in methodical, repeated violence targeting a specific group, in this case young women. What we've previously seen in these sorts of cases is that the killer, generally speaking, has endured some trauma that convinces them the murders they perpetrate are justified. It may not be a rational situation to any of us, but viewed through the lens of the perpetrator's trauma, it makes sense. If we assume the killer is male—which is a logical assumption not only because of the nature of the targets but because most murders are committed by men—then I would hazard to guess TCK endured abuse either at the hands of one of the women in his life, a mother, step-mother, or grandmother, maybe, or that he witnessed abuse to one of those same women that he was powerless to stop."

"I have to think there's a third option," said Dean. "That the killer is angry at the world, and at women especially. Someone who's been belittled, demeaned, and slighted his whole life and has decided to take out his frustrations on those who can't effectively fight back."

Mason pursed his lips. "I suppose that's possible, but it doesn't fit with my experiences. Angry men are often criminals, sometimes abusers, but there's a key psychological difference between a rageful man and one who becomes a serial predator."

I chewed on my lip, still thinking about Mason's conclusions. "Why would witnessing abuse of someone TCK cared for cause him to inflict abuse? That doesn't make any sense."

"Not to a logical mind," said Mason. "But the individual we're dealing with isn't logical. They're broken by trauma. Perhaps they witnessed a murder of a caregiver or loved one and in their mind, that solidified the idea that people who are worthy of love deserve to die. Perhaps TCK is targeting young women because he cares for them rather than the opposite. Maybe in his mind, he's setting them free."

Dean's lifted an eyebrow in consideration. "The crimes haven't been sexual in nature, so I suppose that's plausible, if disturbing."

"I'll have a better idea of who we're dealing with once I review the evidence," said Mason, "but something else

that seems obvious is the killer is careful. That's not necessarily a trait you'd expect to find in someone who's been
severely traumatized, unless they had to be careful to avoid
harm themselves. Still, the crime scenes prove TCK is
meticulous. The crimes are never committed in the presence of witnesses, and he's never left any physical
evidence. It's incredibly hard to pull that off even once,
more so when you have the full weight of the NWPD
coming after you. That said, for as intelligent and cautious
as the killer is, he's also someone who craves validation of
his intelligence almost as much as he craves the violence
itself."

"What makes you think that?" I asked.

Mason steepled his fingers. "Several things. First and foremost is the presence of the tarot cards. Someone who only
craves violence will kill. Someone violent and cunning will do
so without leaving evidence, but only someone who enjoys the
thrill of the chase will leave evidence behind on purpose.
Besides, this case is now personal. It has been ever since the
killer phoned Detective Dean."

I recalled the previous evening, as I'd been getting ready to
leave and Dean had received the phone call. I could see every
crease in Dean's brow as he understood who he was speaking to,
see the haunting pain in his eyes as the killer told him he
intended to strike again.

An echo of that same pain passed across Dean's face.
"You're right. It's about more than the murders now. It's a game,
one upon which lives depend. But the call fits your profile,
Mason. Whoever was on the other end muffled their voice so I
wouldn't be able to recognize them, and they only spoke for a
few moments, leaving me no clues as to their intents. They

knew exactly what they were going to say, and they stuck to the script."

The door creaked, and in walked Moss and Justice. The big guy looked worn around the edges, but Moss looked no less chipper than she had in the morning. She scanned the contents of the room, taking in Mason but lending most of her attention to the cardboard boxes.

"I guess we're moving in," she said. "No cots yet, so it can still get worse."

Dean stood. "I wanted a dedicated base of operations, and yes, bringing in pillows and blankets is a distinct possibility. This is Virgil Mason, a criminal profiler from HQ. Mason, these are detectives Moss and Justice."

Moss eyed him with trepidation. "HQ, huh? We'd heard rumors of changes..."

Mason gave a stiff nod. "I'm here by the chief's orders. I'm not taking over."

Justice cast a cautious look at Dean. "So we didn't get muscled out? What are all the case materials doing here then?"

"We're still working TCK," said Dean. "MCD just has the lead now. I can fill you guys in later, but we didn't get pulled. What about you two? Any new leads from The Library?"

Justice sighed and took a seat. "I wish. Officers are canvassing local businesses and residences, but so far with no luck, and they're only getting further and further from the crime scene. Moss and I have been sifting through the list of regulars we got from Nance, but if I'm being honest, that's a dead end. Those guys are sad sacks, every last one. If any of them are serial killers, I'm a gnomish ballet dancer."

Moss shrugged. "We didn't expect much, and we're still disappointed. That should tell you something."

Dean shook his head. "It was an avenue we had to pursue. I'm guessing Miss Breen has been transported to the morgue?"

Moss nodded.

Dean chewed his lip. "I feel like I'm missing something. I'm going to head back to the scene. Either of you want to come with?"

Moss and Justice shared an incredulous look, then Moss took a deep breath before answering. "We've been out there all day, but I could tag along if you like. It's always good to have someone to bounce ideas off of."

"What about Phair?" asked Justice. "She was only there for an hour."

"We need to provide MCD with copies of all the case reports," said Dean. "I was planning on leaving Phair behind to get everything prepped. You want to give her a hand?"

I don't think I'd ever seen Justice shoot out of a chair so fast. "Now that you mention it, I was thinking about heading back to The Library myself. There's got to be some more regulars we haven't milked yet."

Dean smirked. "No doubt. Guess you're on your own, Phair. We'll need copies of everything for the new leads, preferably by the end of day. Got it?"

My stomach sunk as I snuck a glance at the mountain of boxes in the corner. "I'll do my best."

CHAPTER FOURTEEN

I expected the process of collecting copies of the TCK case files to be a miserable slog in every way, and the actual experience didn't disappoint. Luckily, almost all the reports had been prepared in triplicate using carbon paper, both the handwritten reports and the typed ones, but just because there were multiple copies didn't mean they'd been separated and organized. For each box I had to separate out the copied pages, put them in back in order, and collate them before placing them in a new box in an order that approximated the original.

If that was all the work on my plate, it wouldn't have been so bad, but the boxes I'd lugged up from the basement didn't only contain reports. There were photographs: of the victims, their apartments, the crime scenes, most of which there were only single copies of, meaning I had to run to the photography lab on the second floor to deliver envelopes full of negatives in need of duplication. Needless to say, the middle-aged man in charge of development quickly determined I was not someone worthy of befriending. There was bagged evidence in the boxes as well, none of which could be feasibly split, so I moved it to the boxes to be delivered to MCD. The worst were the handwritten notes, most of which had been taken in the field when carbon paper hadn't been available. That meant I had to copy each by hand.

Luckily, Mason took pity on me and helped. He needed to go through the reports in more detail anyway, so it made sense for him to help organize, collect, and copy as I waded through the piles. Good thing, too, otherwise my hand might've cramped into a hideous claw from all the scribbling.

Mason took notes as he worked, sometimes asking questions, most of which I didn't have answers to seeing as I was roughly as knowledgeable about the case as he was. His forehead wrinkled as he peered at a report about the third victim, Maggie Richards.

He flipped a page and grunted, shaking his head. "You know the strangest thing about these killings, Officer Phair? It's how different they are. All the murders have been violent, but we have two distinct bodily assaults, one strangulation, and one stabbing. That's not typical behavior of a serial killer. Most of the time, they have one method they prefer. And the targets themselves, while young and female, don't appear to have been cast from the same mold. As I mentioned, the killer we're seeking was probably traumatized during a formative event. Normally when that happens, the trauma imprints itself on the mind. It makes the killer feel as if the victims they target need to be punished or rewarded, depending on how they view their crimes. But these women don't have a lot tying them together in terms of their jobs, social circles, or backgrounds."

I looked up from my repeated efforts of tearing and stacking carbon paper, my hands stained dark with the sooty coating.

"That's bothered Detective Dean for a while, too. He's convinced there's a thread connecting the victims."

Mason lifted a thick eyebrow. "What evidence is he basing that on?"

I pursed my lips. "I'm not sure it's an evidence-based assumption, to be honest. More of a hope. If there's nothing tying the victims together, we have little hope of finding the killer."

Mason cocked his head. "I'm not sure I agree with that."

"Really?" I set the stack of carbon paper aside. I still hadn't figured out if the copies should stay with us or go to MCD. "I figured as a criminal profiler, you'd think identifying common themes between murders would be our best chance of catching this guy."

"I do," agreed Mason. "My point was simply that the common thread doesn't have to run through the victims. How much effort has Detective Dean put into studying the fragments of tarot cards that have been left behind?"

I felt my brow furrow. "I don't know for certain, but knowing Dean, he's dissected them six ways to Sunday. The cards were identified in the reports, I know that much."

Mason flipped through his notes. "I can see that. The Star Card, the Ten of Pentacles, and the Queen of Wands. Not sure what card was on today's victim. I'll ask Dean. What's important is deciphering the reason each particular card was left."

"You don't think it's random?"

Mason gave me a look that suggested he was reevaluating my intelligence. "I'd bet against it. How much do you know about tarot?"

I shrugged. "Extremely little. I know they're playing cards and they come in a bigger pack than your standard fifty-two card deck. I know some people play games with them, but I never have. Couldn't even name any of the games you *could* play with them."

"Neither could I," said Mason. "I doubt my knowledge of tarot extends much beyond yours—something I'm going to need to remedy—but the larger use for modern tarot isn't in playing games. It's for divination."

"You're talking about fortune-tellers," I said. "That's all bunk, you know?"

Again, Mason shot me a disapproving look. "Of course it is, but people still believe in it. Beyond that, they believe the individual cards that are drawn have meaning. Clearly, Dean has already considered this, as some of his notes in the reports indicate." Mason ran his finger down his notes. "Star Card: themes of hope, inspiration, blessings. The Ten of Pentacles: wealth, success. Queen of Wands: courage, confidence, inspiration. According to the reports, cards that are played upside down can have the reverse meaning, though, which opens a new world of possibilities." Mason frowned and rubbed a couple fingers against his forehead.

I almost admitted that tarot sounded more complex than I'd realized, but I didn't want Mason to shrivel me into a prune with another withering gaze. "So you think TCK is using the tarot cards to... what? Explain why each victim was targeted? Is each card a prediction? Or are the cards part of some larger, more complex narrative? A trail of breadcrumbs that's meant to frustrate and infuriate us?"

Mason nodded as he scanned his notes. "Yes."

I cocked my head at him and gave him my best piqued glance.

Mason was nonplussed. "I wasn't being dismissive. All of

those are possibilities, none of which are any more likely than the others. Given the disparities between these murders, it's just as possible the cards contain a more pedestrian connotation based upon their suits or ranks or perhaps no connotation at all. It's possible the killer placed them on his victims simply to confuse us."

My stomach dropped at the notion. "You think the killer is messing with us?"

Mason stroked his chin. "I know he is, but I refuse to accept the cards don't have any meaning. Not yet. In that sense, I suppose I'm similar to your boss."

The conference room door rattled, popped open, and Moss waltzed through. She paused in front of the table, eyes flitting from the disorderly piles of boxes to the stacks of papers to my carbon stained hands.

She planted her hands on her hips, and a look of concern spread across her face. "Dean sent me to see how things were going."

I smiled, trying to put more cheer into the act than I felt. "It's going great. Can't you tell? We're almost two-thirds through."

One of Moss's eyebrows crept toward her hairline. "You realize it's almost five, right?"

I glanced at the clock. "Dean didn't mention a deadline. Was I supposed to get this to MCD by the top of the hour?"

"Only if you wanted to get off work before dinner." Moss stripped off her jacket and sighed as she sat down. "Come on. Let's get this over with."

I smiled as she pulled a box next to her. Despite her lack of enthusiasm, I was glad to have her, not only because the work would get done faster with her help. Simply put, Mason wasn't much of a chatterbox, and he was too intense for my liking. In the hours I'd spent with him, I don't think he'd cracked a single joke. Even Dean made a light-hearted jab every now and then.

So we delved back into the work, and my hands got even messier.

CHAPTER FIFTEEN

Dawn light filtered through the windshield of Moss's Howardson Hornet, bouncing off the dash and into my eyes. Instead of waking me, it did the opposite, triggering a mild yawn that slowly morphed into a muscle-crippling battle. It was only with a shake of my head, half a dozen blinks, and a severe exertion of will that I was able to overcome it.

Moss glanced at me from behind the wheel, her eyebrows arched. "Doing okay there?"

I blinked a couple more times for good measure and took a sip of coffee from my travel mug. Moss's brew made the stuff at the station seem like bathwater. "I'll survive."

"What time did you get back to the condo last night?"

I tried to think, but my brain wasn't fully operational yet. "Hard to say. After midnight?"

Moss glanced my way again, with sharper intent this time. "What in the world kept you?"

Though Ginger stayed true to her word and helped until the files had been copied and sorted, she let me deliver the duplicates to HQ. Given it was after hours by the time we finished, there weren't nearly as many able-bodied officers around to lug boxes as there'd been when Dean first ordered them brought up. To make matters worse, there were enough materials that I wasn't able to get them all packed in a single squad car, meaning I had to make two trips to and from the Fifth to HQ and back. To my surprise, Detective Glenwell had been in her office during my first delivery, but that only added to the amount of work on my plate, as she requested I get after the technician from our photo studio to get the negatives developed. He hadn't been in when I arrived back at the Fifth, of course, but the delay combined with my second trip and a late-night diner meal followed by my subsequent subway ride to Moss's place had all taken their toll.

I sighed, figuring it wasn't worth rehashing everything. "Took time to get the work done. Hopefully today's efforts will be less mind-numbing."

"And more fruitful," added Moss.

The car jostled as she turned into the 5th Street garage. Moss parked her car, and we headed inside, each of us clutching our travel mugs of coffee as if they were purses filled with jewels. After changing and taking the stairs to the third floor, I headed to the conference room rather than our cubicles. En route, I ran back into Moss, on her way over after listening to her morning messages at her desk.

Despite the early hour, Dean and Justice were already in the war room. If not for their new clothes—Dean had switched into a pale blue suit and Justice had pivoted from solid black to pinstripes—I might not have guessed they'd even gone home. Justice sat low in his seat, his arms and shoulders sagging as much as the chair did under his weight, but it was Dean that surprised me. He looked haggard, with rumpled hair, collar askew, and honest to goodness wrinkles in his shirt. There might've even been bags under his eyes, though his dark skin made it hard to tell. I knew Dean worked as hard as anyone in the precinct, but I'd never really *seen* it.

In addition to Dean and Justice's presence, the conference room had changed in a few more ways. While reports and photos still littered the table, the boxes from which they'd come had been relegated to the corners. Two phones had been connected and added to the party, and on the far side of the room, one chalkboard and one cork board, each of them on casters, had been wheeled inside. For the moment, the cork board was empty, but a list of names had been scrawled onto the blackboard.

Dean gave a tired wave as we came in. "Morning, Moss. Phair."

Moss eyed the changes, same as I had. "You guys are in early. If the whole detecting business doesn't work out, you can always open a bakery."

Dean's brow furrowed. "Pardon?"

Moss gave a dismissive wave as she sat. "Bad joke. Don't worry about it. I doubt anyone would've found it funny even if it wasn't half past dawn."

Justice eyed Moss's travel mug. He crooked a finger as she set it down. "That from your own private stock?"

Moss slid it across the polished hardwood. "Don't drink it all. I don't want to refill from the communal jug any more than you do."

I took a seat next to Moss, not feeling the same flair for banter she was. I think it was Dean's haunted look that was bringing me down. It was hard to smile when he looked like that. Then again, maybe that's why Moss was trying to lighten the mood.

"As you probably noticed, I got copies to MCD last night," I said. "Everything but the photos. I should double check on those, but I doubt the technician is in yet."

Dean nodded as he gestured to one of the phones. "I talked to Glenwell first thing this morning. She was appreciative of our speed, so thanks for the hard work. We'll have someone run them over as soon as they're ready. And Mason?"

I shrugged. "He left about an hour before Moss and I finished. He wanted to conduct some independent research on the tarot card angle."

Dean pursed his lips. "Good. I'll touch base with him."

Justice slurped on the mug, emitting a pleased sigh.

Moss gave him a withering glance. "I said easy there, big guy. So what did the two of you get done last night?"

Justice cradled the travel mug and smiled. "Oh, we got plenty done. Doesn't mean we got any results for our efforts, though. The status quo is unchanged. Nobody saw or heard anything, and none of the regulars from the bar are likely targets. Heck, they're not even outside targets."

"You agree?" Moss eyed Dean.

Alton nodded, the bob of his head less crisp than usual. "I thought as much yesterday morning before we even met Nance, but having interviewed them, yes. None of the barflies should be considered suspects. Also, Justice and I touched base with CSU. The bar is a mess, and the surfaces in the alley behind The Library are mostly rough, but the technicians were able to print the entirety of Miss Breen's apartment. They found nothing but Lacy's prints."

"Nothing?" said Moss. "That by itself is surprising. An

attractive young woman like her must've had friends, maybe the occasional gentleman caller."

Justice shrugged. "Surprising, maybe, but it tracks with what we've seen at the other ladies' homes. They're all clean as a whistle. Maybe that's how TCK picks his victims. He chooses them based on how germophobic they are."

I cradled my mug of coffee protectively, and a thread of yesterday's conversation with Mason floated through my mind. "Or he divined the information."

Dean regarded me with his ice blue eyes. They had more bite to them than I'd expected. "You're talking about telling the future? Via tarot?"

I felt the weight of everyone's eyes on me. Though I'd come to suspect our last major case had supernatural elements to it, I wasn't normally one to believe in things that went bump in the night. How had it fallen upon me to make the argument? "It's something Mason wanted to look into. The meaning of the tarot cards, the potential for divination. I'm not saying I believe it, only that it's an option. TCK could've just as easily cased each victim the old fashioned way."

Justice took another less audible sip of Moss's coffee. "Regardless of how he picked them, to not have left prints anywhere proves he's meticulous as well as disciplined. Which we already knew..."

Dean's eyes lost their edge, but he didn't move them off me, almost as if he thought I hadn't fully expressed my thoughts. "We talked about it briefly yesterday, but I'll run it by Mason when we speak."

Moss reached over and snagged her mug back, shaking it to see how much of the drink was left. Her frown said it all. "So what's the plan, Dean? Are we waiting on orders from Glenwell or acting on our own?"

"Yes and yes," said Dean. "If Glenwell tells us to jump, we're supposed to, but I think she's content to let us do our thing so long as we share what we find. Hawkins might not be, but that old sloth in detective's clothing can stuff it in his ear. He might have seniority, but at least the chief was smart enough to put Glenwell in charge."

My eyebrows rose. Calling someone a sloth wasn't exactly a devastating burn, but it was the worst I'd heard Dean call anyone nonetheless.

He continued. "To be honest, I'm not entirely sure what the plan should be. Every investigative avenue I've pursued has hit a dead end. That doesn't mean I intend to give up. I'm not a fan of criminal profiling, but perhaps Mason's approach can bear fruit. Justice and I have talked about putting together more thorough dossiers on the victims to see if we can find any common threads we've missed. To that end, I think it would be worthwhile to start from scratch. Deconstruct each murder book. Revisit each home, search them for clues again. Repeat every step we've taken. Maybe with Phair's fresh eyes on the data, we'll come across something new."

Even though I hadn't pored over every detail in the pages I'd collated the night before, I'd nonetheless had my fill of reports. Besides, Dean's spoken summary had been as useful as all the documents I'd scanned put together.

"I've never claimed to be an eagle eye, but I wouldn't mind visiting some apartments," I said.

Moss smirked. I couldn't imagine she was any more excited about rereading reports than I was. "I'll come with you. Together, maybe we can figure out what we've been missing."

CHAPTER SIXTEEN

Moss pulled her Hornet into a short, narrow parking spot that was more dirt than gravel. If not for the twin parallel stripes free of weeds, I would've thought it part of the yard of the home next to us.

The automobile grumbled and quieted as Moss pulled the keys from the ignition. Moss climbed out her side, but I had to work for my freedom as the passenger side was only a foot or two away from a rusted chainlink fence. As I got free and sidled my way to Moss's side, I took stock of our surroundings. The neighborhood wasn't the worst I'd ever seen, but it wasn't the sort of place where police officers received a warm welcome. Windows on homes were as likely to be covered by iron bars as they were to be boarded up, lawn sculptures mostly consisted of broken down cars on cinderblocks, and the road had more gaping holes than imported cheese. A charcoal scent from an outdoor grill wafted over from a nearby home, and a half dozen dogs could be heard trading barks in the distance.

"Nice place, huh?" said Moss.

The neighborhood wasn't, but by comparison, the small

two-story duplex in front of us was. The lawn, more weeds than grass, had actually been mowed within the last two weeks, there were drapes in the windows, and someone had bothered to repaint the wooden siding within the last generation. There was a porch small enough to fit a single wicker chair, and on the side of the home, a rickety-looking staircase led to a second-story door.

"Split top and bottom level?" I asked.

Moss nodded. "Sherryl Towns lived in the loft."

The stairs groaned as Moss led the way up. A couple strips of police tape had been stapled across the door. Moss plucked them free from one side, letting them hang across the frame before unlocking the door with a key from her pocket. Like the stairs, it too creaked as we pushed inside.

Despite the rough exterior, the inside of the home was quaint. The rooms were small, as they had to be given the house's footprint, but they weren't overly furnished. I caught glimpses of polished wood, footboards and bookshelves and round tables, the latter spread with crocheted doilies. The drapes I'd noticed filtered the morning light, turning it shades of pale blue and purple and sending long shadows stretching across floors worn smooth from age. If all I'd seen of the place were photographs, I would've thought it the home of a loving older couple, but there was more to the loft than eyes alone could convey. A stale must hung in the air, as if the windows hadn't been cracked in months, and an eerie quiet suffused the home. No voices carried through the air, no hum of refrigerators or fans or buzzing lights, only the creaking of the floorboards as we walked. It was a place of stillness and death.

I stepped into the small communal space in the center of the home, out from which branched bedrooms and a kitchen and a bath. The sink was free of dishes, the dining table free of plates, the backs of chairs free of clothes. "Did someone clean this place after you collected evidence?"

Moss shook her head as she joined me by the dining table. "Miss Towns must've been a neat freak. This place was clean as a whistle when I first arrived with Dean. The bed's even made. Who makes their bed in the morning, honestly?"

I glanced around, noting the lack of photos and wall art. "Seems like she was a minimalist, too."

"Seems like," said Moss. "Though whether by choice or by circumstance is an open question. She was a hairdresser. Can't imagine she made a lot of money. Rents can't be too high in this neighborhood, but still. I have to think most of her free income went towards housing."

I nodded. "As small as it is, it does seem like a little much for a single woman. We're sure she lived alone?"

"All the people we talked to confirmed it," said Moss. "Though if you find anything that suggests otherwise, I'll be interested in seeing it."

"What exactly are we looking for?" I asked.

"You read the initial search report, right?"

We'd brought the copy in the car. I'd perused it while Moss drove. "We're looking for discrepancies?"

"Those, omissions, oversights," said Moss. "Anything that wasn't in the report, or anything you think might be significant even if it was in the report. Anything that suggests TCK might've been here."

I crossed to the street-facing window, pushing the drapes to the side. "I have to admit, as glad as I am not to be stuck re-reading reports, I don't get Dean's insistence we revisit all the victims' abodes. None of the women were attacked at home. Why is Dean so convinced TCK was ever here?"

Moss pulled gloves onto her hands as she walked into the kitchen. "It's a combination of hope and conviction, I think. There's no way the women were picked by chance. They were vetted. They'd likely been stalked. TCK knew when they'd be alone. Because of his meticulous nature, Dean's certain TCK researched each and every one, probably by breaking into their homes. That and Dean isn't convinced the tarot cards were placed post-mortem."

Right. I'd forgotten that piece of information. "TCK could've scouted these women without breaking and entering. Has there been any effort into looking into the owners of nearby buildings?" I pointed out the window. "Most of the information TCK needed probably could've been obtained by a peeping Tom with a good set of binoculars."

Moss's glove snapped as she finished pulling it on. "That's possible, but—"

A floorboard creaked, and a tired but stern voice called from behind the door. "Might as well get out now. I've already called the cops. They'll be here any minute."

Moss turned toward the sound, and I took a few steps to get into the line of sight. An elderly orcish woman with long graying hair stood in the open door, a faded flower print muumuu hanging over her broad frame. Her face was lined with wrinkles, and small tusks protruded from behind thick lips.

Her stance was tense, but she sagged as soon as she saw the distinctive blue of my uniform. "I should've known you'd be cops. Most knuckleheads know better than to break into my home."

It was only as her shoulders dropped that I noticed the tip

of a wooden bat peek from behind the hem of her dress. The woman had come prepared in case her threat didn't do the job.

"My apologies," said Moss. "We should've announced ourselves. I'm Detective Moss and this is Officer Phair. I take it you live downstairs?"

The orcish woman snorted and frowned, leaning against the frame. "Of course I do. This is my house. I own the place."

"You were the landlady to Miss Towns?" I asked.

"Sure was." The orc's frown deepened. "Nice young woman, too. Still have a hard time believing she's gone—or at least I do when there ain't heavy feet creaking the boards above my ears."

"We're investigating her death," said Moss. "Do you mind if we ask you a few questions about her?"

"*Investigating her death...*" The woman sighed. "Sure you are. Been investigating it for, what? Two months now? And ain't nobody been here since the eve of her death when half the damn department descended on my poor home." She hefted her bat and grabbed it in the middle, gesturing to the undersized dining table. "You mind if I sit down? I'm not as young as I used to be."

"Actually, this is still an active crime scene," said Moss. "You could contaminate it by entering. We could head downstairs if you prefer."

"I wouldn't," the landlady said. "In my experience, things either go missing or illegal items mysteriously appear on my shelves when I allow your type in. I'll stay here unless I see a warrant, thanks."

The woman came across as more than a little jaded, but I couldn't blame her. I hadn't expected any different as soon as we crossed the invisible railroad tracks into her neighborhood. "Could you tell us your name, ma'am?"

"Gharol Lorne. That's Gharol with a Gh, not a C. I ain't some dandy from Brentford. And how many questions are you going to ask, anyway? I already spent a couple hours with you folks when this all went down."

I recalled the report I'd sifted through, remembering mention of Gharol, though I hadn't read any of her testimony. I think Dean interviewed her.

Moss bailed me out. "We won't keep you long. Just wanted to confirm a few things about Miss Towns. According to our records, she wasn't married, and it seems she didn't have a boyfriend. Is that right?"

Gharol stuffed the baseball bat under an armpit as she crossed her arms. "She was the only applicant on the lease agreement, I can tell you that much. If you're wondering if she had a gent over all the time, the answer is no. She was quiet. Kept mostly to herself. One of the reasons I liked her so much as a tenant, especially one that lives upstairs from me."

"No pets?" said Moss.

Gharol shook her head. "Not in my house, not without a sizable deposit. Dogs ruin floors, and cats leave a stink, trained or not."

"What about friends and the occasional caller?" asked Moss. "Surely Miss Towns wasn't always alone. She must've had people over."

"Sure, every now and then," said Gharol. "She wasn't a hermit. She had friends. Don't ask me when the last time any of them were here, though. I tried to answer that question the last time, and my memory was two months fresher then. The point is, she didn't have many people over often, at least not while I was at home. Might be she had folks over during the day, but I doubt it. She worked, too, you know."

"You work during the day?" I asked.

Clearly that was the wrong question. Gharol's brow furrowed. "'Course I do. How old do you take me for? I ain't retirement age yet. Even if I was, I don't have some fancy police pension comin' my way. I work for my crowns. Speaking of, when am I going to be able to rent this place again? It's been two months, and I need the income from this apartment to pay my mortgage."

"Soon, Ms. Lorne," said Moss. "We just need to gather as much evidence as we can to help solve Miss Towns' murder. That's why we're here."

"Seems to me you're just banging around," said Gharol. "Besides, how much evidence do you think you're liable to find? It's not as if Sherryl was murdered here—and thank the gods for that. Can you imagine the hit I'd take on rent if I had to scrub blood out of the floors? And yet I'd *still* take that to not getting any rent at all." Gharol cleared her throat loudly for emphasis.

Before we could reply, a distinctive snap split the air, like a distant whip crack. Or more accurately, a gunshot. I turned toward Moss as another one followed the first.

"You hear that?"

Moss didn't waste any time. "Let's go."

We darted outside, pushing Gharol onto the landing as Moss locked the door behind her. The stairs creaked as we rushed down them, Gharol's frustrated voice following us. "Hey! I want answers, you hear? I need a date I can list this place!"

We ignored her as we hopped into the Hornet. Moss picked up the radio receiver and clicked it on. "Dispatch? This is

Detective Moss. I'm at the intersection of Thirty-Seventh and Cherry Trail. We've heard two gunshots. Can you confirm?"

A voice crackled through the radio. "Just a moment, Detective. ... Yes. We've received a call about a domestic incident at Thirty-Ninth and Everly. I'm diverting officers who were en route to a reported breaking and entering."

"The ones Lorne called on us," Moss said to me with a roll of her eyes. She clicked the receiver on again. "We're responding to the call, dispatch. Keep us appraised on backup."

Moss stuffed the receiver back into the console, turned the keys in the ignition, and as the motor rumbled to life, she punched her foot onto the gas.

CHAPTER SEVENTEEN

Our siren wailed as we raced down 39th, the entire car jostling as we bounced over potholes. The radio crackled, barely audible over the siren and the roar of the car. "Dispatch to Detective Moss. Backup is three minutes out."

Moss was fully focused on driving, so I grabbed the receiver. "Copy, dispatch."

As I returned the receiver to the console, Moss cried out. "There!"

She didn't point, but she didn't have to. Ahead, I spotted a house similar to the rest: single story, shabby, with a chainlink fence on one side and a battered wooden one on the other. What stood out was the man sprawled on the front lawn, clutching his stomach and squirming about, a dark reddish stain seeping onto the lawn beside him.

Moss pumped the brakes and cranked on the steering wheel. The car shuddered and tilted. The deceleration pushed me against my seatbelt and sent blood rushing to my head. The

Hornet jostled and caught a smidge of air as the front wheel lifted onto the sidewalk before settling onto all fours.

Moss flicked off the siren. My heart beat hard in my chest and I felt a nervous tingle overtake me. I reached for my door handle, but Moss grabbed my shoulder. "Crawl out my side. Keep the car between you and the house. We have to assume the shooter is inside."

I nodded, my heartbeat rising another dozen beats per minute. Moss hopped out her door and hunched behind the Hornet's engine block. I crawled over the console and out behind her with as much grace as I could muster.

Moss pulled a pistol from her waist holster and gripped it tight in both hands. I pulled my own sidearm, crouching low to keep my body shielded by the car. Now that the siren had been silenced, I noticed the cacophony of other sounds around us. The guy on the lawn was groaning in pain. Shouts and cries, both male and female, were coming from inside the house, the front door of which stood open. The gunshots and sirens had also aggravated the local canine population, as the occasional barks I'd heard at Gharol's had turned into an aggressive campaign similar to what a fireworks display might invoke.

Moss shuffled forward, peeking around the front of the Hornet. She called out, her voice firm and commanding. "This is the NWPD. Come out with your hands up!"

The man on the lawn contained to groan and bleed, the dogs continued to bark, and there was another shout and crash from inside the home. I peeked over the top of the hood to get a better look, but I couldn't see any obvious motion through the windows.

Moss waited for a lull in the cries to try again. "Police! Come out and surrender!"

The dogs took enough of a break for me to catch a snippet of a response from inside the home, but I don't think it was directed at us. Someone shouted in a strained voice, "You see! You see what you've done!"

Another shout, a heavy masculine one, followed. "Shut up, I said!"

Another snap of gunfire split the air, then another. *Crack crack*, in quick succession. I ducked, as did Moss. A crystalline ping joined the bursts, followed by the melodious tinkle of glass dancing across concrete. I took another peek over the Hornet. It didn't seem as if the car had been hit, but one of the windows of the home had been been blasted apart. Glass shards glimmered across the porch in the bright morning sun.

Moss pulled me back down and tapped her ear. "Hear that?"

It took me a second to realize what she was talking about. Another siren. I'd tuned it out with all the other noise. "The other officers should be here soon."

Moss nodded. "We'll wait for them before we move. I'll stay here. You sneak around and cover the back." She pointed to the wooden fence at our side. "Stay low. Don't show yourself or speak up. I'll signal you when the officers arrive."

My heart rate spiked again at the thought of splitting up, but I'd known what I signed up for when I'd joined the police academy. Getting transferred into Dean's investigative squad didn't absolve me of my duty to protect and serve.

I nodded. With my pistol gripped tight, I hustled to the back of the Hornet and darted to the relative safety of the fence. I doubted the weather-worn thing would save me from a bullet, but at least it kept me hidden from view. I ducked low and crab walked along its edge, trying to avoid stepping in the wilted

lilies the neighbor had planted there. As I reached the back of
the property, I took a quick glance at the home before hopping
the fence into another neighbor's yard. Unfortunately, the back
fence was chainlink, not wood, but there was a detached garage
in the corner I was able to hide behind.

I hunched there as I listened to the swelling wail of the
siren. My heart beat hard against my ribs, and I had to wipe my
palms against my uniform to keep the sweat at bay. I peered
around the edge of the shed toward the back of the home, eyeing
the screen that hung from the back door, partially shredded at
the bottom by cat's claws. There was a window in the back, too,
but it was barred, same as the ones in front had been. If anyone
were to make an exit, it would be through the door.

The siren reached a crescendo, and underneath it, I heard
the screech of tires on asphalt. The siren abruptly stopped,
followed by the clang of car doors. I expected to hear Moss's
shout, but for a moment all that hung in the air was the dogs'
barks, now renewed by the second siren. Perhaps Moss was
hatching a plan of attack with the newly arrived officers.

After a long, tense minute, I heard Moss's voice carry across
the property. "This is your last chance. We have the home
surrounded. Come out with your hands up!"

I'd been so focused on Moss's cues I'd almost missed that the
inside of the home had gone quiet for the last minute, too.
Almost as soon as Moss's threat carried through the air, the
screen door popped open, clanging off the house from the
momentum it carried. A man surged through it, balding, wide in
the shoulders but overweight, wearing a stained undershirt and
jeans with tears across the knees. His focus wasn't on the back
of the lot but the woman he was dragging along with him.

She was short, only an inch or two above five feet, with long dark hair that fell haphazardly across her knee-length nightgown. Her eyes were wide, and she struggled against the much larger man's grip.

"Please! Please!" she cried.

The man shook her as he backed away from the house. "How many times I got to tell you to shut up?"

My instincts kicked in. I popped around the edge of the shed, my pistol trained on the man. "Hands up!"

Everything happened quick as a wink. The man's head spun toward me, his eyes widening. His arm whipped up. The morning sun glimmered off something metallic in his hand.

I fired.

The pistol's crack filled the air, louder than any I'd heard, and the scent of spent fireworks filled my nostrils. The man made a pained gurgling sound and stumbled. The weapon in his hand discharged, a fiery crack splitting the air a second time, before falling from his limp hand. His hostage screamed and pulled free from his loosening grip, falling to the ground as she tried to scramble around the side of the house.

All the while, I kept my pistol trained on the man. I kept it on him while his knees buckled and he fell onto his back. I kept it on him as I hopped the low chainlink fence and approached him and while I kicked the revolver he'd dropped out of reach. I kept it on him as I heard more shouts and Moss's voice, as I saw her and another officer round the corner with their pistols drawn. The officer shouted at the hostage not to move and cuffed her. It was only as he did so that I holstered my sidearm.

I pushed the man onto his stomach as he groaned weakly in pain, cuffing his arms behind his back as Moss approached.

"Phair," she said, her pistol still gripped tight. "What happened? Are you hurt?"

I shook my head. "He came out the back with that woman in hand. His gun went off, but it must've gone into the dirt."

Moss bobbed her head. "Stay here. Watch these two. Officer Brownsborough? Move to the porch. Sweep the house. I'll come in from the back."

The officer who'd arrived nodded and ran around to the front of the home. Moss hustled to the screen door, which now hung from the frame by a couple overworked screws. She paused, listening for a moment before diving inside.

I stood in the back of the lot as the former hostage begged and pleaded for help, talking about how none of this was her fault. I didn't pay her much attention. My eyes were on the man I'd shot. A pool of blood was spreading onto the cracked paver stones underneath him, and his pained groans had ceased. His arms weren't moving, so I focused on his chest. There was a hole in his undershirt, the back of which was now a dark burgundy in color, but I wasn't focused on that either. I was focused on whether his chest rose and fell.

Far in the distance, I heard Moss's voice. "Clear." Then another voice, maybe Brownsborough's. "Clear." Moss again. "Clear." The handcuffed woman kept babbling. Her lips moved, but I didn't hear what she said. I had eyes only for the man I'd shot. The pool of blood kept growing, and he wasn't moving. *At all.*

I blinked, and suddenly, Moss was there. She was grabbing me by the shoulder and giving me a shake. *"Phair?"*

I turned toward her with my mouth open, but I didn't say anything. My tongue felt thick and dry in my mouth.

Moss's face was twisted with concern. "Can you hear me, Phair? Are you okay?"

The words felt like someone else's as they pushed past my lips. "Ginger... I think I just killed a man."

CHAPTER EIGHTEEN

I sat in the back of an ambulance on the thin uncomfortable mat that passed for a bed, my back hunched and my head scraping the molded metal roof. A paramedic sat across from me on a padded bench, a young woman about my age but half my size. She had a stethoscope around her neck, a clipboard in one hand, and a pencil in the other.

She flipped a page over the top of the clipboard. "How about chest pain?"

I sighed. "I'm telling you, I feel fine. I don't even know why I'm here."

The paramedic looked at me over her rectangular glasses. "You don't know why you're here?"

"Don't twist my words. I'm not confused or disoriented."

"I don't know that," said the paramedic. "I'm trying to determine it. It's my job, and doing it properly would be a lot easier if you'd answer my questions, Officer."

I turned to look out the open back of the ambulance. The vehicle had parked a home's length away from the crime scene, though I'm sure they would've parked closer if they could've. The house at which the shootings had taken place was a zoo. Besides the paramedics, one set of which had already come and gone with the victim from the front lawn strapped in back, there were additional cops, a coroner, and a crime scene unit waiting impatiently for the crowds to die down so they could get to work. Moss's Hornet was still parked on the lawn where she'd left it. For the time being, she was in charge of the investigation, but I didn't know if that would change once the chain of command had their say.

I sighed and turned to the paramedic. "Fine. I'll answer the questions. Let's get this done with."

The paramedic gave me a dubious glance as she turned back to her clipboard, as if she'd believe me when she saw it. "Do you have any chest pain?"

I shook my head. "Not any more. A little bit during and after the incident."

"I'm only interested in how you're feeling at the moment, thank you. Are you experiencing any dizziness or light-headedness?"

"No."

"Do you feel clammy?"

"No."

"What about confusion?"

I thought back to when Moss materialized in front of me, but the paramedic had said she was only interested in the present. "Not at the moment, no."

She nodded and stood. She put her clipboard and pencil next to me on the mat. "Can I see your hand?"

I held it out. She pushed my sleeve up and pressed a couple fingers to the inside of my forearm. After a few seconds, she pulled them away and jotted a note on her clipboard. "Eighty to ninety beats per minute. A little high, but in the normal range."

She proceeded to open one of the cabinets underneath the bed and pull out one of those blood pressure monitors that goes around your arm. I didn't know what the name was. A pressure-ometer? Regardless, she wrapped it around my arm, pumped it a few times, and watched the dial on the handle while keeping an eye on her watch. After about fifteen seconds, she unwrapped the thing and lay it on the bed. "One thirty over eighty-two. Also a little high, but not abnormal given the circumstances."

The paramedic was quiet as she jotted a few more things down. I was ready to ask her if I was going to live when I heard a rap at the side of the car.

Moss stood at the back door. She looked expectantly toward the paramedic. "How is she?"

"I'm fine," I said. "Also right here."

Moss shot me a fierce look that made it clear she hadn't asked me. "I'd like the medical professional's opinion."

The young woman flipped the sheets on her clipboard back into place. "Physically, she's fine. A little amped from the inci-dent, but nothing serious. Emotionally? That's a different story, one I'm not qualified to evaluate."

"*Emotionally?*" I said. "Trust me, when I say I'm fine, I'm fine."

The paramedic didn't say anything. She also made a point not to look me in the eye.

Moss waved me down. "Thanks. Come on, Phair."

I didn't need to be told twice. I pried myself off the bed and crawled outside, thankful for the headroom. Moss led me to the sidewalk, but she stopped after only a few paces toward the scene.

"Seriously," she said in a low voice. "How are you feeling? Not physically. Overall."

I rolled my shoulders. They were tight. "I wasn't spouting bravado. I really feel okay."

Moss lifted her eyebrows. "Hopefully, that's true, but the simple fact is you're not the best judge of that right now. It's okay. We'll get you looked at. That's why we have protocols regarding officer-involved shootings."

I watched the house as a coroner wheeled a gurney with an empty black bag on it across the grass toward the back. My throat tightened at the sight of it, and I recalled the smell of gunpowder and the whip crack of my pistol.

I swallowed and averted my eyes. "Speaking of, what happens now?"

Moss sighed. "You're going to be busy, to put it mildly. You'll have to give your statement on what happened, multiple times. So many times your throat will get sore and you'll get tired of the sound of your own voice. Don't let it bother you. Tell the truth, be patient, and don't get frustrated. It's part of the process. You'll meet with your union rep, maybe a lawyer, and eventually a psychiatrist."

"*Lawyer?*" I said.

"Purely a preventative measure," said Moss. "One assigned to you by the union. But nobody's going to charge you with anything, trust me. This is as open and shut a case as they come. The evidence in your favor is overwhelming. Besides, District Attorney Bogart is a fair man. He wouldn't touch this with a ten foot pole, even if he wasn't friends with Detective Dean."

"Speaking of..." I glanced down the street to where a distinctive emerald green Howardson Viper was approaching. It slowed as it reached the crime scene, then sped up again before pulling over and parking in front of the ambulance. The passenger door opened. Justice worked on folding himself out of the car while Dean came around the driver's side.

Dean stuffed his hands in his pockets as he reached us. "This is not the call I expected to get this morning."

"We were at Towns' loft when we heard the shots," said Moss. "We were first on the scene, but we waited for backup. We played it by the book."

"I have no doubt," said Dean. "Doesn't mean this won't become a distraction, though."

I swallowed back a lump in my throat. "Dean, I'm sorry. Neither one of us was trying to pull resources away from the TCK case. Moss gave me orders and I followed them as best I could..."

Dean held up a hand, and his face softened. "Don't apologize. If what I've heard is accurate, none of this was your fault. More importantly, you made the right choice when faced with a difficult situation. Not every officer does. If I came across as frustrated, it's with the situation, not you. But this is a fact of life. The city doesn't go to sleep because we have a case we're focused on. Crime doesn't stop. We have to roll with the punches, adjust and adapt and keep going when we can."

By this point, Justice had joined us, though he was rolling his shoulders to get the cricks caused by Dean's small Viper out. "He's right, Phair. We've always got multiple cases going, but they all come to a halt when there's an emergency. We might be detectives, but we're officers of the law first. Lieutenants, captains, even the chief is, too. Your duty never goes away, no matter how far up the ladder you climb."

Dean nodded. "Well said, Ogden. Moss, I'm guessing you've been leading the investigation?"

"Such as it is," she said. "Seems pretty clear cut. A dispute between exes and a new boyfriend that turned violent. Phair put a stop to an emergent hostage situation."

"Because you were involved, you know we'll need to confirm everything independently," said Dean. "Justice, you mind taking a look around, preferably before the coroner moves anyone? I'll be there in a minute."

"You got it." Justice nodded to Moss and me, a smile crossing his lips. "Good to see you're both unharmed."

I bobbed my head in response as Justice left.

As he rounded the fence into the lawn, Dean squeezed my shoulder lightly. "How are you? Honestly?"

My bravado had all been spent on the paramedic. Besides, I couldn't lie to Dean, not when he seemed so invested in my wellbeing. "Physically, fine. The shooter's gun went off, but it hit dirt. Emotionally, I'm a little frazzled. Feels like there's a nervous energy still humming through my body, as if the adrenaline hasn't totally worn off. Mostly, I'm worried about what happens now, from the department's perspective."

Dean sighed. "It's a process, but not one to be feared. Go through the steps and be patient. You'll be out of commission for a while, but there's nothing we can do about that."

"Out of commission?" I said. "I'll be taken off duty?"

"It's standard procedure," said Dean. "Minimum one day, usually a few."

"What about the TCK case?" I said. "We've got so much work to do. I don't want to get pulled off it."

"It's not your call, or mine," said Dean. "And it's for the best. You need to process what happened today. The only way for that to happen is to give it time."

My face fell. It wasn't that I thought I was integral to Dean's investigative team, that between Dean and Moss and Justice and now Glenwell and Hawkins that I'd somehow be the one to bring TCK down, but I'd nonetheless become attached to my new role in the department. "Please, Dean. I could stay at the office. Work on the reports."

Dean gave a reluctant smile. "Your commitment is commendable, but your health is the most important thing. I'll talk to the captain, but it's his call. In the meantime, you should get back to the station to give your statement. Moss, you're driving, right?"

She nodded, and Dean waved us off. "Good. Time to go then. Best of luck, Phair."

CHAPTER NINETEEN

O nce I arrived at the Fifth Street Precinct, I lost track of time. A representative from the union was already waiting for me. He led me to a small, windowless room on the first floor, nicer than our interrogation rooms but not by much. There, he explained what would happen, laid out what rights I had as a result of collective bargaining, and told me he'd be available in case I had any questions. Frankly, I was confused enough about everything that I didn't know what questions to ask, but the rep told me he wouldn't be going anywhere and if I thought of anything, I could ask later. I did wonder about the lawyer Moss had mentioned, but the rep assured me it was better not to involve one at this stage of the process as it would only muddy the waters, something I didn't want to do. He then gave me a stack of forms and instructed me to start filling them out.

I'd only gotten halfway through when a pair of detectives from internal affairs arrived. They seemed intimidating as they entered, two men in their forties or fifties, both with similar crewcuts and crisp suits. I'd heard the same stories about internal affairs as everyone else. The rank and file mostly hated or feared them, sometimes both, viewing them as providing only unsatisfactory resolutions to situations to which they were summoned. I didn't have any personal distaste for IA, however, as I figured self-policing was an important departmental role. If anything, the police probably needed to conduct more internal investigations, not fewer.

Of course, that didn't change the fact that Detectives Taylor and Grunfeld were about as impersonal and aloof as individuals came. The pair of them seemed to have been drained of all emotion, as if a machine had sucked it out of them and replaced it with ice water. They approached our meeting with a collective cool that I envied as I sat there with sweating armpits and a thumping heart, but the pair couldn't have been all bad. They brought me a doughnut and coffee when they arrived, at least.

The interviews with them went about how Moss said they would. They asked me to describe the incident in my own words. When I was done, they asked questions to clarify, delving into every detail, making sure my every action was specified. They'd take some notes, ask me if I wanted more coffee or a bathroom break, and we'd start over. Once we broke to give me time to finish my written report, and another time we broke just to stretch our legs for ten minutes. Sometimes the questions changed and Taylor and Grunfeld thought of new things they hadn't bothered to ask before, but mostly it was an exercise in repetition. I knew what they were after. They were ferreting out any inconsistencies in my story, same as Dean might with a suspect in interrogation, but I took Moss's advice. I told the truth, same as I remembered it, every time. I don't think I contradicted myself at any point, but if I did, Taylor and Grunfeld didn't show their hands and call me on it.

I didn't know what time it was when we finally wrapped. All I knew was my throat was sore, I was starving, and my bladder was ready to burst. A quick glance at the windows while on my way to the ladies room made it clear morning had passed into late afternoon, but when I exited, feeling relieved, I found the union rep waiting for me outside. I sighed, asking what we needed to do next, but he assured me that as far as he was concerned, we were done for the day. He was just passing along word that the captain wanted to see me.

I found Captain Ellison in his office. He wore the same starched shirt he always did, with its epaulets and the curved breast pockets tightly buttoned. He looked up as I knocked on his door. "Sir?"

"Officer Phair," he said. "Come in. Have a seat."

He didn't tell me to close the door, so I didn't. I sat down and gave him a nod. "What can I do for you, sir?"

Captain Ellison had always come across as calculating and political, but there was a grandfatherly look to him as he leaned forward in his chair. "I wanted to let you know I've spoken to your colleagues while you were with IA. Detectives Dean, Moss, and Justice, as well as Officers Brownsborough and Hunt who responded to the call alongside you. All of them tell the same story, that of an officer who responded to a tense, dangerous situation with bravery and action. I know it's never easy to use deadly force, but because of your quick thinking, you saved a woman's life today. You did your badge proud, Officer."

I wasn't sure I believed that. As I repeated my actions over and over again for internal affairs, I couldn't help but wonder if there was anything else I could've done. If there was a different path I could've taken that wouldn't have resulted in a man losing his life today, yet also me not losing mine. I wasn't sure there was, but that didn't make accepting the results of my actions any easier.

I bobbed my head, appreciative of the captain's candor. "Thank you, sir. That means a lot."

Ellison leaned back in his chair. "So how are you feeling? Meeting with IA can be exhausting on a good day. It's several times harder when you're under duress."

Over the course of the day, I'd gone from not wanting to admit how I felt to wanting to be honest to not wanting to talk about it any more from simple exhaustion. "I'm tired, sir. I want the day to be over, if I'm being honest. Other than that, I feel pretty good."

The captain pursed his lips. "I understand completely. How many days would you like to take off?"

"*Days off?*" My brow furrowed. "Sir, I think I might not have expressed myself properly. I'm physically tired, but after a good night's sleep, I'll be right as rain. I don't want to be taken off duty. There's too much to do."

"There's always too much to do, Officer," said Ellison. "That's why we employ so many people. We work together so that if any one individual gets knocked out of commission, justice marches on. The department never sleeps."

Everyone had told me I'd miss at least a day or two, but with the moment at hand, it felt more real. Strange how a few months ago I'd never even considered joining the force, and now the thought of spending a couple days away from my job had opened a gaping pit in my stomach. "Sir..."

The captain held up a hand. "Save your complaints, Officer. I already know what you're going to tell me, mostly because Dean stopped by and briefed me. You're not the only one who wants to resolve the TCK case, and frankly, you taking a step back for a few days isn't going to make a difference. That said, I will admit I'm not the best person to determine your fitness for duty. If you're determined to get back to work as soon as possible, report tomorrow morning at police HQ to the psychiatrist's office. If they clear you, I suppose we can let you back, at least in a limited capacity."

A weight lifted off my chest, and I sat up straighter. "Thank you, sir. I'll be there first thing."

The captain smiled, as if he knew how I'd react. "Just know you're welcome to change your mind between now and tomorrow. And if you need anything, don't hesitate to reach out. We're here for you, Officer. Dismissed."

I nodded and headed for the exit.

"Oh, one more thing," said Captain Ellison.

I paused at the door. "Yes, sir?"

"Dean wants you to check in with him before you head home. Said he had something important to share."

I nodded again and headed toward the stairs. I figured I'd find Dean in the war room, but the conference room had been locked and the lights were off. I tried his desk, but that too was empty, as were Moss and Justice's workspaces. I ventured into one of the nearby clusters and found someone, Detective Valente from burglary, but he wasn't sure where Dean was. The break room, perhaps? I tried that, too, but failing to find him, I set out on my own. After making a pass through the pit on the main floor, I figured it made sense to check if Dean was still at the station, so I headed into the attached garage. It was there I found him, leaning against the concrete twenty feet from the door. His tie was loosened and a cigarette that was little more than a filter smoldered from between his fingertips. He waved as he saw me.

My nose wrinkled at the intense smell of the Slowburn Lights. "You wanted to see me, Dean?"

He breathed out a cloud of smoke as he snubbed his cigarette butt on the ashtray top of a nearby trash bin. "I did. How did everything go? You're still in once piece, so IA couldn't have treated you too badly."

"They were professionals," I said, fanning away the smoke. "Extremely *thorough* professionals, but they didn't pressure me or trick me in any way. They were just doing their jobs."

Dean nodded. "They get a bad rap, but they have the department's best interests at heart. What kind of an entity would we be if we weren't beholden to the same rules we enforce upon others? I think officers think negatively of them because we usually face them at our worst, when we're defensive and tired and angry."

"*We?*"

Dean gave a reluctant smile. "I've been in your shoes, Phair. I didn't mention it this morning because... well, it didn't seem like the right moment. I just wanted to make sure you were prepared for what was to come."

"I was, thanks." I chewed my lip, thinking about the best way to phrase what I wanted to say. "So... you've killed someone in the line of duty, too?"

Dean took a package of cigarettes from his pocket and spun it between his fingers. "Only once, thankfully. It was during a raid on a suspect's home, someone who was wanted on kidnapping and sex trafficking charges as well as murder. Kind of a similar situation as what you went through this morning. The suspect was armed and tried to take a hostage. I fired. He bled out at the scene."

I wasn't sure what to say, but to be fair, I wasn't even sure how to feel about my own shooting.

Dean stared longingly at the cigarettes in his hand. "It's a tough thing to go through. You can feel fine one day only to find yourself riddled with guilt the next, even when you know the actions you took were a hundred percent justified. I think it's a survival mechanism. Our minds prioritize immediate physical concerns over emotional ones, but once you've gotten home and relaxed and you're on your own, that's when it can hit you. The mind's a complicated organ in that regard." Dean pursed his lips and stuffed the cigarettes back in his pocket, almost angrily.

"Well," I said after a pause. "Maybe it's a good thing I'm staying at Moss's place. Means I won't have any extended time to myself, even after I head home."

Dean's face relaxed as he pulled his attention away from the cigarettes. "Indeed. But what's important isn't simply being around others. The mind is good at putting off reflection until there's an opportune time. You have to know when to ask for help, and to be willing to accept it when it's offered."

I thought back to the conversation I'd had with Moss over coffee two morning ago. "We support each other, and we work as a team..."

Dean smiled. "That's right. It's important to pick each other up when we fall, but sometimes you have to let others know *when* you fall. They don't always notice."

I nodded. I honestly felt pretty good other than being tired, but it was nice to know I had friends there to help me if I needed them. "I'll try to be as honest with myself as I am with you and the gang."

Dean smirked, as if he already saw the logical loophole in

that statement. "There's one other thing you have to accept besides help though."

"Being?"

"A hot meal." Dean dug his keys out of his pocket. "You hungry?"

My stomach growled at the mere mention of food. "You weren't lying. You *have* been through a session with IA, haven't you?"

Dean's smile widened into something more genuine. "There's a taco truck that usually parks up the block on Seventh. I'm buying."

If I'd thought a weight had been lifted from my shoulders when the captain told me to report to HQ, then something even more magical happened as I walked to Dean's Viper. I'd had fanciful thoughts about Dean since the moment I laid eyes on him, with his broad shoulders and debonair style, but here he was, taking me out to eat, not on a date or as co-workers but as friends.

And I couldn't be more pleased about it.

CHAPTER TWENTY

The door was open when I arrived, so I knocked upon the closest bit of exposed wood. "Excuse me. Dr. Nelson?"

The man inside the office was of late middle age, with dark skin, a shaved head, and a beard that contained only a few brown hairs among the gray. He wore a sweater vest over a dress shirt and slacks, and there was a single golden earring in his right ear. He sat in an oversized blue suede chair with a book open in his lap. He lifted his head and gave a reserved smile. "You must be Penelope Phair."

I took a step inside the office, which almost perfectly resembled what I imagined a psychiatrist's office would look like. There were matching bookshelves against opposite walls, each filled with all manner of tomes: fat, skinny, paperbacks, leather-bound doorstops, some dog-eared, some pristine. There was a desk against the far side, but most of the room was open, populated only by the doctor's chair and another similar one, this one more green than blue. "Yes, sir. Officer Phair reporting."

The man's eyes twinkled. "Please, don't call me sir. I may be

surrounded by police, but I'm not a member of the department.
In here, you're not Officer Phair. You're Miss Phair, or Penelope
if you prefer. You're welcome to call me either Gerrold or
Doctor Nelson. This is an informal setting."

The office around him supported his position, but the rest of
police HQ outside made a different argument.

Nelson sensed my hesitation. "Come in. Close the door and
have a seat."

I did as the man asked, settling into the large blue-green
chair opposite him. It looked stiff and uninviting, but upon
settling myself into it, I found it was anything but. It was the
perfect reading chair: comfortable, supportive, with just the
right amount of give.

Dr. Nelson placed his book on a side table to his right.
"Have you ever had a session with a psychiatrist, Miss Phair?"

I pulled my eyes from the diplomas and framed photographs
hanging from the walls. "Ah... no. It's not an experience I've
ever craved. No offense."

"Why is that?" asked Dr. Nelson. "You don't like to talk
about your feelings?"

"Not particularly, but more importantly, I don't want
someone to tell me I should be medicated because of circumstances outside my control. I didn't grow up in the most
nurturing environment, and I came out okay without drugs,
thanks."

Nelson pursed his lips. "A troubled childhood. A clear
distrust of authority. You're not the sort who normally joins the
police department, Miss Phair."

"I guess I'm an anomaly."

Nelson smiled and held up a hand. "My apologies. It's in my

nature to analyze, but the past isn't why you're here. I'll do my best to determine your state of mind and let sleeping dogs lie. And you needn't worry about me forcing medications on you. Some psychiatrists rightfully receive bad reputations for attempting to solve all psychological problems with drugs, but I don't adhere to that school of thought. I think most problems can be solved by talking through them. Medication is a last resort."

I settled further into my seat, Nelson's mellow voice putting me at ease. I wondered if it was his natural tone or if he'd perfected it through years of practice. "So what do I need to do to convince you I'm fit for duty?"

Nelson snickered. "As the tough cop might say in interrogation, I'll be asking the questions here, Miss Phair. Why don't we start with last night. How did you sleep?"

"Fine," I lied. I'd actually tossed and turned for hours, but it wasn't entirely because of the shooting. I couldn't get TCK off my mind, either.

Nelson's lips turned slightly toward the floor. "Hmm. Do you have a headache?"

I shook my head. "No." Though in truth, I didn't feel that great due to the poor sleep.

"What about nausea?" he asked. "An upset stomach? Loss of appetite?"

"I didn't feel like eating much this morning, but I think that's mostly because I was nervous about coming to this session."

Nelson brightened. "At last, a truthful answer. Feels good, doesn't it? Perhaps we can funnel that newfound honesty into the rest of our conversation, hmm? If nothing else, it would make things go quicker."

I sighed, only mildly surprised. "You've been doing this a long time, haven't you?"

"Thirty years next month."

I rolled my eyes. "Fine. I don't have a headache, but I'll admit I didn't sleep great last night. But it's not just because I, well... shot someone yesterday. I'm part of an investigative team. We're working a big case. It's weighing on all of us. I feel pressure to make breakthroughs. Plus I'm not even sleeping in my own bed. I just got out of a relationship, and I'm crashing at a co-worker's place. There's a lot going on."

"Indeed." Nelson crossed his legs, eying me with fatherly concern. "Why don't you tell me about the incident. In your own words."

I took a deep breath to keep my frustration at bay. At least I'd already honed my story from repeating it to IA a million times. "At nine twenty-three yesterday morning, Detective Moss and I heard two shots fired while at the former home of Sherryl Towns. We returned to our squad car and called dispatch—"

Nelson held up a hand. "Sorry to interrupt. I'm actually familiar with the details of your response. I received a copy of the report this morning and perused it before you arrived." He flicked a finger toward his desk. "What I meant was if you could expound upon how you felt, during the call and after the shooting. What thoughts crossed your mind, what your emotional state was. My apologies for being unclear."

"Oh." I blinked. The IA detectives had never once asked about my emotions during their interview. They'd purely been concerned with my actions. "Well, I suppose I was excited and nervous as Detective Moss and I responded to the call. I remember my heart beating hard in my chest from the adrenaline, and that only increased when the suspect fired shots into the lawn. I remember being very focused as I got into position at the back of the home. Time seemed to slow as the suspect emerged from the house with a hostage in his arms, and when I told him to freeze... I don't know. I don't remember thinking at all. I saw the flash of his gun and I reacted. I shot him without making a conscious decision to."

Nelson gave me a moment. "And afterwards?"

I found myself back in the moment without trying. "Moss came around the side of the house to check on me. I was in a bit of a daze, but my training kept me grounded. I didn't do anything to put myself or anyone else at risk. I holstered my weapon and cuffed the suspect while Moss cleared the home, and then... I lost track of things for a bit. I was in shock. I'd never shot anyone, and I'd certainly never..." I licked my lips, my tongue suddenly dry. "I'd never killed anyone."

I took another deep breath. Nelson didn't interrupt.

When I was ready, I kept going. "Moss helped me to the front of the house. Made me sit while additional backup arrived. She checked on me a few times as she took the lead on the case, but it's a bit of a blur. I started to come out of it as the paramedics arrived. My brain firmed up, for lack of a better term. Memory cleared as well. I was nervous at that point. That lasted most of the day, but it was mostly due to my interactions with IA. Now as I think back, the shooting seems... distant, if that makes sense. But I'm not wracked with guilt or fear or regret. I made the right call. I did what I had to do."

Nelson rapped his fingers against his knee. "The report suggests that, too, but being correct in your actions doesn't absolve you of guilt. It's not how the brain responds, at least not in the majority of the population. It's why soldiers who come back from war, even the ones who followed the rules, often deal with post-traumatic stress disorders, or why drivers involved in fatal car collisions often slide into depression."

"I don't think that's going to be a problem with me, Doctor," I said. "I'm way too busy to slide into anything at the moment."

Nelson lifted an eyebrow. "Is that so?"

"Absolutely. My team needs me. Well, maybe they don't. I'm an officer, after all, and they're detectives, but this case is..." I didn't know if I should share that I was working on the TCK murders. That seemed like need to know information. "To put it mildly, the case my team has been assigned is important. Please, Doctor. I need to get to work. I'll deal with this stuff once we close the case, I promise."

Nelson snorted and shook his head. "The funny thing is I'm certain you're still telling the truth, and yet you don't find issue with your proposal."

My brow furrowed. Had I accidentally said something psychologically taboo?

Doctor Nelson picked up on my confusion. "There are three types of reactions to traumatic events, Miss Phair. Mild or transitory reactions, where the individual involved is able to self-cope, largely by talking to friends and family. Intermediate, where post-traumatic symptoms can last for weeks or even months, and severe physiological disabilities, what is often referred to as a mental breakdown. Do you know which of those categories you fall into?"

"The mild one?"

"Incorrect," said Nelson. "At this point, it's impossible to classify your reaction because you're working so hard to suppress it. You haven't allowed yourself to face the reality of what you went through because you're so convinced there are other, more pressing concerns in front of you."

The doctor's words closely mirrored what Dean had told me the afternoon prior. "Isn't that a good thing, though? That I'm able to compartmentalize?"

"Maybe," said Nelson. "But maybe not. It kicks the can down the road. Ultimately, you have to face a problem to solve it, and you have to be honest with yourself and others to resolve it."

"Some problems go away on their own," I said. "Unreturned phone calls, for example…"

If Nelson wore glasses, he would've looked over them at me. "Not emotional problems, Miss Phair."

I sighed. So much for acing my interview with the one person who could decide to let me stay on the job. "Does this mean I have to stay at home and stew until I reach some sort of epiphany? Or have a breakdown?"

Nelson shrugged. "Given your condition, I don't see how isolating you would help in any way. Right now, what you need is a support system ready and willing to offer aid if and when you're ready to deal with the emotional aftermath of your actions."

I blinked. "So… you *are* sending me back to work?"

Nelson rose from his chair and moved to his desk. "If you were experiencing even intermediate symptoms, I wouldn't recommend it, but under the circumstances, I don't see the harm—provided you stay away from stressful situations. I'm recommending you return to desk work only. No responding to active calls, and defiantly no taking part in situations where you could be a danger to yourself or others. I'll be sure to stress that when I speak to Captain Ellison over the phone."

I shot to my feet. "Really? Thank you, Doctor! I mean, I'll be sure to do that. Not put myself or others at risk, I mean."

Nelson regarded me with another of those concerned, fatherly glances. "To be clear, Miss Phair, I'm not giving you a clean bill of health. I'll want to have more sessions with you in the future to check on your progress. I'm simply saying that continuing to work in a supportive environment won't hinder your progress. But progress *does* need to be made. Sooner or later, you'll have to confront what you did, and only then will we be able to see how deep the wound is."

I swallowed and nodded. It wasn't exactly the diagnosis I was hoping for, but it would have to do.

CHAPTER TWENTY-ONE

I headed for the war room as soon as I arrived at the precinct, but I didn't find Dean, Moss, or Justice there. Virgil Mason sat at the center of the conference table. A rust-colored suit hung over his broad frame, and next to him on the table rested a dark brown trilby hat. A number of reports were spread around, as were several photos plucked from their midst.

He glanced up at the sound of my entrance. "Morning, Officer."

"Morning, Mason," I said. "Just you here this morning?"

"For the time being." He flipped a page on his report, seemingly in no rush to make small talk. "I heard about the call you responded to yesterday. How are you holding up?"

I sighed. "Everyone and their mother has asked me that over the past twenty-four hours. Not that I don't appreciate your concern, but I'd rather not keep regurgitating the same canned response over and over again. No offense."

"None taken," said Mason. "When too many people show

concern, it can come across as perfunctory rather than genuine, and there are few things worse than false empathy. I'll get out of your hair in a moment. I was about to head over to MCD to share some theories with Glenwell and Hawkins."

"*Theories?*" I leaned over the table. "What sorts of theories?"

A smirk grew over Mason's face, almost as if he knew how I'd respond to that lure. "About the relevance of the tarot cards. Pull up a chair."

I headed around the conference table and took a seat next to him. He pushed his chair out so he could watch me as easily as the evidence in front of him. "You'll recall I wanted to delve into the nuances of the tarot deck."

"Yeah. You said you were going to study the meanings of the cards, see if you could spot a pattern between the cards left at the murder scenes and the victims."

Mason nodded. "I spent the rest of that first day gathering resources and most of yesterday reading. As I'd suspected, tarot is richly steeped in meaning, at least the divination side of it is. There are competing schools of thought about what the cards symbolize. Some argue the meaning of each card is rigid, while others think each card can have different meanings depending on when it's played, how it's played, and its proximity to other cards. That made me start thinking if the order in which the cards were assigned to the victims was important, or if the placement of the cards on the victims was a clue. Face up, face down, facing the victim, facing away. It was too damn confusing. And then, this morning, I developed a compelling new theory."

I leaned in. "Which is?"

Mason watched me intently, his eyes as flay and gray as

ever. "That the killer doesn't know a damned thing about tarot, or at least not much more than I did two days ago."

I deflated a little. "You think the cards are being placed randomly? That they're another red herring?"

Mason wagged a finger. "Not necessarily. What I'm saying is the cards might've been picked based upon superficial, exoteric qualities rather than anything more nuanced."

I frowned.

Mason plucked a report and some photographs and pushed everything else out of the way. "Consider this. Victim number one. Sherryl Towns. Left with a corner of the Star Card on her body." Mason took a card from what appeared to be a brand new tarot deck and laid it next to the rest. "This is the same type of deck as the one TCK used, so we should be able to compare apples to apples. As mentioned previously, the Star Card is known for conveying themes of hope and inspiration. Putting that aside, what do you see?"

"In the card?" I asked.

Mason nodded.

I picked it up. "There's a naked woman on it. She's next to a pond, cupping the water. It's nighttime, and the stars are out."

Mason tapped one of the photos he'd left before him. "Now what do you see in this photograph?"

It was one of the images of Miss Towns. I swallowed hard, trying not to focus on the unnatural twist of her head. "I see the victim. She's clothed, wearing a dress. Lying on concrete, next to some bushes. She was murdered at nighttime, but these photos were taken in the morning."

"Look closer. In fact, there's a better photo. A closer view. Here." Mason plucked another photograph and handed it to me.

This photo was a closeup of one of Sherryl's hands. I wasn't sure why the crime scene photographer had been interested in them. Perhaps they'd been trying to determine if she'd fought back against her attacker. "I'm not sure. Her hands look to be in good condition. Skin is a little pale, but I'm not an expert on lividity."

"The dress, Officer."

I blinked, surprised I hadn't noticed before. "There's a star motif on it."

"Star Card, star print fabric," said Mason. "As I said. Superficial."

I set the photograph down, thinking. "So he chose the Star Card for her because of her dress? Everything we know about TCK suggests he's devious and clever. This seems... too simple."

"Perhaps TCK intended the tarot as a red herring, but he's subconsciously picking cards for each victim based on aesthetics or obvious traits. Everyone has blind spots, even meticulous individuals."

"What about the other women?" I asked. "Were they all wearing clothing with a connection to the tarot cards left to them?"

Mason frowned. "Unfortunately, no. Victim two, Ellowyn Farview, was left the Ten of Pentacles. The card itself depicts an old man with dogs at his feet, none of which matches anything found at the scene, but as I mentioned, the most common theme associated with that card is wealth. And..." Mason held out a hand.

"Miss Farview was a wealthy socialite," I said. "It's a superficial attribute."

"Exactly."

I cast my eyes across the reports. "What about the third victim? Miss Richards?"

Mason flicked though his tarot deck and handed me the Queen of Wands. "That's where I'm hitting a wall. The obvious themes with that card aren't particularly tangible, and the card itself shows an abundance of items. A queen, a sunflower, a staff, a cat, statues of lions. Nothing I've seen of Miss Richards suggests a connection to those items. Similarly, Lacy Breen was left with the six of cups, which features flowers and children on the card. Again, there's no obvious link there."

I pursed my lips. "There's got to be a connection. We just haven't found it yet."

Mason blew out a slow breath. "Or TCK realized his subconscious was influencing his choice of cards, and he put a stop to it."

I froze, his words cutting like a knife. "You believe that?"

"Doesn't matter what I believe," said Mason. "What matters is there's no evidence one way or the other, which means more investigation is needed. Are you going to continue your search of the victims' homes?"

I relaxed a little. Apparently, even the suggestion of another dead end was enough to put me on edge. "I don't know. It's up to Dean, or maybe Glenwell."

Mason gathered his tarot cards and stood. "Well, I'd like to tag along if possible. One more set of eyes couldn't hurt, and it's possible we could find the connection we're missing with the third or fourth cards. I'll touch base with Dean later, see if he's okay with it."

"Speaking of Dean, do you have any idea where he is?"

Mason headed toward the door. "Sure. Last I know he was

headed to the morgue to get a report on Miss Breen. He only left a few minutes before you arrived."

I shot to my feet. As enthralling as Mason's theories might've been, I wouldn't have sat through them if I'd known doing so meant missing out on new evidence. I thanked Mason and hustled past him toward the stairs.

CHAPTER TWENTY-TWO

There was a chill in the air as I reached the morgue, but that wasn't anything new. The entire basement of the Fifth was perpetually cool no matter the season, but the morgue was a few degrees cooler than even the records room or the mysterious, dark sections of the basement populated by bats and gremlins. Perhaps the architects who'd built the place had known more about air flow and thermodynamics than their successors gave them credit for. Then again, maybe the chill was more mental than physical. There was something undeniably creepy about being in a room filled with dead people, after all.

I found Detectives Dean and Justice alongside Coroner Jowynn, all of them standing next to one of the morgue's gleaming stainless steel examination tables. The table itself was covered by a white sheet, but the topography of the sheet made it clear there was a person underneath it. Lacy Breen, perhaps?

"Detectives," I said, somewhat out of breath from my quick descent. "Emmett. Sorry I'm late."

"Technically, you can't be late if you're not invited in the first place," said Justice.

I blinked, taken aback. "Sorry. I didn't realize I wasn't supposed to be here."

Dean rolled his eyes in the big detective's direction. "Don't mind Justice's lack of decorum. What he meant to say is none of us expected you back at the precinct today. The psychiatrist cleared you?"

"To a degree. I'm not cleared for active duty, just investigation, and I'm supposed to avoid stressful situations." *And at some point, I'm supposed to face myself and confront the reality of what I did,* I thought, *but there would be time for that later.*

"No stressful situations?" said Justice. "That rules out pretty much everything that happens within these walls. Even getting the coffee maker started in the morning qualifies."

Emmett Jowynn smiled. He didn't look as mussed as he usually did, though he still looked underdressed in his white lab coat next to Dean and Justice. "Well, I for one am glad to see you back. I heard about things yesterday. Must've been tough."

I was glad he hadn't asked me how I felt. "Thanks, Emmett. So, did I miss anything?" I glanced at the sheet covering the table next to us.

"Coroner Jowynn gave us his full report on Lacy Breen's death," said Dean. "We were bouncing some ideas around."

My shoulders sagged. I hadn't been quick enough. "Oh."

Emmett might've been scatterbrained, but he picked up on my emotional cues. "I could give you a quick recap. Wouldn't take but a minute."

"Might as well," said Dean. "We need to be on the same page if we're to advance the investigation."

I brightened, and Emmett smiled. "Perfect. First things first, as I initially suspected, Miss Breen was stabbed to death. Her official cause of death is massive hemorrhage combined with organ failure as a result of trauma, specifically hemopericardium. That occurs when blood fills the pericardial sac of the heart. Based on the size and nature of the wounds, it's clear a pointed, non-bladed instrument was used. An ice pick is the most likely culprit, but there are any number of items that could've been used, from over the counter tools to improvised weapons. Further examination of her body beyond the stab wounds didn't reveal additional injuries that would normally be associated with a violent struggle: no bruising, no scratches, no fractures, not even any skin under her fingernails beyond her own. Well, that's not entirely true. There was some bruising on the back of Miss Breen's skull and in her gluteus, as well as a fracture in her coccyx, all of which is consistent with Miss Breen falling backwards to the concrete upon being stabbed. None of the wounds appear to have occurred post-mortem, and CSU's parallel investigation didn't find any physical evidence of her attacker on her, so no hair, blood, et cetera. Am I missing anything?" Emmett glanced at Dean.

"No evidence of sexual assault," said Dean. "Which is consistent with the rest of TCK's murders."

Emmett bobbed his head. "Right. I was filing that under no physical evidence, but it's good to clarify. One thing I'll add that the detectives and I were discussing is how abnormal it is to have a stabbing such as this without those additional signs of struggle. Miss Breen suffered a total of twenty-seven puncture wounds to her torso and abdomen, none of which seemed to have grazed her anywhere else. To land even a few hard thrusts upon a victim who is struggling for her life without catching a stray arm or shoulder is hard enough, let alone over two dozen. It suggests Miss Breen's attacker caught her off guard and stunned her with a fast initial strike, which then caused her to fall and hit her head. Perhaps she was disoriented enough from that for the attacker to fall upon her and deliver the rest of the blows without disruption."

"It makes sense," said Justice, "but Coroner Jowynn wasn't able to identify any blows among the twenty seven that hit the heart or another spot that would cause such a severe initial shock, nor was he able to conclusively prove most of those stabbings came after Miss Breen fell to the pavement."

Emmett shrugged apologetically. "There are limits to forensic science, I'm afraid. I wish I could be of more help, but my work is limited to interpreting medical results, not inferring anything beyond that." Emmett smiled as he turned to me. "Since you're here though, Phair, have you given any thought as to what you'd like me to do with the rat?"

Despite his stoic demeanor, Dean had an expressive face. Still, I'd never known his eyebrows could rise *that* high until now. *"The rat?"*

Between the case being handed to MCD and the shooting, it had slipped my mind. "Right. One of the CSU techs found a dead rat up the alley from where we found Miss Breen. She couldn't exactly box it up with the rest of the evidence, so I asked Emmett if he could hold it in cold storage."

Justice's face wasn't as limber as Dean's, but his eyebrows had also gone through some gymnastics. "The better question is why you considered a dead rat in an alley evidence."

Dean and Justice's confused looks made me feel foolish for thinking I'd stumbled across something worth investigating. "A dead rat by itself isn't anything notable, not in this city, but I remembered after the murder in Miller's Creek Park you mentioned a dead squirrel had been found near the body of Miss Richards. You made a point of asking about it because I'd seen a squirrel run across my path the night before. I know a squirrel and a rat aren't the same, but they're both small rodents. Maybe it's not a coincidence."

Justice didn't look convinced, but Dean's brow drew down. "You know, there was a dead bird found not far from the scene of Miss Towns' murder. Something small, I think. Maybe a sparrow. I didn't see it myself, but someone photographed it. It made its way into the murder book."

Now Justice turned thoughtful, too. "What about near Ellowyn Farview's car crash?"

Dean shook his head. "Nothing that was reported, but that murder hasn't fit the mold of any of the others. It's still the biggest mystery, in my mind. This dead animal business might be worth looking into. Maybe we're grasping at straws, but there could be a connection there..."

Dean drifted off, his eyes focused far away.

Emmett looked at us expectantly. "So, ah... should I hold onto the rat then?"

Dean blinked and turned toward the coroner. "No. We need to investigate it. Figure out if there's anything suspicious about its demise. Are you able to perform an autopsy on it?"

"Necropsy," said Emmett.

Dean lifted an eyebrow. "Huh?"

Emmett's face went through some contortions. "Sorry. Autopsies are performed on humanoids. Necropsies are performed on animals. But to answer your question, I suppose I'd be *able* to. In terms of the cutting and prodding. But I'm not trained in rodent physiology. I wouldn't know what to look for to see how it died. I could call a veterinarian friend, though. I know a couple."

Dean tapped his middle finger against his thumb, his look still distant. "Do that. I don't want to leave any stone unturned... or any rat undissected."

"So what's next, Dean?" asked Justice. "Do you have a plan of attack while we wait on the, ah, rat necropsy?"

Dean nodded, his visage becoming more focused. "Yes. Phair was working on re-cataloguing the victims' homes, looking for evidence that might've been overlooked. That got pushed to the side because of yesterday's call, but I still think it's a decent avenue to pursue. Phair, I want you to keep at it. Moss is otherwise engaged, but Justice could go with you. I've got a few more details to pursue regarding Miss Breen."

Justice gave me a nod, and together we headed toward the parking garage.

CHAPTER TWENTY-THREE

J
ustice's boat-like Phantom rumbled and groaned as we pulled up outside the compact fourplex that was the former home of our third victim, Maggie Richards. The building itself was quaint, a red brick structure with two basement apartments and two surface ones that were elevated four or five feet above street level. Something other than the building itself drew my attention, though. A conspicuous Howardson Crown Royal was parked in front of the structure, the same model as for police cruisers but painted a flat brown instead of the traditional black and white.

Justice killed the engine and we got out. As we did so, a man emerged from the Crown Royal, his rusty suit looking particularly red against the mocha of the car.

"Mason," said Justice as we reached the sidewalk. "What are you doing here?"

Virgil Mason bobbed his head as he joined us, but he didn't remove his hat. "Waiting for the two of you. Detective Dean said you'd be here soon, if you weren't already done with Miss Farview's apartment."

"He supported you being a part of the search?" I asked.

"He didn't have a problem with it," he said. "More importantly, Detective Glenwell wanted me present. She thinks my theory about the tarot cards might have teeth."

Justice's brow furrowed. "I feel like I missed something."

"Mason might've found a link between the tarot cards and the victims," I said. "Miss Towns was left a piece of the Star Card while wearing a star print dress. Miss Farview was left the Ten of Pentacles, which symbolizes wealth, and she was a wealthy socialite."

"Speaking of," said Mason. "Did you find anything at her home that exhibited a connection to the card? Anything stronger than the theme of her wealth? Pentacles or pentagrams? Imagery of dogs or old men?"

"Dogs and old men?" said Justice. "Not unless you count her part-time boyfriends or the pictures of her dad."

Mason didn't laugh. He didn't even smile. I wasn't sure he understood the concept.

"Nothing that hadn't been catalogued in the reports," I said. "Honestly, it was a boring, dispiriting exercise."

Mason grunted. "Maybe I'll head there myself later, see if I can pick up on anything the two of you missed. In the meantime, let's focus our attentions here. I already told Phair, Detective Justice, but I haven't been able to match any element of the card to Miss Richards' murder." He dug in his jacket pocket and produced his tarot deck. He opened it, slid out the cards, and picked one of the ones on top. "For the record, we're looking for anything represented on the card. Anything related to royalty, sunflowers, staffs, cats, or lions could be a clue."

"A clue to what?" asked Justice.

"That's to be determined," said Mason. "While the cards

could be a red herring, it's possible TCK is picking his victims to fit a narrative. If we can understand the narrative, there's a chance we'll be able to predict the next victim."

Justice didn't look convinced, but I think he was just grumpy he had to postpone his lunch to search homes he'd already gone through. "Alright. You know the drill, and I assume everyone has read the reports. Glove up, and be thorough."

We descended to the basement apartment on the right side of the building, brushing the police tape aside as we headed in. Whereas Miss Towns and Miss Farview's apartments had been diametrical opposites—one small and old and minimally furnished, the other sprawling and dripping in luxury— Maggie's apartment was somewhere in the middle. There was a new matching fridge and stove set in the kitchen. A lacquered radio acted as a centerpiece in the living room, and thick rugs had been placed over much of the cold, polished concrete floor. Miss Richards had clearly made choices about where to spend her budget, though, as many of the furniture pieces were second-hand.

Justice spoke over his shoulder. "I'll start in the bedroom. You guys tackle the living room and kitchen."

I slid into the living room before Mason could claim it as his own. I'd been stuck with kitchen duty in Ellowyn's apartment, and I didn't relish going through the same space again. Kitchens weren't known for being great hiding places of incriminating evidence, other than bodies stuffed into ice chests.

There was an oval-shaped coffee table in the living space, and a glass, now empty, rested upon a cork coaster. The sides were dusty, still coated with a fine layer of the powder CSU applied before looking for prints. A couple half-height bookshelves stood against the walls, each of them two-thirds full. One of them appeared to hold nothing but legal texts, which made sense given Maggie's profession, but the other was filled with fiction, romance if the titles were any indication. I spotted *The Passionate Embrace, The Burning Flame,* and *A Heartfelt Flutter,* among a few more scandalous titles.

I knelt and brought the novels off the shelf one at a time, inspecting each and every cover. It wasn't a particularly tedious chore—many of the covers featured illustrations of handsome men in various stages of undress—but I didn't look at them to be titillated. The point of the search was to be thorough, and as Mason had emphasized, everything could be a piece of evidence. The law texts mostly had leather bindings, but there was imagery galore on the romance novels. First, I set aside a book titled *Tonight, A Knight,* the cover of which featured a woman in a flowing dress laying by a moonlit pool with a knight in armor kneeling beside her. A knight wasn't precisely a royal theme, but it was close enough that I figured it deserved extra attention. Then I set aside a book titled *The Woodsman.* The shirtless man on the cover had a full beard and a bow slung across his back, but it was the walking stick in his hand that made me pause. Did it qualify as a staff, as on the Queen of Wands card? Another book made the pile, this one titled *Adventure in the Jungle.* It featured a muscular man in a loincloth protecting a woman from an advancing lion in the deepest heart of a tropical forest. Either the cover artist didn't know or didn't care that lions don't live in the jungle, but regardless of the geographical inaccuracies, I put it with the rest because of the feline themes.

I stood, giving my knees a needed break. I stared at the

books I'd set atop the shelf, as well as the shelf I'd yet to get to. "Mason."

The criminal profiler looked up from the drawer he had open. He responded by grunting.

"I might've found something. Three somethings, to be precise, and I'm not even close to done."

He came over, looking at the books I'd set on the shelf. "The imagery is a possible fit." He grabbed *The Woodsman* and flipped it to the copyright page. "Published seven years ago. Book doesn't look new. Clear signs of wear at the edges. Have you flipped through these to see if there are any notes written in the margins?"

"Not yet," I said.

"Do that. If you find something, we'll go from there, but I don't think these mean anything."

"Is that a gut feeling?" I asked.

Mason looked at me with mild disdain. "If I'm right that the tarot cards have been picked for each victim rather than left randomly, then it stands to reason TCK picked the cards based on traits he was able to discern, like Miss Towns' dress or Miss Farview's wealth. These books don't fit that profile, not unless he spotted Miss Richards reading one in public, which I doubt given the nature of the novels. Besides, if a romance novel was the motivation behind this kill, why not pick a different card? The Lover, or perhaps the Two of Cups? This doesn't feel right to me. I'm looking for something more visual."

I stared at the books. My gut told me Mason was right. "Dean thinks there's a possibility TCK visited his victims' apartments. That's why he asked me to search them, but you seem to think he picked his victims based on what he saw on the street, when they were out and about. Are we wasting our time here?"

"I wouldn't be here if I thought that," said Mason. "For TCK to have pulled off each murder as cleanly as he did, he had to have planned thoroughly. Part of that is knowing your victim. Stalking them. It's entirely possible he was here, or at least in the near vicinity. What I'm trying to understand is what he saw that might've influenced him."

Justice's deep voice echoed throughout the apartment. "Phair. Mason. Come check this out."

I followed the sound of his rich basso into Maggie's bedroom. There, Justice stood in front of a dresser, on the top of which was a jewelry box. The box had been opened, and before it on the dresser was a small, rectangular container.

"What did you find?" I asked.

"Could be nothing. Then again..." Justice trailed off as he lifted the rectangular cardboard box. It was edged with golden trim and the brand, Virginia's, was embossed on the side. "Hard to know the age of something by looking at it, but the box is pristine. No wear on the edges at all."

"So?" said Mason. "I'm not seeing any of the imagery we talked about."

Justice lifted a finger and opened the box. He rotated it to show us the contents. On a thin cotton pad lay a silver or white gold necklace with a fine chain. No jewel hung from it, though. Instead, the pendant was cast from the same metal as the chain, forming the shape of a cat. Not any cat, either. It sat on its hind legs, ears perked, staring straight forward—just as the one on the Queen of Wands was.

"Now that," said Mason, reaching out to take it, "is what we're looking for. Something visual. Wearable. Something TCK might've spotted on Miss Richards."

"The box looks brand new," said Justice. "If she'd worn this, I imagine she'd only done so once or twice."

"Which suits us perfectly," said Mason. "If she'd only worn this necklace in public a couple times, that allows us to narrow the opportunities for TCK to have crossed her path. Maybe she'd never worn it at all. Perhaps TCK saw her purchase this at a jewelry store. Regardless of the details—" Mason smiled as he lifted the necklace. "This could be our first genuine lead on TCK."

CHAPTER TWENTY-FOUR

I sat at the war room conference table, phone in hand. Next to me, a crumpled sandwich wrapper crinkled as it slowly expanded. A waxed paper soft drink cup that had once held cola tinkled as the last clump of ice inside it collapsed into the pool of melted ice at the base. Sweat ran across my ear. It was hot and tender from where I'd been pressing a receiver against it for the last hour.

The speaker crackled and a voice came on the line. "Hello, Officer Phair?"

"Yes?" I responded.

"We have a copy of *Tonight, A Knight,* but I'm afraid *Adventure in the Jungle* is out of stock and we don't carry *The Woodsman* at all."

I sighed. I'd been on hold for close to ten minutes. "There seems to have been a misunderstanding. I'm not interested in purchasing any of these books. What I need to know is if you carry them and when you last sold any copies. You've answered the first question, but the second question is more important."

"Oh." The woman on the line's voice drooped. "Well, that's

trickier. I'll have to dig through our receipts. I could probably find our purchase orders a little easier. Let you know when we last received orders from the printer."

On the other side of the table, Virgil Mason spoke into his phone, giving details about the necklace to jewelers. Despite the fact that he thought the pendant was the more enticing clue, he didn't want to dismiss the romance novels entirely, so I'd been tasked with contacting booksellers to try and trace who might've purchased the novels. Frankly, I didn't think I had much of a chance of getting anywhere. Maggie's books hadn't appeared brand new, and even if I did track down the bills of sale for years old novels, how was that supposed to lead to the Tarot Card Killer? Books were mass-produced. These titles had undoubtedly sold thousands of copies. Maybe more.

I reminded myself I'd specifically requested to remain on the case in lieu of resting at home and getting some reading done. It was enough to suppress a growl of irritation. "Once again, ma'am, the purchase orders aren't going to help. I need to know when you sold them."

"Okay, well, I can dig up the receipts, I guess. But it'll take some time..."

I lost track of the conversation as Justice barged into the room, file in hand. He carried it high, fanning it as he moved. "Guys. Think I might've found something."

I spoke into the receiver quickly. "Um, sure, sure. Have the results sent to the Fifth Street Precinct as soon as you have them, attention Detective Dean. Thanks."

I hung up the phone. Mason's conversation met a similarly rapid demise. He pushed his phone to the side as Justice closed the door behind him. "What have you got?"

Justice opened the beige folder and set it on the table

between us. "A police report from a few weeks ago. A pawn shop got hit six days before the murder of Maggie Richards. Seaside Pawn. Name's a misnomer. Place is actually on First and Crabtree, but that's besides the point. What matters is what got taken."

Mason grabbed the file before I had a chance to do the same. He scanned the report, his eyes darting across the text until he got to the bottom of the page. "A collection of Virginia's Jewelry was stolen. Condition: new, still in box. Specifically, the items included a fourteen karat gold ring with a sapphire gemstone, a floral brooch inlaid with garnets, and a white gold necklace with a pendant in the shape of a cat sitting on its hind legs." Mason looked up from the page, his eyes slightly wider than before. "Of course. TCK stole the necklace. He wouldn't risk leaving a paper trail of the purchase."

I blinked. "Wait... Maggie didn't buy the necklace herself? We're now assuming TCK planted the necklace in her apartment?"

Mason's brow furrowed in thought. "It makes sense from a profiling perspective. Each of TCK's murders has been meticulously planned and executed. It takes time to do that. Chances are he picks his victims first and, as he comes to know them, assigns them a specific tarot card that fits the narrative he's created for them. If no narrative presents itself, though? He writes his own."

"I don't think we should assume the necklace was planted," said Justice. "He could've mailed it, presented it as a gift from an admirer. Or he could've given it to her in person. I doubt that, but if TCK did meet Miss Richards before the murder, that would be a huge breakthrough for the investigation."

The entire premise that Maggie hadn't bought the item

herself seemed off to me, but it seemed like too big a coincidence to think the precise item we found in her home had been stolen a few days before her death. Then again, it seemed as if I was the only one to question why TCK had broken into any of his victims' apartments, and apparently I was wrong about that, too. "We should look into the break-in. I'm assuming there haven't been any arrests in the case, yet."

Justice shook his head. "Burglary hasn't even touched this one. I'd guess there's either a backlog of cases or this pawn shop is on someone's shit list."

"Not the shit list," said Mason. "More like the do not touch list."

Justice and I gave him our best confused frowns.

Mason took our looks with the same impassiveness he took everything else. "Seaside Pawn is owned by the Keymoiras. It's a mob business. I figured you guys knew. The detectives who were assigned the case probably knew better than to bother." Mason flipped through the report. "The patrol officers did their due diligence, though. They canvassed the scene. Even got a witness who claims to have seen the break-in."

"A vagrant, yes," said Justice with a nod. "But the description is vague. Human male, five-eight to six-two. Dark hair. Possible beard. I mean, really? *Possible?* That makes everything in that description suspect."

"We have to follow it, though." Mason picked up the phone. "I know some people in burglary, including down at the Old Town Precinct where this occurred. Hello, Operator? Get me Detective Blackmaul at Old Town."

Justice finally took a seat, the chair squealing in misery as he settled into it. "I guess we could try to find the vagrant. See if we could get a more concrete description out of the guy."

"Things may not be as hopeless as they seem," said Mason. "The fact that it's a mob owned pawn might help narrow the field. I have to think only a select crew of guys would be willing to hit it, perhaps from rival gangs. Hello? Blackmaul. It's Virgil Mason from profiling."

I leaned across the table as Mason settled into his conversation, speaking low to Justice. "Are we really going to spend time and effort tracking down this vagrant? You yourself said the description is probably bogus. Do we really think a random hobo is going to be the key to taking down TCK?"

Justice shrugged. "Major criminals have been taken down by lesser infractions than breaking and entering. Fact of the matter is, law-breakers don't stick to one type of crime. I may not put a lot of stock in that description, but this lead is the real deal."

Mason's phone clattered as he tossed it onto the base. He pushed himself from his chair and grabbed his hat. "I think we might be on to something. I'm off for some files. Be back in an hour."

Mason didn't invite either of us to come with him, and the door clattered shut behind him. I grabbed my drink and slurped up the cool water left at the bottom of the cup. "What do you want to do in the interim? Find this vagrant? What's his name?"

"I don't know," said Justice. "It's in the report somewhere. If I'm being honest, I don't feel much like trolling the streets with my eyes peeled for this guy. I'm going to get a coffee instead, maybe touch base with the gang unit, see what they can tell me about the Keymoiras." Justice glanced at my empty paper cup. "You want anything?"

I shook my head. "I'm reasonably awake. Thanks, though."

Justice nodded and headed out. I busied myself with

reading the burglary report, hoping to find something Justice and Mason had missed. Unfortunately, I failed. The description of the stolen necklace seemed to match the one we found, but none of the other goods rang a bell.

When I finished with the report, I tried to make myself useful, calling homeless shelters and the other precincts to see if they had the named vagrant in custody. Patrolling the streets wasn't the only way to find the homeless after all, and this seemed like a more fruitful avenue than the bookstores. I'd made it through all the shelters I could think of and a couple stations when Justice returned, this time with Dean in tow.

It was immediately obvious a change had occurred within Alton. Gone was the sense of tired uncertainty I'd noticed in him since Lacy's death. In its place the focused, intent Dean had returned. He wanted us to share every detail with him about our trip to Maggie Richard's apartment, not just the necklace but the romance novels, too. He took it all in quietly, only asking questions to clarify details, nodding throughout.

We'd almost finished discussing the Seaside Pawn report when Mason returned, a cardboard filing box in hand. He nodded. "Dean. Good to see you back. Have Justice and Phair brought you up to speed?"

Dean eyed Mason's armload. "Mostly. What's in the box?"

"Leads, hopefully. You're just in time to help sort through them." Mason deposited the box on the table and tipped open the lid. "Detective Blackmaul at Old Town wasn't as useful as I'd hoped, but he agreed that if we focus on rival gang members, specifically those with known feuds with the Keymoiras, we might be able to find someone who fits the bill. I don't even know if all these guys fit the description the vagrant gave, but it's somewhere to start." He pulled out as many folders as he could grab. "Everyone take a stack and start reading."

Justice passed out stacks to me and Dean. I accepted mine, looking at it dubiously. "I'm not entirely sure I understand the plan. We know the suspect's description is suspect, no pun intended, so how are we supposed to narrow the field? We can't exactly bring all these guys in and question them about where they were the night of the pawn shop burglary."

Mason smiled, I think for only the second time since I'd met him. "That's the beauty of profiling. We don't need a physical description. What we're looking for is a certain type of individual. Someone violent. Careful. Probably a loner. If they have mommy issues, that's a plus. These records won't tell us everything, but with luck they'll tell us enough. Let's get to work."

We all dove in with as much enthusiasm as could be hoped for in reading reports. Justice left and came back with more coffee. This time, I accepted some, but I'd only gotten halfway through my mug when I arrived at the last file in my stack. My brow creased as I read the report, and my throat went dry.

I didn't bother reaching for the coffee. "Guys?" I croaked. "I might have something."

Dean looked up from his literature. "Yes?"

"Gregory Lloyd Cassman," I said. "Ex-military. Dishonorably discharged after getting in an altercation with a commanding officer, then he went to prison on domestic assault charges. Put his girlfriend in the hospital for three weeks. Once he got out, he fell off the map—until he showed up working for the Treyvell crime family a couple years ago. And this is his mugshot."

I held out the photograph for everyone to see. Cassman was

human. Tall, but not too tall, with dark brown hair, and at the time, a closely cropped beard.

Mason looked at the photograph almost reverentially. "Dean. This is it. This is our guy."

Dean's eyes didn't stray. "I know. Give me the phone. I need to call a judge about a warrant."

CHAPTER TWENTY-FIVE

The sun had dipped below the horizon, but a purplish haze lashed with streaks of fading pink still hung in the sky. Far in the distance, the moon glowed a pale yellow, the same color as the streetlights overhead. Cassman's home sat in the middle of my field of view, an old single story flat with a mottled brick exterior and overgrown bushes in front. Dean, Moss, Justice, and a patrol officer by the name of Hutchison huddled in front of a detached garage one house over, their cars parked a block away. They waited as their clocks ticked toward seven thirty, at which point they would move in, as would the team in position around the back of the home. Meanwhile, I sat in an unmarked car five houses down, watching the whole thing with bated breath as Officer Hutchison's partner, Loudon, watched over me.

I'd pleaded with Dean to let me come—heck, some might say I'd begged—but he wasn't swayed by my emotional appeal. He made it clear I wasn't supposed to be at work at all. It was only because he and the captain went out on a limb for me that I wasn't stuck at home, missing everything entirely, and even if he wasn't concerned with breaking protocol, he wouldn't let me join out of concern for my wellbeing. Though he didn't come out and state it explicitly, I think he feared the apprehension of Cassman could turn violent, and he didn't want me in any position where I could hurt myself or others. I suppose I should've been happy Dean had acquiesced to me waiting in a car under supervision while the others moved in, but it was hard to feel as if I wasn't being chastised, even if I understood his point of view.

I stared intently at Dean's squad, only looking away to glance at my watch. We'd all synchronized our timepieces before leaving the station, so when my minute hand pointed straight down, Dean, Moss, Justice, and Officer Hutchison moved in. They moved quickly but deliberately, their pistols drawn and held at their sides. They hopped the low chainlink fence by the sidewalk and surged up the steps to the front door. No one knocked, nor did they announce themselves, as the judge had granted Dean's request for a no-knock warrant. Justice merely kicked the door open with a powerful blast of his foot and they all poured inside. Beams of lights shot out the windows as the detectives and patrol officers switched on their flashlights. After a couple moments of silence, I heard muffled yelling, perhaps even a crash, but I was too far away to be certain. No shots were fired, of that I was sure.

I sat in the car, literally on the edge of my seat, as I waited for someone to emerge from the home. The flashlight beams died as the home's lights came on, and shortly after, Moss emerged. She had her pistol holstered, and she walked confidently onto the sidewalk toward our squad car. Once she made eye contact, she waved me over.

I didn't wait for confirmation from Loudon, I just hopped

out and hustled over to meet her. I was out of breath even though I'd only run thirty feet. "What happened? Is everyone okay?"

"Everyone's fine, Phair," she said. "We got him."

I stood there for a moment, the sound of my breathing heavy in my ears. I felt a tingle in my fingertips, the tell-tale prickle of adrenaline. I'd heard what Moss had said. I thought the news of capturing TCK would make my heart soar, but other than the tingle I didn't feel a thing. Perhaps it would take time to process the news. To come to grips with it.

"Is it safe for me to come in?" I asked.

"As safe as a house that age can be," said Moss. "We've cleared the place, and the suspect is in custody. Come on. There's still a lot of work to do."

I followed Moss through the open chainlink gate, up the porch steps, and into the home. The front door spit us into a living space cluttered by milk crates, discarded boots, and empty bottles of Olde Yeoman malt liquor. The place was shabby and felt about as big as a tin can, though the abundance of officers and detectives inside probably contributed to the claustrophobia.

Moss ushered us past two of the officers from the support team into a bedroom. Another officer knelt inside, one hand grasping the cuffed wrists of the man on the floor. His hair and beard were both a little longer than in the mugshot, but it was Cassman, no question about it. Despite the presence of hundreds of tiny shards of porcelain on the floor, he didn't look injured, but he wasn't happy. He clenched his jaw tight, and his eyes burned with unrestrained fury.

Justice, on the other hand, wasn't uninjured. He sat on

Cassman's unmade bed, a handkerchief pressed against the side of his jaw.

I didn't move into the room for fear of stepping on Cassman. Honestly, I felt unnerved just looking at him. "Justice. Are you okay? Moss said no one was harmed."

"I'm fine." Justice pulled the handkerchief back and glanced at it. A streak of blood stained it, but the cut on his jaw looked to be only skin deep. It didn't well up with the handkerchief gone. "The suspect caught me with a right hook as we came in. He got the worst of it."

I'd suspect as much of anyone who got into a tussle with Justice, and the big guy was telling the truth. I'd overlooked an angry red splotch on the side of Cassman's face nearest the floor. His face would be half purple by morning.

I lowered my voice, although it probably wasn't enough to keep Cassman from overhearing. "Have you guys found anything?"

I wasn't specific, but Justice knew what I meant. "The search is ongoing. Officer Hutchison recovered a thirty-eight caliber pistol with the serial numbers filed off from the dresser, and Officer McMurtrey found a heavily wrapped brick of smack. At least a couple pounds worth."

"Nothing else?" I asked. "No rope? No ice pick?"

"Not yet," said Justice, "but we're only getting started. Dean's in the basement with another of the officers. I'd be down there myself if I could fit down the stairs. Probably best we keep at least two pairs of eyes on the suspect, though."

Truer words could not have been said. At least Justice didn't seem the least bit intimidated by TCK. Maybe taking the guy's punch and knocking him on his ass had that effect on a psyche.

Then again, perhaps he didn't seem as intimidating to a six and a half foot ogre as he did to me.

I asked Moss about the basement, and she led me through the living room into a narrow hall near the kitchen. One of the doors in the hall was pushed wide open, revealing a yawning chasm, only a foot and a half across and leading to stairs only slightly less steep than a sheer cliff. The thing wouldn't have been up to code even if there was a handrail, which there wasn't. A single bulb buzzed below, casting light onto the dirt floor of the sub-level.

"After you," said Moss. "Don't break your neck."

I tested the first step. It creaked, but it supported my weight. I braced myself against the wall, keeping a hand on the ceiling for balance as I descended the steps. The ceiling in the basement was quite low, the lowest beams only an inch taller than my head, so I was able to keep hold of them all the way to the bottom. There, I found Dean and one of the other officers between shelving racks piled high with goods.

Dean glanced our way at the sound of the creaking steps. He frowned, first at me, then at Moss who was following me down. "I told you she should stay in the car."

"Be reasonable," said Moss as she jumped the last two steps to the dirt. "She hasn't been on this case as long as the rest of us, but it's safe enough to bring her in. Imagine if I'd been the one to take the shot a couple days ago and I was on probation. You think I'd be waiting in the car?"

Dean pursed his lips. "It's not about what you're willing to do. It's about what the chain of command tells you to. We can't jeopardize this case. Not after everything we've been through."

Moss dipped her head a little. "Sorry. You're right."

"Be safe, is what I'm getting at. Play by the book," said Dean. "That said, since you're here, come and give this a look. You'll want to see this especially, Phair."

I shuffled through the nearest aisle, ducking as I reached a beam that was an inch lower than the rest. Dean had pulled a milk crate from one of the shelves. He held something he'd plucked from it in his gloved hands.

I recognized the packaging immediately. "That's a Virginia's Jewelry box."

Dean lifted the lid. Inside was a brooch in the shape of a rose, inlaid with small red gemstones. "It's the brooch from the police report. The ring is in this box, too."

My breath caught in my throat. "And the necklace?"

Dean shook his head. "Could be somewhere else in this pile, but it's nowhere I can see."

The nervous tingle I'd felt on the street returned, this time in force. My heart beat faster as my brain started to accept the truth before me, and I was forced to still a tremor in my arm by gripping it with the other.

Before I had an opportunity to say anything, the officer in the adjoining aisle came around the corner, something held in his hands. "Detective Dean. You need to see this."

As he came closer, it was obvious what he held. A deck of cards. Not standard playing cards, but *tarot,* the box worn from use.

Dean carefully folded the box open and pulled free the cards. He flicked through them methodically. His brow creased, his eyes steadily growing wider. "Gods above..."

I wasn't familiar enough with tarot to tell one card from another, not at the speed at which Dean flipped through the deck, but I tried to count how many were there. I'd counted seventy-four.

"Dean," I said. "That deck's four cards shy."

He turned to me slowly, his lips parted. "Not just any four cards, Nell. *The* four cards. We got him."

CHAPTER TWENTY-SIX

I stood in the observation room for one of the Fifth's interrogation rooms, staring at Gregory Lloyd Cassman through the one-way mirror. He sat there, one eye swollen shut from the strength of Justice's blow, but he didn't look defeated. He sat with his back straight despite the fact that his hands were cuffed to the table, and the anger I'd seen in him still smoldered.

Moss stood beside me, arms crossed and a look of frustration on her face. There had been a long discussion over whether she or Justice should accompany Dean into the interrogation. Moss had argued her status as a young woman would put Cassman into the frame of mind he adopted as a killer, meaning she should come. Justice agreed with Moss's theory, but he argued that was a bad thing, that TCK was too calculating and shrewd. Better not to include Moss and instead let him in. His blow to Cassman's face had clearly enraged him, and he figured an irate TCK would more easily slip in his testimony.

Ultimately, Mason cast the deciding vote. He'd stayed at the precinct while we raided Cassman's home, but he joined us as soon as he heard we had the suspect in custody. According to Mason, Justice's reasoning was more in line with the profiling, although Mason didn't think Cassman would crack regardless of who went after him. Any admission of defeat on his part, Mason said, would be a surprise. Nonetheless, he wanted to watch as much as the rest of us, which is why he stood staring through the mirror on the opposite side of the room from Moss.

Moss glared at Mason out of the corner of her eyes, but our focus turned to the interrogation room as Dean and Justice entered. Moss flicked a switch on the tape recorder at the side of the room. The reels spun to speed as Dean and Justice took their seats. Dean set a slim folder on the metal table in front of him, whereas Justice tucked a paper bag next to one of the table's legs.

Dean's voice crackled through the observation room's speakers. "You're Mr. Gregory Lloyd Cassman, is that correct?"

Cassman didn't say a thing. He glared at Dean with his one good eye.

"This'll go faster if you make an attempt to answer our questions," said Justice. "Not that it matters much. We've been itching to talk to you for a long time, and we've got the whole night in front of us."

Cassman snorted. His voice was raspy and gruff when he spoke. "You want this to go faster? How about you assume I'm not going to tell you jack shit. Whatever you think I did, I didn't. End of story."

Dean and Justice shared a glance, but I couldn't get a feel for what was conveyed with their backs turned to me.

Dean opened the folder and produced four photos. He lined them up on the table. "Tell us about these women."

"What do you want me to tell you?" said Cassman. "They look pretty dead."

Justice tensed. "How about you start with why you murdered them, you sick bastard."

Cassman rolled his one eye. "What is this, some kind of joke? Some tough cop routine? Get out of here."

Dean's voice was cold. Emotionless. Clinical. "Take a closer look."

Cassman's jaw muscles tightened. "I didn't murder anyone."

Dean's finger crept across the table. "This woman was Sherryl Towns." His finger moved to the next in line. "Ellowyn Farview. Maggie Richards. Here's Lacy Breen. She was murdered a few nights ago. They were all young. Vibrant. Hopeful. They had their whole lives in front of them—until you killed them."

Cassman shook his head and looked away.

"Where were you three nights ago?" asked Justice. "Around two to three A.M?"

"Asleep," said Cassman. "Like any normal person."

"And before that?" asked Justice.

"I don't know," said Cassman. "Out. With friends. Not murdering young women."

"What about the night of August thirteenth?" asked Dean.

"At three in the morning?" said Cassman. "Sleeping. And earlier? Probably out with friends. Still not murdering people."

"The night of August twenty-ninth?" asked Dean.

Cassman pursed his lips. "Let's assume, for the sake of moving things along, that I was asleep by two every night, and that I didn't murder anyone while I was awake."

Dean and Justice shared another look. Dean collected the photographs, sliding them back into the folder as Justice picked up the bag from the floor. He opened the top and set the two boxes of Virginia's Jewelry on the table in front of him.

"We found these in your basement after taking you into custody," said Justice.

"Nice work," said Cassman with a smirk. "Did you find the note next to them telling you to piss off?"

Justice's shoulders tensed again. Dean must've noticed his irritation, too, as he took over. "These pieces were reported stolen from Seaside Pawn several weeks ago. These two items as well as one more. A necklace with a pendant in the shape of a cat."

Cassman's one eye narrowed slightly. "Were they? Interesting. I didn't steal them, if that's what you're implying."

Dean continued. "The necklace wasn't recovered from your home. It was found in the residence of Maggie Richards. One of the young women who was brutally murdered."

It might've been my imagination, but it seemed as if Cassman paused before answering. "I don't know anything about that."

"So how did these pieces of stolen jewelry get into your house?" asked Justice.

"I don't know," said Cassman. "They're not mine. Maybe someone planted them there. Like a cop, maybe."

"Like they planted the thirty-eight caliber Rossman Special revolver?" asked Justice. "Or the forty ounce brick of opiates we found?"

Cassman's brow furrowed. He didn't say anything.

Dean gave Justice another nod. Justice reached into the bag and produced the deck of tarot cards the officer had brought us. "And these? I suppose they're not yours?"

Cassman clenched his jaw. "No."

"Planted as well?"

"Must've been."

"I don't suppose you can explain why four cards are missing? The exact four cards we found left on those four dead women that you *definitely* don't remember murdering."

The fire returned to Cassman's lone eye. "Seems to me there should've been a lawyer here for most of this. I think I'm going to wait until they arrive. Wouldn't want them to miss anything important."

Dean and Justice shared another long look, then Justice swept the evidence into the bag, and both of them stood. It was a simple motion, but Dean gave it such gravitas. As he stood there, he towered over Cassman, more so even than Justice. He radiated an energy and passion I'd never before seen.

Moss stopped the tape recorder, and we met Justice and Dean in the hallway.

"Well," said Moss after they'd closed the door. "What do you think?"

Dean shook his head. "I don't know. He's not the person I'd built him up to be in my mind. He's flippant and cocky—"

"He's a prick, is what he is," said Justice.

"—but," continued Dean, "if this profession has taught me anything, it's not to be surprised. Sometimes an unassuming street rat turns out to be an accomplished thief. A soft-spoken matron can hold onto as much hatred as a gang enforcer, and sometimes a serial killer turns out to be a brash prick who makes a dumb mistake."

"He's never going to admit to being TCK, you know," said Mason. "You'll have to pin him on the evidence."

My brow furrowed in thought. "I don't get it. You said this had become a game to TCK. That it was no longer just about the murders. That's why he called Dean. It seems so strange he'd engage in a battle of wits only to clam up once caught."

"It makes complete sense," said Mason. "As Detective Dean pointed out, we caught him because he made a dumb mistake, planting evidence that he stole. He would never admit to that. In his mind, we didn't beat him. We didn't outwit him. We're not worthy adversaries. We caught him on a technicality."

"A technicality we need to back up with more evidence," said Dean. "The fact that we found the jewelry and tarot cards in his home will go a long way toward a conviction, but without murder weapons, he still has some wiggle room. We'll need to dig into his life. Track his every movement. The ice pick in particular will be key. That murder is recent enough that we should be able to find it if we track..."

Dean trailed off, his eyes drifting down the hall. I turned to find Detective Glenwell walking toward us purposefully.

"Detective Dean? A word." She crooked her finger toward him as she arrived. "Mason. You can join us."

Glenwell cracked the door to the observation room and, seeing it was empty, ushered Dean and Mason inside. Justice, Moss, and I exchanged confused glances as the process unfolded.

I broke the silence first. "Do either of you have any idea what's going on?"

"Nothing good," said Moss. She didn't put her head to the door, but she nonetheless turned toward the room, ears pricking in curiosity.

The door muffled the conversation within, but within a minute, we heard Dean exclaim loud enough for us to hear, *"Are you kidding me?"* That was followed by a similarly loud curse, a choice word I'd never heard out of Dean's mouth before. The door to the observation room wrenched open, and Dean stormed out. He pushed past us without a word, heading toward the stairs.

Mason, normally so unflappable, followed him into the hallway, looking dazed.

"Mason." Justice glanced at Dean's rapidly receding form. "What the hell happened?"

Mason lifted a finger, staring at the wall as if we didn't exist. "I... need a minute. Maybe a coffee. Something..."

He wandered off. Moss, Justice, and I shared a quick glance before darting toward the stairs. We caught sight of Dean in the stairwell, exiting on the third floor. From there it was easy to track him to the war room. He stood in a corner, hands on his hips, staring at the wall, breathing heavily.

Moss took a step forward as Justice closed the door. "Dean. Are you okay? Talk to us? What's going on."

Dean turned, his face flushed from anger. "What's going on is we failed. We didn't catch TCK."

An icy hand gripped my heart. "No. Did someone else get murdered?"

Dean shook his head. "No, thank goodness. But Cassman isn't the killer. He's a CI, working with the narcotics detectives at MCD to help take down the Treyvell crime family."

Moss blinked. "He's a *criminal informant?*"

Dean shrugged. "Apparently. The hit on Seaside Pawn was part of his ongoing initiation into the family business, and by arresting him, we've jeopardized the entire investigation. *Damn it.*"

"I don't know about this Dean," said Justice. "That explains why he was in possession of the jewelry, but it doesn't explain the tarot cards or how the pendant came to be in Maggie Richard's apartment. He may be a criminal informant, but that doesn't mean he can't also be the killer. His profile fits the bill, and I might burn HQ to the ground if they try to provide immunity to a CI who's a serial murderer."

Dean sighed. "That's pretty much what I told Glenwell, but she assured me it's not Cassman. As part of the investigation into the Treyvells, the detectives are keeping in regular communication with him. They have eyes on him. Specifically, he was meeting with department operatives the night of Lacy Breen's murder. He was on the other side of the city at two A.M."

Justice slammed an open hand against the wall, making a loud bang. *"Damn it!"*

I couldn't quite wrap my head around what I was hearing. "But... the tarot cards we found in his basement. I don't get it."

Dean's hand fidgeted nervously, and he stuffed it in his pocket. When he pulled it out, he was gripping his pack of cigarettes. "I don't know. It must've been planted, just like Cassman said." He stared at the pack. "I need a smoke. I'll be back."

We all stared at him as he walked past us. As he reached the door, Justice shrugged. *"Shit.* I'm going to join him."

The pair left, leaving the door open. I stood rooted in place, feeling as empty as a wrung-out dishrag. "I didn't know Justice smoked."

"I don't think he does," said Moss. "That's how bad this is."

My insides were hollow. When I'd seen Cassman on the floor, I'd felt fear staring into his eyes. I felt the rage pouring off him, and when we'd found the tarot cards, I knew we had him. I'd known it deep in my core, but that knowledge had been ripped out, replaced with a gaping maw. "We had him, Moss. We had him..."

Moss sighed. "No, Nell. We never did. He outsmarted us. Again." She clapped me on the shoulder. "I'm going to get some coffee. Want some?"

"Sure," I said numbly. I settled into a chair, staring through the wall into the distance. For a few minutes, I floated powerlessly in a sea of my own emotions, tossed to and fro by alternating waves of doubt, fear, and disbelief, but I'd never been one to fall deep into wells I couldn't pull myself out of. Even as the emotions washed over me, I started to wonder where we'd gone wrong. We'd found the tarot cards at Cassman's home—well, technically, one of the supporting officers had—but they'd been there. If Cassman wasn't the murderer, they must've been planted, and yet the jewelry he stole from Seaside Pawn hadn't been. So how was it the cat pendant ended up in Maggie Richard's apartment? Did Cassman have a roommate? Probably not, given the size of the home. Someone must've set him up, but who? Had one of the Treyvells figured him as a CI and planted the evidence? That implied one of them was the Tarot Card Killer. That might make sense. If anyone had the criminal knowhow to pull of a series of murders where no evidence was left behind, it would be a gangster. Maybe losing Cassman as a suspect wasn't as catastrophic as it seemed. If he'd truly been framed, that presented a limited list of other suspects...

The wheels on one of the chairs next to me squeaked, and a mug clattered against the table. Moss settled herself into a seat, pushing the coffee toward me. "You doing okay?"

I blinked. I hadn't heard her come in. "Deep in thought, that's all."

"Well, I barely got to the percolator in time," said Moss.

"This guy almost cleaned it out." She shot a thumb over her shoulder as Mason walked in, his own mug in hand.

Mason still looked dazed as he took a seat at the end of the table. "Caffeine is my one vice. I won't apologize for it."

"If coffee counted as a vice, the entire police department would have to confess their sins," said Moss.

I couldn't believe Moss was tossing jokes around. "You're surprisingly chipper given we just learned we arrested the wrong man for a string of violent murders."

Moss took a sip of her brew and made a face. "The longer you spend in this profession, the more you realize one of the best qualities you can have is a short memory. Forget your failures and put your nose back to the grindstone. You won't catch any criminals moping about."

I frowned. "Long memories are useful when you're attempting to piece together evidence."

"My apologies," said Moss with a wave of her hand. "I should've said *selective* short term memory is important. That and getting pissed off when someone beats you so you come back fiercer than before."

Mason lifted a finger. "That last part I can agree with wholeheartedly."

I shook my head. I wasn't in the mood for banter. "Can we focus for a minute? I've been thinking about the implications of Cassman not being our guy. It's not all doom and gloom."

Moss sat up in her chair. "See? What did I say about noses and grindstones?"

I pursed my lips.

"Again, my apologies," said Moss. "Go ahead."

"Okay. As I see it, Cassman—"

One of the two phones on the conference table rang, the one

closer to me. Annoyed at the interruption, I sighed as I picked up the receiver. "Yes?"

A muffled voice crackled through the speaker, deep and dark and mechanical in nature. It was a voice as cold as death. *"You're not Detective Dean."*

CHAPTER TWENTY-SEVEN

My blood ran cold, and my breath caught in my throat. I knew who this was. I'd heard the faint rasp of his lifeless voice when he'd called Dean a few evenings ago.

The voice crackled in my ear. *"Who is this?"*

I swallowed, trying to generate some saliva. "Ah... Officer Phair. I work with Detective Dean."

The voice on the other end of the line laughed, a sound like ice cracking. *"An officer? Is that what he's stooped to? Drawing anyone he can in hopes they'll have a revelation he's failed to? What's next? Does he plan to catch me by consulting a horoscope?"*

Moss and Mason were both looking at me with furrowed brows. I waved them closer, as a bit of anger at TCK's insults had loosened my tongue. "What do you want?"

"What a foolish question. Detective Dean has yet to determine what I'm after, so what chance do you have? But if you meant to ask why I'm calling, that I will tell you. I want you to pass along a message. Are you ready?"

Mason leaned into the table, and Moss had closed to within a foot of me. "I'm listening."

"Tell Detective Dean, tell everyone you work with and everyone who will listen, that you've failed. To say you've played into my hand is an understatement. You are chess pieces on a board, and I am the hand above that moves them. You are but marionettes to me. You will never catch me. I am ten steps ahead of you, and I always will be. Tell him."

I heard a click, and the line went silent. I pulled the receiver from my ear and set it on the base, my fingers numb at the tips and my heart beating hard.

Moss put a hand on my shoulder, her fingers like steel. "Phair...?"

"It was him." I drew a ragged breath. "It was TCK."

Mason's hand tightened into a fist, and he growled. "The nerve of that bastard. The longer this goes, the more of a game it becomes..."

The door creaked open, and I smelled cigarette smoke. I was too numb to turn in my chair, but I heard Dean's voice. "You all look like a ghost floated through here."

"He just called, Dean," said Moss. "Phair spoke to him."

Dean swore again. He thumped into the chair next to me and pulled up close. He looked me square in the eyes, his intensity of focus that seemed to ebb and flow now back in force. "Tell me, Phair. Every word, while it's fresh in your mind. This is critical."

I took a sip of the coffee Moss had brought to lubricate my throat, then I launched into it. I might've replaced a word or three with similar ones, but overall, I think I managed to repeat TCK's conversation verbatim. It's not that I had a photographic memory, but his words had etched themselves onto my mind. His icy, metallic voice would stick with me for a long time.

Dean was quiet as he listened, as were Moss and Mason. He waited a couple seconds after I finished to make sure I didn't have anything else to add. "He didn't make any mention of killing again? No mention of retaliation?"

I shook my head. Even after repeating the conversation, my lungs felt taxed, as if I'd run a mile. "No."

Dean leaned back, his chair squeaking. He nodded slowly, his face relaxing ever so slightly. "Good. This is good."

"Good?" said Moss. "You call having a serial killer phone us to gloat over his murder spree *good?*"

"He's scared, Ginger," said Dean. "We're getting closer. We must be."

Mason's brow furrowed. "How do you figure that? The man just ran circles around us. He made us look like fools."

Dean shook his head. "He didn't call to gloat. He may have wanted us to think that, but it's not the reason he called. He called for validation. I didn't realize it after his first call, maybe because I was too close to it, but this time, it's clear as day. He needs us to feel lost and powerless. It feeds him. Drives him. And like any need, it's a weakness. A weakness we can exploit."

Mason chewed on his lip. "I'm not sure I agree with that, Detective. I still think TCK views this as a game. The murders satisfy a part of his psyche, and these interactions with you satisfy another. He mentioned chess in the call. I think he sees this as a match. A test of wits, one he thinks he'll win."

"But he needs the game, otherwise he wouldn't play," said Dean. "Either way, it's a weakness. A mistake. *And mistakes are where we thrive.*"

CHAPTER TWENTY-EIGHT

I thanked Moss for the ride to work as we parked in the 5th Street garage. I balanced a paperboard drink tray laden with two tall cups of coffee in my hand as I headed to the locker room to change. Once in uniform, I took the stairs down to the morgue. When I arrived, I found Coroner Jowynn seated at his small desk in the corner of the room, sandwiched by filing cabinets on one side and a glass-doored chemical cabinet on the other. His fingers clacked on the keys of his typewriter, filling the air with a staccato mechanical rhythm.

"Morning, Emmett. Wasn't sure if you'd be in yet." Although it wasn't exactly the crack of dawn, it was still pretty early.

Emmett jumped at the sound of my voice, but a smile spread across his face as he turned. "Officer Phair. Morning to you, too. I usually get in early when the schedule allows it. I find it's easier to work when no one's around."

"I personally find it easier to get work done when I'm awake, which if it was up to me wouldn't be for another hour or two, but to each his own." I smiled and held out the tray. "I didn't know if you liked your coffee black or with milk, so I got one of each. Although if you're the sort who doesn't like coffee, I'm afraid you're out of luck."

Emmett chuckled under his breath. "I do like coffee, thankfully. With or without milk is fine, although technically we're not supposed to have food or drink in here. It is a morgue, after all."

"Right. The dead people could make things unsanitary and all that."

Emmett pushed his glasses further up his nose as he stood. "Well, it's quite sanitary, for the most part. Cleanliness is a critical part of mortuary work, you understand. If we didn't adhere to strict health and safety guidelines, not only would I be putting myself at risk, but we'd be risking the health of everyone who passes through here, from officers to families of the deceased. Not to mention the smell would be awful. The cool temperatures down here only do so much to prevent decay on their own. But when it comes to food and drink, or anything that will be ingested, we have to be more careful. Food-borne illnesses can be nasty. *Salmonella. Botulism. Escherichia coli?* Not good." Emmett's face drooped as he took note of my furrowed eyebrows, and he chuckled nervously. "But... that's probably not what you want to hear, given how you're planning on drinking one of those coffees yourself."

I couldn't help but shake my head. Emmett was adorable in his own nervous, rambling way. "If you want, we could take these to the hall and drink them there. As long as you don't think they've been contaminated simply by being brought into the room, I mean."

Emmett brightened. "That's a wonderful idea."

I handed Emmett the coffee with milk and kept the black one for myself. We headed toward the doors, side by side.

"So, ah... what brings you downstairs this morning?" asked Emmett. "And bearing gifts, no less?"

I popped the top off my cup and blew on the coffee within. Steam poured off it, and a rich, earthy smell tickled my nose. The coffee at the precinct might've been free, but you got what you paid for. "I was wondering if there'd been any more news about Lacy Breen. I heard we were still waiting on a toxicology report?"

Emmett nodded, following my lead with the coffee. "It came overnight. She had traces of a recreational drug in her system, which was a bit of a surprise, but it doesn't appear as if she was dosed with anything that would've made her less able to defend herself."

I hummed. "And I don't suppose CSU has uncovered anything else? No more physical evidence?"

Emmett shrugged as he replaced the lid onto his cup. "Not that I know of, but I'm not in regular communication with them. You should ask them."

"Right." I nodded a few times, letting my cup warm my hand. "And... any news on the rat?"

Emmett's grin returned. "The truth about the coffee finally comes out."

I smiled sheepishly. "Sorry. I know you're probably busy performing autopsies on people, and I know this isn't your wheelhouse, but I can't help but think the rat might be important. After the events of last night, we have a lot of new leads to look into, but I don't want to forget about this one."

If Emmett knew about Cassman, he didn't question me about it. Instead, he nodded knowingly. "I understand. I get sucked into rabbit holes myself, and I dislike coincidences. It's why I called my vet friend Veronica after you left yesterday. I was with her while she performed the necropsy."

I straightened. "You got it done?"

Emmett smiled. "Rats aren't that large. It doesn't take too long to dissect them."

"What did you find?"

Emmett sighed. "I'm sad to say... nothing."

"Nothing?" I blinked. "Nothing at all?"

Emmett gestured with his cup, carefully so not to spill. "Not really. As you already saw, the animal didn't have any external injuries that suggested it had been attacked. We didn't uncover any masses or tumors, so it doesn't appear as if the rat died of cancer. It wasn't malnourished. If anything, it was on the large side. It had probably been feasting off food scraps tossed out by the bar. I suppose the thing could've been poisoned, but usually there would be traces of rodenticide left in the stomach. Neither Veronica or I were able to identify anything of the sort."

"But... finding nothing is itself suspicious, isn't it?"

"Not necessarily," said Emmett. "Animals die of all manner of things, same as people. It's entirely possible the rat died of a heart attack or an infectious disease."

"Wouldn't you be able to tell if that were the case?"

"In the case of a heart attack, I'm afraid to say our analytical techniques are not that advanced," said Emmett. "Remember, rats are small. Their cardiovascular systems are even smaller. And in the case of disease, that's disease dependent. If it died of the plague, that would be different than if it died from a respiratory illness in terms of the damage done to the major organs."

I stood with my coffee, thinking over Emmett's claims. "So there's no obvious reason it died?"

"None that I or Veronica could identify, I'm afraid."

"But what's the likelihood animals would pass away in the near vicinity of each of our murder victims?" I asked.

Emmet shrugged. "I really couldn't say. If you want that question answered, you might want to talk to a statistician, not a coroner."

I rubbed my chin. Maybe I would, at that.

CHAPTER TWENTY-NINE

I sat in the war room, the murder books from the first three TCK slayings stacked beside me. I'd gone through each of them as I'd gathered the duplicates for MCD, but I hadn't studied the books closely. I still couldn't say I'd read every detail, but I'd sifted through them, searching for any mention of dead animals, pulling the photographs, and trying to recreate the positions of the animals with respect to the victims.

First of all, Dean had been correct. No dead animal had been discovered near the scene of Ellowyn Farview's murder—which didn't mean there hadn't been one. Given Farview's car had crashed into a drainage ditch that extended into the sewer in one direction and an unkempt field in the other, it wasn't hard to imagine a dead animal might've gone overlooked.

Regardless of what might or might not have transpired in the vicinity of Farview's car crash, all I could do was focus on the evidence from the other murders scenes. In the murder of Miss Towns, a blackbird had been found near her body, behind the bushes into which Towns had stumbled. I wasn't a birder by any means, but the animal in question seemed too small to be a raven or a crow. Perhaps it was a cowbird. More important than its species, however, was its condition. Though a few of its feathers protruded in awkward directions, the bird itself didn't look as it had been mauled by a cat. In fact, it didn't appear to have suffered any wounds at all. I suppose the thing could've flown into a window and broken its neck, but the photographs of the side of the bowling alley showed nothing but a long stretch of brick. I couldn't spot any blood around the bird either, though the photographs weren't close enough to the animal for me to make any firm conclusions.

Similarly, the dead squirrel found near the scene of Maggie Richards' murder didn't look as if it had been bitten. It lay on the forest floor in the photograph, legs splayed and eyes bulging but without any wounds to speak of. If anything, its eyes were the only thing that struck me as odd. If the squirrel had died from natural causes, wouldn't its eyes be closed? It only made sense for the eyes to be open if the death was sudden, right? Perhaps I should pose the question to Emmett.

The door creaked. I looked up to find Dean entering. He wore an indigo suit with a crisp shirt underneath that matched the color of his hair.

He gave me a nod. "There you are. When I spotted Moss but not you, I thought you'd run off."

"If I didn't take the day off yesterday, I don't know why you think I'd do so today," I said. "I went down to visit Coroner Jowynn. Had some questions for him."

Dean peered at the photographs in front of me. "Questions about the dead rat?"

"Yes."

"Did he have anything notable to say about the creature's death?"

"I guess that's open to interpretation," I said. "Jowynn performed a necropsy on the rat with the aid one of his veterinarian friends, but they didn't find any obvious reason for its death. That in and of itself isn't notable, but when you combine that observation with what we see in these photographs, the picture gets more interesting. Come take a look."

I waved Dean over, and he skirted the table to my side. I pulled some of the photographs to the side so he could get a better view. "Ignore for the moment Ellowyn Farview's murder. At the scene of the other three TCK killings, in each case, a small animal was found dead near the murdered woman. While we've only performed a necropsy on the rat, photographic evidence shows all three animals as unharmed. And if my estimates are correct, each one was found within twenty-five feet of the murdered victim. Doesn't that strike you as odd?"

Dean pursed his lips. "It hardly seems like a coincidence."

I took a deep breath. "I know this seems like an odd detail, but its been bugging me ever since CSU found the rat outside The Library. Heck, even before that. It bothered me when Justice told me about the dead squirrel in Miller's Creek Park. Something tells me it's important. I don't know how it'll lead us to TCK, but it means *something*."

Dean nodded a few times before saying anything. "I agree. I came in here to see if you wanted to accompany me to the phone company, but you should follow this. It's not the sort of lead Glenwell and Hawkins are going to put any weight behind, that's for sure."

My heart swelled knowing Dean thought I'd come up with an intriguing avenue of investigation, even if I didn't know where I was going to go from here. "What are you going to do at the phone company?"

Dean shrugged. "Waste my time, probably. I'm hoping they'll be able to provide information about the two phone calls TCK placed to the department. I'm pretty sure their technology is the same as the last time I checked, but maybe one of the operators can tell me something. I can't imagine TCK used his voice modulator until we came on the line, but I could be wrong."

I nodded. "Good luck, regardless."

"Thanks," he said, heading back around the table. "Moss and Justice should be around, if you need them. They're meeting with Horace and Kratz from the gang unit, trying to come up with an angle of attack on the Treyvell crime family, but they shouldn't need any help on that front. Glenwell and Hawkins have pretty much called dibs on that line of investigation, anyway." Dean paused as he reached the door, his brow furrowing.

"Something wrong?" I asked.

He shook his head. "No. It just occurred to me some killers start out torturing animals. It's a telltale sign of cruelty in children and can act as a gateway drug to future murders, in a sense. Might be worth touching base with Mason. He'd know more of the psychology, I imagine. It could be something to use when cross-referencing arrest records in search of TCK." Dean waved a hand. "Just a thought. It's your call how you want to pursue this, but make sure whatever path you take, it's fruitful. We need to make progress. TCK's call last night proves he's afraid, but caged animals are the most dangerous. Something tells me he's going to strike again—and we need to stop him before he does."

CHAPTER THIRTY

I paused as I stepped into the University of New Welwic veterinary lab, thinking I'd gotten bad directions. The laboratory looked more like what I would've expected from the chemistry or biology departments with lots of glassware on shelves, chemical cabinets full of labeled jugs, and microscopes everywhere. Fume hoods hummed in the corners, their grills pulled down low, and a centrifuge rattled as its internal drum spun samples at high speed. Despite initial appearances, though, I must've been in the right place. The posters on the walls showcased the musculoskeletal systems of dogs, cats, and horses.

A middle-aged woman wearing a white lab coat and with her brown hair held in a ponytail stood in front of a pair of students, one a tall elven girl and the other a mixed race bloke, a bit taller than your average dwarf but with coarse auburn hair and tan skin. Both of them wore white coats, too, but none of them wore safety glasses, so I guessed it was safe for me to enter.

I caught the middle-aged woman's eye. She held up a finger

in my direction. As she finished speaking, her students nodded and headed toward opposite sections of the lab.

"Doctor Diana James?" I asked as she approached.

She smiled, causing small creases to form around her eyes. She extended a hand, which I shook. "That's right. You must be Officer Phair, Victoria's friend."

We'd spoken over the phone. "To be accurate, Victoria is a friend of a friend. I don't know her personally, but my friend speaks highly of her. She's been helping us with an investigation."

Doctor James stretched her eyebrows. "Well, I was going to ask how Victoria was doing, but I guess you wouldn't know. I'm glad to hear she's being of service to the city, however. It doesn't surprise me. She was always an excellent student. Very progressive."

I didn't know if helping Emmett qualified as providing aid to the city, but if her expertise helped us catch TCK, nobody would argue against it. I nodded.

James continued. "So what can I help you with?"

"I understand you're an expert on veterinary pathology."

James nodded. "Mammalian pathology, specifically. You mentioned over the phone you're looking into some mysterious animal deaths?"

"Correct," I said. "That of a small black bird, a squirrel, and a rat."

The doctor's brow furrowed. "Are you tracking some sort of animal killer?"

"Not exactly. This is part of a bigger case." I pulled out the folder I'd been holding under my arm. I opened it and pulled out a few items. "Each animal died under strange circumstances. Specifically, none of them seemed to have sustained any injuries much less life-threatening ones. The first two animals passed away some time ago. At the time, their deaths weren't considered suspicious. It was only a few days ago that we found another and caught wind of the connection. This is the report Victoria put together after performing a necropsy on the rat. As you can see, she wasn't able to come to any definitive conclusions."

Doctor James glanced at the report. "Without seeing the body myself, I couldn't make any judgements about her summary. That said, Victoria was very capable. I'm sure she was thorough." She looked back up. "Can I ask what this is all about?"

"I'm afraid I'm not at liberty to discuss the case," I said. "What I came to ask is this. Victoria didn't determine any particular cause of death for the rat. She suspected it might've died of heart failure or perhaps an infectious disease. Let's assume however, just for the sake of assumption, that all three animals died in the same manner. Can you think of anything that could've killed them, suddenly and without leaving evidence?"

"Well, heart failure or disease could've indeed done that."

"Assume someone killed them," I said. "That their deaths weren't natural."

James sucked on her lip as she closed the folder. "Did you perform a toxicology test on these animals?"

"No, but Victoria looked in the rat's stomach. She didn't find any traces of poison."

"Ingested poison," corrected the doctor. "If the rat had been killed via an inhaled poison, it wouldn't have left traces. An injected poison probably would've caused bruising and local trauma, but gas wouldn't have."

I thought about that. While tox screens hadn't been performed on the dead animals, I knew they'd been completed for the murdered women. None of them had come back positive for poisonous gases, and if the animals had all been murdered within twenty-five feet of the women, it seemed likely traces of the gas would've been found on our victims.

"Circumstantial evidence suggests it wasn't gas," I said. "Can you think of anything else?"

James crossed her arms. Her brow furrowed. She opened her mouth only to close it a moment later. "You're certain someone killed these creatures? That they didn't die from natural causes?"

"It's statistically unlikely they all died naturally in the spots we found them."

James continued to think. "If we rule out fast acting poisons, that leaves few other possibilities. One is a slow acting poison. Think of lead poisoning, for example. Low-level exposure over time can add up, and levels that wouldn't be detectable in humanoids could be fatal for small animals. That leads to a second option which is a nutritional deficiency. If these animals were raised and fed diets that lacked specific nutrients, they might die while appearing otherwise well fed."

That was a decent point. I hadn't considered the animals might've been planted rather than killed on the spot.

"Apart from that," continued Doctor James, "the only other thing that makes sense is heart failure or seizure."

"We're assuming someone murdered them," I reminded her.

"I know," said James. "While rare, heart failure can be caused by extreme shock or even fear."

I squinted a little. *"Fear?"*

James smiled. "It sounds silly, but consider when you experience a terrible surprise. Your heart seems to freeze inside your chest. It can be hard to breathe. Those reactions aren't exclusive to people. Animals feel them, too. There's a species of goats that are well known for fainting when they're surprised. Other animals seize up. It's quite common in small mammals, actually, when they're set upon by a terrifying predator. Instead of fleeing, as would make sense, they're frozen by fear. I've witnessed it in mice and chipmunks, but I suppose the same could happen to squirrels or rats."

"Really...?" I trailed off. "So you think a predator could've been responsible for their deaths after all?"

James shrugged. "I'm saying it's a possibility, if a slim one. But I think you'd be hard pressed to find a predator so terrifying it managed to scare a blackbird, a squirrel, and a rat all to death. While two of those creatures are mammals, all three live in different environments. In the air, on trees, and on the ground. That means each animal has a different flight response. What predator could terrify each one so fully?"

It was a valid question. Even considering it forced me to challenge assumptions I'd held about the murders. Specifically, what if TCK wasn't a person, *but a creature?*

CHAPTER THIRTY-ONE

I sat at one of the long reading tables on the main floor of the University of New Welwic's Library of Art and History. A curved lamp with a green glass shade hovered to my side like a shrub leaning under a heavy breeze. The yellow glow of the bulb lit the book I had open in front of me, a text on mythology entitled *Hideous Beasts and How to Avoid Them: A Multicultural Treatise on Mythological Creatures and the Legends Surrounding Them.* While the title was sensationalist, it was both well-written and in-depth, something I couldn't say for either of the two books the librarian at the front desk first retrieved for me. One of those was overblown drivel posing as non-fiction, and the other was so dry that even if good knowledge resided amongst its pages it would take someone with a less acute sleep reflex than me to find it.

I'd pushed them both to the side to make space for *Hideous Beasts,* through which I now searched for every myth and fairy-tale I could find about creatures that used fear to assault and immobilize their prey. The first creature I investigated was one I was already familiar with: the gorgon. Physical descriptions of the beasts varied: some referred to creatures that were half man and half snake, with an oversized snake bottom that replaced the legs and hips, while others referred to human-like animals with living snakes for hair. The gorgons apparently possessed such a horrifying visage that one look into their eyes would turn the beholder to stone. Most often, mythology referenced gorgons as female, but I didn't put too much faith in that. If that were the case, men who saw them never would've been petrified, as they'd be too busy staring at their bare tits to bother looking into their faces. While myth after myth spoke of them as terrifying, I couldn't bring myself to think they might've played a role in the deaths of the small animals or the women targeted by TCK. The myths were specific about the victims turning to stone, after all, not them dying of fright.

The next creature I gave serious consideration to was the minotaur. Fabled to be a massive, muscular man with the head of a bull, the minotaur certainly cut a terrifying figure, with the ferocity of a raging bull but the visceral cruelty of man. Certainly, a minotaur would've possessed the strength to snap Sherryl Town's neck as if it were a twig, or to beat Maggie Richards to a pulp, but as much as I wanted to make the mino-taur theory work, I couldn't fit the pieces together. While I could imagine the fearsome minotaur making quick work of TCK's victims, I didn't see how animals would be intimidated enough by the thing's presence to drop dead on sight. The crea-ture didn't have any preternatural ability to inflict fear according to the mythology, and my disgust was probably unique to the fact that I was human. Seeing unnatural muta-tions in your own kind is disconcerting, after all.

That led me to the creature I was now reading about: the wendigo. Sometimes described as a malevolent spirit, other times described as a fearsome beast, the wendigo appeared to people as a tall, emaciated humanoid with bones pushing against its skin, sunken eyes, and teeth like knives. Supposedly they possessed an insatiable hunger and a heart of ice. They reeked of death and decay, and they were well known not only for their malevolence but their cannibalistic nature. Quite frankly, the beasts sounded like something out of a nightmare. Because of their supposed supernatural powers, I could see how they might freeze creatures and humans alike in fear, but I couldn't see them as the culprit, either. Every tale told of their cannibalism, and though TCK's victims had been horribly murdered, none of them had been eaten, thank the Gods.

A speaker crackled overhead, echoing throughout the cavernous reading room. "Call for Penelope Phair. Please report to the librarian's desk."

I closed *Hideous Beasts* and tucked it under my arm as I headed across the floor to the entrance. I wasn't surprised to hear my name called. In fact, I'd been expecting it. When I first arrived at the library, I'd phoned Detective Dean, but having not been around, I'd been forced to leave a message.

The elderly woman at the front desk regarded me with a look of withering indifference as I arrived, the phone held nonchalantly in a limp grip. "Do try to keep your voice down."

I hadn't given the woman any reason to hate me when I arrived, so I assumed her ire was part of her regular persona. I nodded as I picked up the phone. The cord wasn't endless, but I was able to pull the unit to the end of the curved desk. "Officer Phair speaking."

"Hey, Phair. It's Dean. You called?"

"I did." The librarian glared at me, and I lowered my voice. "I was able to meet with Dr. James at the vet lab. She's the professor Emmett's friend who did the rat necropsy recommended."

"Was she able to shed any light on the death of the animals?" asked Dean.

"To a degree," I said. "In her mind, the most likely causes of death are either poison, malnutrition, or shock. I think we can probably rule out malnutrition. The rat didn't show any signs of that, and the photographs of the other animals didn't suggest it, either. Poison is plausible, but it would've had to have been delivered via gas or injection, neither of which we found evidence for. Which leaves shock, which is what I'm trying to investigate here in UNW's Library of Art and History."

I could almost hear Dean's brow creasing. "Wouldn't that be something you'd research at a medical library?"

"Sorry," I said. "Let me back up. Dr. James said a possible cause of shock could be from fear. They literally might've seen something so shocking, so terrifying, they keeled over and died. I know that sounds like a stretch. Murder may be terrifying for us, but an animal wouldn't react to human on human violence the way we do—unless it wasn't human on human violence."

"What are you getting at?" asked Dean.

"That perhaps we've been making an incorrect assumption that TCK is humanoid," I said. "Think about it. Both Sherryl Towns and Maggie Richards' deaths suggest their attacker had supernatural strength. Maybe even Ellowyn Farview, too, depending on how quickly and violently you assume she was strangled. The attacker also exhibited a knack for disappearing into the aether as if they were never there, almost as if they had supernatural powers. So what if we're not dealing with a person but with a *creature*? That's what I'm researching. Beings with preternatural powers, those who are known for their ability to inflict fear and human suffering. So far, I've been reading about gorgons, minotaurs, and wendigos, but none of them fit the bill. The key is finding a creature that would be terrifying not only to young women but to small animals, too. Once we have a solid theory in place, we can try to answer some of the thornier questions, like how it is this creature was able to survive into the modern era? And without attracting attention, in an urban environment no less. Not to mention—"

Dean's voice cut across the line. "Phair."

"Yes?"

Dean spoke slowly and carefully. "I think you may have veered off track. Don't get me wrong. Dr. James' analysis raises interesting questions, but there's no reason to think some supernatural monster with the power to inflict debilitating fear is behind the tarot card murders. I know our last case was a little off the wall, but you can't assume every murder we solve will have elements of the inexplicable to it."

"But then how did the rat die? And the squirrel?"

Dean sighed. "Phair, TCK called us. He spoke to us on the phone. How could he do that if he were some mindless, bloodthirsty creature? Trust me, I've been in your shoes. Sometimes it's easier to create fantasy scenarios rather than accept the hard truth: that the most frightening monsters in life are people like you and me."

My stomach fell out from under me, and I felt foolish.

Dean sensed my shift in mood. "I still think the animal deaths are important, and if you want to continue to pursue them, that's fine. But we have to make sure your efforts aren't wasted. We need our investigation to be productive. If you find that's not the case, I'm sure Moss and Justice can put you to work."

"Got it," I said. "I'll be back soon."

I hung the phone on the receiver, though I let my hand linger atop it. Dean hadn't been sharp or cruel, yet I unmistakably felt as if I'd been reprimanded. To be fair, Dean had a point. I'd spoken to TCK. He wasn't a hideous beast. He was a hideous person. And yet, I couldn't shake the feeling I was onto something. A mysterious phenomenon had killed those animals, something science was having a hard time explaining.

On a whim, I picked the phone back up and held it to my ear. "Operator? Could you connect me to Shay Daggers." I gave her an address.

The librarian gave me a cold look, as if I was inconveniencing her by continuing to use the phone. Well, what was she going to do? Call the police?

The phone clicked a few times then rang. After the fifth ring, someone picked up. A familiar warm yet tired voice. "Hello?"

I'd half expected to have my grandmother's manservant Baul answer, but I was glad to be wrong. "Nana. It's me. Penelope."

Nana's voice brightened. "Oh, good morning, dear. How are you? It's been a while since you called."

"I know. I'm sorry about that. It's been busy at work, and then I moved out of my apartment—"

"You did?" Nana's voice grew stern. "Are you having boy problems again? I thought you'd found someone you connected with."

"Well, we did connect, in several senses of the word. Just not on a deep mental and emotional level..."

Nana snickered, as if she knew exactly what I was referring to.

"But it's fine. I'm staying with a friend from work now, a female friend. I'm going to try to find a place closer to the Fifth Street Precinct. It'll make my morning commutes a lot easier. And really, moving out was for the best. But that's not why I'm calling."

Some of Nana's laughter lingered on the line. "Well, I think it's rather mature of you to realize a relationship wasn't working and to have ended it proactively. It shows growth, and I know it's not always easy for you to keep a clear head when handsome men are involved. But, as you said, that's not why you called. So what can I do for you?"

I was glad Nana wasn't pushing. As much as I loved her, I wasn't ready to go into the details of my love life with her. "You dealt with a lot of crazy, paranormal cases when you were a detective in the force, right?"

Nana hummed. "And here I thought you might ask me for money. To be honest, I did. But if memory serves me right, you don't much believe in that sort of thing."

"I'm believing more and more with each case I work on."

Nana laughed. "Doesn't that sound familiar. What's twisting your mind into knots?"

"I'm trying to figure out if there's a mythological creature so frightening that the very sight of it kills small animals. Birds, rats, squirrels. That sort of thing."

"You're on the hunt for a supernatural animal murderer?"

"Not exactly. I..." I glanced at the librarian. She wasn't glaring at me anymore, but I nonetheless pulled the phone a bit further into the corner and dropped my voice even more. "I'm working the Tarot Card Killer murders, Nana."

Her voice lost its mirth. "I see. And he's been killing his victims with fear?"

"Well... no. Just the animals. I mean, we've found a dead animal at the scene of each of his murders. A different kind each time. Not killed via the same methods as the women."

Nana cleared her throat. "Well, that doesn't make much sense does it? He's killing women and animals at the same time but via different techniques?"

To be fair, it didn't. "I guess not."

"How were the victims killed, if you don't mind my asking?"

I took another glance toward the front of the desk. "The first victim's neck was snapped. Twisted clean around. The second died by strangulation. The third was beaten to death, and the fourth was stabbed, either with an ice pick or something else long and thin."

Nana hummed again.

I waited a few seconds for more, but nothing came. "What does that mean?"

"Have you asked yourself why each murder has been committed in a different manner, Nell? Serial killers usually have a modus operandi, don't they?"

"Sure. And TCK does. He leaves a piece of a tarot card on each victim."

Nana sniffed. "Beyond that. I mean specifically in the way the victims are killed."

I shrugged, even though I was on the phone. "I don't know. It's something we've talked about. Our prevailing theory is that TCK doesn't want to repeat himself. By attacking in new and unpredictable ways, he keeps us from establishing a consistent profile we can use to track him."

"I guess that's a possibility," said Nana.

"Do you have an alternate hypothesis?" I asked.

"Depends," said Nana. "Do you want the logical explanation or the supernatural one?"

I kept Dean in my mind's eye. "Let's start with the logical one."

"Well, it seems to me this killer is playing a game with you," said Nana. "It could be the mechanism of the murders is a message. Clues meant to lead you in a certain direction, if not necessarily to him then to the next piece of the puzzle. Same as the tarot cards he leaves behind."

"You sound like the profiler who's been working with us. And the supernatural explanation?"

"Well, the murders make more sense if you consider how they all tie together. A broken neck, strangulation, broken bones, and being stabbed with a needle?"

I blinked. "I didn't say needle. I said we thought he'd been stabbed with an ice pick."

"An ice pick to a person is about the same size as a needle is to a doll."

My mouth slowly fell open, threatening to catch flies. *"What?"*

"Are you familiar with effigy magic, dear?"

"I'm not familiar with any kind of magic," I said.

"Effigy magic involves casting spells upon poppets, which are dolls that have been made to resemble real individuals. Most of the time effigy magic is sympathetic, but it can be used for nefarious purposes. In those cases, it's... dark stuff."

My mind raced. "Might the sort of person who performs effigy magic also be the sort who dabbles in tarot?"

"Perhaps," said Nana. "Tarot is used in divination, after all. Or it could be the cards are a red herring."

"But you don't think they are," I offered.

"You're the one investigating the case," said Nana. "What do you think?"

I gave myself a moment. "I think it would be extremely helpful if you knew someone who could give me more information on dark magic."

Nana snickered. "Perhaps it would at that. Do you have a pen?"

CHAPTER THIRTY-TWO

I rang the doorbell and waited. A voice called out from within the apartment, muffled by the door. "Coming." I waited another thirty seconds, wondering if perhaps I'd been lied to, when finally I heard the clink and clack of chain locks and deadbolts being released. The door creaked as it opened, revealing an elderly fae woman dressed in a pale blue shawl that fell to mid thigh over tailored navy slacks. Though she had a collection of wrinkles on her brow and around her mouth, her eyes were large and bright, and her hair, white as freshly fallen snow, was dense and lustrous. I'd assumed she was my Nana's age, but either I'd been wrong or I needed to ask about her beauty regimen.

"Miss Islespring?" I asked.

"You must be Shay's great-granddaughter, Nell." She smiled in response to my furrowed brow. "Don't worry. She called ahead, but to be honest, I might've noticed the resemblance even if she hadn't. You have her eyes."

I cocked my head. "I'm sorry, Miss Islespring, but I think

you're confused. My great-grandmother has azure eyes. Mine are hazel."

The old fae woman's eyes twinkled. "Indeed, but there's much more to a woman's eyes than their color. Please, come in. And call me Ocean."

Ocean retreated into her apartment, and I followed her, closing the door behind me. In terms of layout, her flat wasn't particularly out of the ordinary, but the way she'd decorated it made it stand out. Rather than featuring a single flat color, the walls had been painted into elaborate murals of natural landscapes. The living room was an underwater wonderland, with schools of fish, octopuses, sharks, and eels all swimming among rolling hills of coral. It didn't appear as if the décor was purely based on her name, though. The kitchen was painted to resemble a wide-open grassland, the snippets I caught of her bedroom revealed a forest shrouded in shadow, and the bathroom appeared to be patterned after a clear night's sky. The murals weren't two-dimensional, either. Artwork mounted on the walls projected out, giving the scenes a sense of depth and realism that was almost uncanny. The abundance of potted plants in each space, each picked to resemble what might be found in the associated biome, only added to the effect.

Ocean sat in a wicker chair with blue cushions that looked as if it belonged in a seaside cabin, waving toward a couch of a similar construction. "Have a seat, dear. Can I get you some tea?"

An eel with a malicious smile stared at me through a sea of seaweed-like tendrils as I sat. "Ah... no thank you. I'm more of a coffee person, to be honest. But don't make any on my account. I've already had plenty."

Ocean followed my gaze. "You appreciate my décor?"

"It's lovely," I said, tearing my eyes from the eel. "And oddly realistic. It's like visiting a natural history museum."

"If I must live in a city of concrete and steel, then at least I can bring the natural world into my close surroundings," said Ocean. "I find it helps me attune myself to the natural energies of the world. It makes certain seances and spells easier to cast."

"Right. Nana did mention you were a..."

Miss Islespring smiled. "A witch?"

I nodded.

Ocean tucked her feet underneath her on the couch, showing more flexibility than I imagined she had. "You needn't fear saying it. There are no inherent negative connotations to the word, only those the fearful and ignorant ascribe to it. Us witches are in fact quite proud of our abilities. It's not a common trait, after all. Not anymore, with so much of the world's magic having faded..."

I lifted an eyebrow. "The world's magic is fading?"

Ocean took a deep breath. Her hair cascaded across her shoulders like molten silver. "That, my dear, is a *very* long story and not one I suspect you came to hear. I'll save it for another time, should we meet again. In the meantime, what can I do for you?"

Focus, Phair. Don't get sucked into magical tangents. "I was hoping you might be able to provide me with some information about tarot and poppets."

Ocean smiled. "Well, which one? Those are very different disciplines."

"I suppose we can start with either. How about tarot?"

"Of course," said Ocean. "While there are games that can be played with tarot decks, I'm assuming you came to me regarding its occult uses. In that sense, tarot is primarily used in divination, also known as cartomancy. There are two groups of cards in the deck, the Major Arcana and the Minor Arcana. Many fortune-tellers will only use the Major Arcana, but those seeking true divinations will use the entire deck. As with most forms of divination, cartomancy is much more of an art than a science. Nuance is everything. Every draw can imply multiple predictions, and sometimes you only know which one is true when one comes to pass."

"You make it sound less like a prediction and more like a guess."

"I would disagree," said Ocean. "Knowledge properly divined is accurate, just not precise."

"What's the difference?" I asked.

"If I say a man will die at the stroke of midnight as he crosses the East Bay Bridge, and it comes to pass, then I've made an accurate prediction. But if I'm unable to tell you *who* that man is, then the prediction is not very precise, is it?"

I chewed my lip. "That makes sense. So could tarot—I mean, cartomancy—be used to track someone's movements? Could it be used to know their intentions?"

"Track their movement?" Ocean shook her head. "I doubt it. That's a precise prediction. But their intentions? Most definitely. That's where divination shines. In determining upon which path someone lies. It can be used to predict what sorts of actions people will take, which directions they will go. It simply doesn't do it *precisely*. So, for example, it might predict you will go on a journey tonight, maybe even where that journey will take you, but not the things that will happen along the way."

I wasn't sure I bought into the whole concept of predicting the future, but if Ocean was telling the truth, then it had some implications for TCK's murders. Perhaps he could've used cartomancy to tell when his victims left their homes or when they would've been alone. Or was that too precise?

I moved on. "Tell me about poppets."

Ocean leaned back in her chair. "That's a much more traditional sort of magic. Much older than cartomancy. Its origins date back millennia, back to when the world's highest cultures still lived in caves and spoke in little more than grunts. Essentially, it involves the formation of an effigy of someone followed by the casting of magics upon the effigy to influence their future. Usually, the magics are sympathetic in nature. Spells are cast to heal broken bones, cure sickness, promote fertility, or bring good luck, but the poppet can be used for evil. The spells can be destructive, though there is a cost to such things..."

Ocean trailed off, her brow furrowing. I gave her a moment, but only one. "What sorts of costs?"

Ocean looked up, meeting my eyes for the first time. Hers were a pale green in color, like sea foam and every bit as frothy. She didn't stare *at* me. She stared *inside* me, past the hazel coloration of my irises into the core of what made me who I was. Suddenly, I felt naked, in both body and mind, and a shiver ran through me.

"This is why you're here," said Ocean. "Someone is using poppets to hurt people."

She could've inferred it from my body language. I tried to convince myself that was the truth. "I believe so."

Ocean took another deep breath. She turned and stared at her bathroom, the one painted like a midsummer's midnight. "Sympathetic magic, generally speaking, is easy to perform if you have the knowledge and skill required. It builds positive energy, what some people refer to as chi or life force. It creates strength in the universe. Black magic is altogether different. It drains life force rather than building it. It goes against the natural order of things. Because of this, it takes a toll on those who partake in it. Sometimes the toll is physical, sometimes mental, emotional, or spiritual. Eventually, it will tax all four. It's incredibly dangerous to use, but to someone who doesn't understand the dangers, or worse, doesn't care?" Ocean shook her head.

I had many questions, but I couldn't get past one thing Ocean had said. "Black magic *drains* life force?"

Ocean turned toward me. "Indeed. Most black magic requires a blood sacrifice. One life traded for another, or in some cases, one life spent to end another. Death begets more death. It is a wicked, wicked thing."

I thought of the dead animals we'd found near the slain women, pieces of the puzzle coming together in my mind's eye. "Could such a thing be done remotely? Could you trigger the effects of a spell by engaging in blood sacrifice from afar?"

Ocean shook her head sharply. "You ask the wrong person. I don't know many details when it comes to dark magic. I also can't point you toward someone who can answer your questions, not only because I don't know who you should ask but because even if I did, I wouldn't tell you. The world would be a better place if all black magic was extinguished. In this and only this it is good that magic is fading."

The old fae woman had adopted a sad look, the look of someone who had seen too much pain throughout her years. I needed to tread carefully, as I still had questions in need of answering. "How does magic with a poppet work?"

Ocean let out a heavy breath. "You start with a doll. The poppet itself. In the olden days, the poppet might be made of anything. Carved from wood or a root or a vegetable. Fashioned from sticks and corn husks. The poppet itself isn't important. It need not be representative of anyone in particular because its appearance will not affect how one binds it to the target."

"And that is...?"

"You imbue the poppet with three essential elements of the target," said Ocean. "Something of the head, something of the thread, and something of the dead. Plainly speaking, you need a hair from the body, a piece of clothing, and a memento that ties the target to their past. Older cultures would use a tooth or piece of bone from a dead relative, but strictly speaking, that isn't necessary. An emotional connection to a lost loved one works as well as a physical one."

"And the poppets? You said they could be made of anything?"

"Traditionally, yes," said Ocean. "But I doubt anyone but fae girls living in huts in the forest would still do so. It's much easier to buy a doll in this day and age."

I frowned. "There are stores that supply goods for spells?"

Ocean smiled. "Of course there are, but as I said, one needn't go to one of those to buy a poppet. Any old doll would do."

I thought about that. "I don't suppose you know anyone who's actively engaged in effigy magic?"

Ocean shook her head. "I do not. Fewer and fewer witches practice with every passing year, but if what I suspect is true given your line of questioning, there is at least one witch still active in the city."

I nodded and stood. "Thank you very much for your time, Miss Islespring. This conversation has been extremely enlightening."

"You're very welcome," said Ocean, joining me in standing. "And Nell?"

"Yes?" I said.

Ocean's eyes threatened to delve into me again. "Be careful. Black magic is not to be trifled with."

I swallowed, *hard*. "I'll do my best."

CHAPTER THIRTY-THREE

I found Dean in the war room when I returned to the Fifth, his jacket thrown over one of the chair backs. He was slumped in his seat, his hair rumpled and the second topmost button on his shirt unbuttoned.

"Rough day?" I said.

He flicked a few fingers at me weakly. "You could say that. My trip to the phone company was a total waste. They confirmed what I already knew: the switchboards they use are automatic. While TCK must've spoken to an operator to place the call to our station and again to have the call transferred to the conference room, there's no way the phone company could tell me where the call originated. The only way to do that is if someone had been watching the switches as the call was placed. Obviously that didn't happen."

"But he spoke to someone," I said. "Presumably without using the voice modulator. That's something, right?"

Dean rolled his eyes. "*Something,* but not much. The phone company had no idea which operator took his call. I did talk to the operator on duty at the station last night. While she remembered putting a call through to us, she didn't recall anything particular about the three second interaction. The voice was male, on the deeper side. That's it. I suppose if we catch TCK, she might be able to recognize him by voice, but we'd have to find him first, and I sure hope we have enough evidence to pin his crimes on him by that point."

"Well, that's not nothing," I said. "We've been assuming TCK is male, but it's good to have a confirmation."

"Hooray," said Dean with a wave. "We've narrowed TCK down to half the residents of New Welwic. Maybe I'd be more excited if Glenwell and Hawkins hadn't constantly been on my ass today, or if Moss and Justice had gotten anywhere in regards to the Treyvells."

"They haven't made any headway?"

Dean shrugged. "Not to my knowledge. What about you? Any progress on the animal deaths?"

I took a seat. "Actually, yes, though I've pivoted away from thinking the deaths are fear-induced."

Dean didn't exactly sigh, but I could tell he was relieved. "It was an interesting thought experiment, but we have to follow the evidence. That's what it comes down to."

"I hope you mean that, because I'm going to need you to keep an open mind."

Dean's brow furrowed.

I pushed forward before I lost my nerve. "Before I dive into the mysterious deaths, I want to touch on the TCK murders. Have you thought about what the different methods of death— broken neck, strangulation, blunt force trauma, and stabbing— all have in common? About what ties them together?"

This time, Dean did sigh. *Heavily.* "Of course I have, Phair. I've thought about it every day for the past six weeks. I've tried to make sense of the differences between the murders, tried to piece them together every which way, but no matter what I do, it doesn't make sense. So if you have a theory, by all means. Let's hear it."

I took a deep breath to still my anxiety. Dean had embraced my crazy theories before, but that was when he wasn't tired, stressed, and pushed to his limit. "It's not easy to twist a woman's head clean around, nor is it easy to beat her savagely enough to break half the bones in her body. But it's easy to do that to a poppet."

Dean frowned. "A what?"

"A doll. After I left the library, I met with a woman, a self-proclaimed witch who told me about effigy magic. Essentially, it's magic you cast upon someone via an effigy. She spoke of casting positive, healing spells, but she acknowledged they can be used for harm."

Dean's jaw muscles worked, and his lips scrunched in displeasure. "Phair..."

"I know. It's ludicrous, but consider the questions this theory addresses. First, there's the issue of how the women have been murdered. Anyone can twist a doll's head around, but how many could do that to a living, breathing adult? It's physiologically very difficult, as you well know. Then we have the murder weapons, specifically that we haven't found any. If TCK was killing women via an effigy, there wouldn't *be* any murder weapons, and it would explain how Lacy Breen was killed: with a needle, not an ice pick. Each murder has been committed without witnesses, which is what you'd expect if TCK was torturing a doll from the safety of his home rather than with his victims in person. And it explains the dead animals. The witch I spoke to said black magic drains life force. It takes life to imbue the effigies with power. I don't know how it works, but TCK must've found a way to pull the life force from animals to fuel his dark magic."

Dean's visage made me think he was growing angry, but when he spoke he just sounded tired. "While I appreciate your willingness to think outside the box, you have to realize you haven't provided one solitary scrap of evidence in support of this theory. It's all conjecture. You're familiar with the difference between causation and correlation, right? Just because evidences line up with your theory doesn't make it right."

"I know that, Dean, but if I'm wrong, there should be *some other* way to explain this string of murders. Effigy magic explains how Ellowyn Farview was strangled *while driving*. How her killer mysteriously escaped the car crash without leaving physical evidence, without being seen by witnesses, without leaving footprints or a scent for bloodhounds to catch. You've been working this case for two months. What other explanation is there for Ellowyn's death besides the killer never being there?"

Dean remained quiet. My heart beat heavy in my chest, and I could hear my own breathing. Perhaps I hadn't realized how animated I'd gotten. Was that part of the problem? Did Dean think I was personally attacking him for not having come up with the solution earlier?

"It doesn't explain everything," Dean said eventually. "It doesn't explain why the first, second, and fourth victims were targeted while alone, outside, whereas Miss Farview was targeted while driving."

"I don't have all the answers," I said. "It's just a theory, but if I'm right, we can use it to produce new leads."

"Let's assume for a moment you're onto something," said

Dean. "How do we use this knowledge to our advantage? Do we start a task force to track users of black magic? How the hell do I sell the captain on that?"

"There might be another way," I said. "You've tracked sales of tarot cards since the first murder, right?"

"Of course," said Dean. "We contacted every store in the city who sells them. We talked to every cashier, every owner, canvassed every location. Nothing. Not a single lead."

"Right. Because TCK knew we'd be investigating the tarot angle. For all we know, he bought them years ago or shoplifted them. He'd know to hide his purchase of the cards. But he wouldn't think to hide his purchase of dolls."

Dean's brow furrowed.

"It's possible he made his own," I said. "But I don't think it's likely. TCK is clever and conniving but also brash. He probably thought he could commit dozens of murders without getting caught. If you were in his shoes, wouldn't you buy dolls in bulk? And wouldn't that raise a few eyebrows at the local toy shop or craft store? A grown man buying dolls by the case?"

Dean cupped his chin in his hand and gave it a rub. Normally, he was smooth shaven, but today he bore a little scruff. "It's not much, but it's not as if any other leads have paid dividends. Have you eaten lunch?"

I nodded. "Picked something up on my way back."

Dean stood and grabbed his jacket. "Alright. Let's hit the road."

CHAPTER THIRTY-FOUR

Dean's Viper purred as we pulled into the parking lot of Garland Arts and Crafts, a big-box store that seemed out of place amongst the convenience stores and mom and pop shops in the neighborhood. The parking lot had room for sixty cars, yet only a half-dozen spots were currently occupied. In a city where roommates often shared three hundred square foot apartments due to cost concerns, I couldn't imagine how maintaining the lot was cost effective for the owners, but then again, there were overgrown fields and abandoned buildings in parts of New Welwic. Maybe it had to do with tax law or depreciation or some other concept I didn't quite understand.

Dean parked near the front, and we walked in. A stale potpourri smell hung in the air as the door chimes rang, alerting the cashiers at the registers in front. One of them hailed us with a cheerless monotone. "Welcome to Garland Arts and Craft. Is there anything we can help you find today?"

"Hopefully," said Dean. "We're looking for plain,

customizable dolls. On the small side, probably, and inexpensive. Do you carry anything like that?"

The cashier Dean addressed, whose name tag read Carl, gave us a confused look, one I'd seen so many times I'd lost track. Six? Seven times? We'd been to a lot of stores.

"Uh, we might," said Carl. "Aisle twelve, next to the yarn and needle art. I can show you, if you'd like."

"Please," said Dean.

We followed the guy as he ushered us down the broad center aisle, right on twelve, and past the aforementioned yarn and needle art to the doll-making tools. He waved to one of the low bins that contained human figures, free of defining features, made of soft gray cloth and tightly stuffed with cotton. "That's probably the closest thing we've got, but if you're looking for something a little nicer, we also carry Girl Nouveau dolls. Some of them are fully outfitted, but there's a customizable line intended for hobbyists."

Dean picked up one of the dolls, turning it over in his hands. "Do you sell a lot of these?"

"Honestly?" said the cashier. "I don't think so, but I don't keep track of stock."

"Who does?" asked Dean.

"Our manager. He's up in his office." Carl shot a finger toward a set of stairs leading to some second floor offices at the side of the building.

"Thanks." Dean gave me a nod and we headed up. I tried not get excited, but to be frank, I didn't have to try hard. We'd found several likely options at other stores, but none of them had sold dolls in bulk in recent months.

Dean knocked on the manager's door before pushing in. The man inside, mid-forties with thinning brown hair and

sagging jowls, looked up from his desk overlooking the floor. He
scowled, but the look melted away after one glance at my
uniform. He sputtered as he pushed himself to his feet. "Good
afternoon, Officers. How, ah... how can I help you?"

"Detective Dean, NWPD." Dean showed his badge before
brandishing the doll. "We need to know how many of these
you've sold and when."

"Sure," said the manager. "Can I ask what's—"

"*How many,* and *when.*"

Clearly, Dean was as frustrated with our progress as I was.
The manager knew better than to test him. "Of course. I'll
check our orders with the distributor. Let me get the stock log."

The manager hustled to one of the filing cabinets behind his
desk. He threw open the topmost drawer and pulled from it a
thick, black binder. He placed it on his desk and flipped through
it. He paused for a moment, looking at the doll. "Could I see
that?"

"By all means." Dean held it out.

The manager plucked it and consulted the tag affixed to it.
He then returned to his binder, flipping two more pages
before stopping. "Here we go. We last ordered a crate of those
about two and a half months ago. Our stock had completely
run out."

Dean gave me a look, his eyes a little wide. My own heart
fluttered at mention of the timing. Two and a half months was
only a couple weeks before the first murder.

"Who bought you out?" I asked. "How many did they buy?"

The manager wrung his hands. "Well, that I couldn't say.
This is just the stock log. We'd have to consult the receipts to
know how many were purchased."

"You have those?" asked Dean.

The manager nodded. "We keep store copies for a year for return purposes. Would it be okay if I asked what the doll—?"

"Show us the receipts," said Dean. "This is urgent."

"Of course." A bead of sweat dripped down the manager's brow as he led us out of his office and down the hall to what looked like a supply closet. He unlocked it. Inside, in addition to a ratty couch and a heavy safe, were a number of cardboard boxes, the same brand as the ones we stored our files in at the precinct. Go figure.

The manger pushed into the stacks. "The receipts should be over here. If we reordered on August tenth, we're probably looking at an early August sale. Maybe late July. We should take both boxes to be safe."

Dean took one box from the manager and handed it to me before taking the second himself. "How are the dolls listed?"

"We use a shorthand," said the manager. "If you bring the boxes to my office, we can sift through them together."

"Let's get to it, then," said Dean.

The manager looked despondent as he locked up and took us back to his office. Undoubtedly, he had better things to do, but he knew better than to point it out. Unfortunately, the pink receipts weren't carefully stacked inside each box, but rather haphazardly thrown together. We had to sift through them by date before scanning them for their contents, so we set up an assembly line, with Dean and I setting aside receipts from the first to the tenth of August and the manager looking through the goods sold. The poor man continued to sweat as we over-whelmed him with slips, but as Dean and I approached the bottom of the first box, the man perked up.

"Ah! Here we are. A receipt for twenty doll-making bases. First of the month, no less."

Dean plucked the pink bill from the man's hands, scanning it. "Twenty... Very good." He turned the bill back to the manager. "Who did you sell this to?"

The man's brow grew more moist with each interaction. "I don't know. We don't include the customer's name, just the items sold."

"Who was working the first of August?" asked Dean.

The manager scurried to his wall calendar. "Let's see... The first was a Monday, so it should've been Carl and William, same as are here now."

"Thanks." Dean tapped me on the shoulder, and we hustled down the stairs to the main floor. The two cashiers were back at their posts at the front of the store, and if any customers had come in our wake, they were currently lost among the sprawling aisles.

Dean held up the pink piece of paper as we approached the pair. "August first, someone came through here and bought twenty of those dolls you showed us, Carl. A man, probably alone. No wife, no children. One of you sold it to him. I need to know anything you can remember about him."

The pair of cashiers looked at each other. Carl spoke. "August first? That was two and a half months ago."

"Which is why I need you to think hard," said Dean. "This is important. Extremely so."

Carl and William started to look as nervous as their manager, though neither started to sweat profusely.

"Sorry, sir," said William. "If it was within the last week, maybe I could remember someone if you showed me a photo, but I don't pay that much attention to the customers. I know that sounds bad, but it's true."

Dean shifted his gaze to Carl. "This person might've been

anxious. Cagey. Do you recall anyone suspicious? Anyone at all?"

Poor Carl wilted under Dean's gaze. "Sorry. I'm with William. All types of people come through here. Everyone's got a hobby. I wish I could be of more help."

Dean's hand tightened into a fist. His jaw muscles pushed against his cheeks, and his nostrils flared. Without saying a word, he turned and stormed out the door, leaving the door chimes ringing in his wake.

Carl and William stood like statues in his wake.

"It's not your fault," I told them. "Thanks for your help." Then I darted out the door after him, before Dean made a choice he'd later regret.

CHAPTER THIRTY-FIVE

I shouldn't have worried. As the afternoon sun greeted me, I didn't hear Dean roaring off in his Viper. Instead, I spotted him about ten feet from the doors, leaning against the Garland facade as he dug his Slowburn Lights and a lighter from his pocket.

He had a cigarette lit and between his lips by the time I got to him. The acrid, slightly sweet smoke blew toward me under an intermittent breeze, filling my nostrils with its unpleasant scent.

I waved a hand to clear the smoke, though the breeze was doing a decent enough job of it for me. "I don't think I've ever told you this, but I don't care for smoking at all. It's smelly and foul and expensive."

Dean took a long drag and blew out the smoke. "I guess we have something in common then, because I absolutely *hate* smoking."

I blinked. "Is that some sort of cop joke?"

Dean flicked the first few nascent ashes from his cigarette to the pavement. "It's not a joke, Nell, just the truth. There are few things I regret in life, but smoking is one of them. I started after Arrwyn's death. I needed something to keep my mind off her, something to do in those quiet moments when all I had were my thoughts. I didn't intend for it to become an addiction, but these damn things have made a slave of me. They've sunk their claws in deep. If I go even a few hours without them, I feel jittery and anxious and paranoid. They're the only thing that calms my nerves, and damnit if my nerves don't seem to be shot constantly. With every passing day it gets worse."

Arrwyn was the detective Dean had been engaged to. She died of an overdose a few years back after falling too deep into the persona she'd adopted as part of an undercover drug operation. "It is just the TCK murders or something else that's causing it?"

Dean snorted. *"Just* TCK. As if a serial killer brutally murdering women, leaving no trace of his presence, taunting us, and making it personal in the process wouldn't be enough to cause me to suffer from severe anxiety." Dean took another drag from his cigarette and blew it out. "Sorry. That's another thing about cigarettes. They make me irritable. It's a vicious cycle. If I smoke, I act like shit. If I don't smoke, I feel like shit and I end up acting the same way."

"It's okay," I said. "It's not you. It's the drug."

Dean shrugged. "Same difference. But to answer your question, yes, it's TCK. This case could make or break my career, but that's not really what's causing my anxiety. I hate being outmaneuvered. Outwitted. What I hate even worse is knowing a killer is loose and I'm powerless to stop him. I've never faced this, Nell. Have I come across tough cases and clever adversaries? Sure. I've seen the whole spectrum. I've caught murderers who couldn't add two and two together and others who'd make college professors seem like dolts. But regardless of who I've gone after, I've always identified enough mistakes to track them down. Not this time. Maybe it wouldn't bother me so much if this was a one-off murder. A housewife who planned the perfect crime and offed her husband for the insurance money, for example. But TCK is going to keep killing until we stop him. Maybe we'll get him eventually, but I can't bear the thought of even one more young lady falling to him..."

I took a step toward him. I wanted to give him a hug, or at least put a hand on his shoulder, but I didn't know if either was appropriate. "The situation isn't that desperate. We're making progress. We're on the hunt."

Dean lifted an eyebrow, the cigarette between his fingers smoldering. "Are we? Seems to me this is another dead end. Even if TCK bought those dolls, we still can't use the knowledge to our advantage. What are we going to do? Stake this place out? Hope he comes back? He bought *twenty* dolls. I'm not willing to sacrifice another sixteen women."

I wasn't either, but Dean wasn't in a mood to be convinced. "Can I see the receipt?"

Dean dug into his pocket and produced it. I took it from his hand, smoothing out the creases. I hadn't gotten a good look at it while Dean and the manager kept possession of it, but there was more than the dolls listed. The shorthand the store used was a little hard to decipher, but I got the hang of it after a few mental gymnastics.

"TCK bought other things, too," I said. "Needles. Thread. Cloth. All items that could've been used to make poppets."

"Or dolls of any kind," said Dean. "In fact, those might suggest someone other than TCK bought these. Why decorate a poppet? I thought it didn't need to resemble the target?"

Dean made a good point, but there was something else at the bottom of the receipt. I tried to decipher the abbreviations. *FE Inc Stick, 50pk, 3.* Incorporated sticks? Ink sticks? A pen?

My eyes widened as I figured it out. "He also bought incense sticks."

Dean sucked on his rapidly dwindling cigarette. "So?"

"So tarot is used in divination. Incense is as well. This was TCK, Dean. I'd bet anything on it."

Dean's eyes narrowed. He pursed his lips as his cigarette burned toward his fingertips.

I knew he was onto something. "What is it?"

Dean pointed at me with the smoldering stub. "Let's say you're right. TCK was careful about buying his tarot cards because he didn't want us to track him through them. But he was sloppy about the dolls. He bought incense alongside them. He let his guard down. So put yourself in TCK's shoes. If you're not worried about being caught, where do you go to buy your supplies?"

I wasn't sure I understood the question. "Uh... to Garland Arts and Crafts, apparently."

"You go to the most convenient store," said Dean. "And for most people, convenient is synonymous with close. TCK probably lives in this neighborhood, Phair! We could finally be onto something."

I felt short of breath at the mere thought of TCK being close by. Had my bet on the poppets really paid off? "So what do we do? How do we track him?"

Dean smiled. "You're not the only who gets to indulge in crazy ideas, you know." He tossed his cigarette to the pavement and ground it out underfoot. "We're going back into Garland. We've got an item to purchase and a few phone calls to make."

CHAPTER THIRTY-SIX

It took several calls, and I got the impression Dean had to put his ass on the line to make it happen, but regardless of the strings to be pulled and the concessions to be made, within an hour, the Garland Arts and Crafts parking lot had another six squad cars in it. Two officers came in each vehicle— well, technically three. The proud-chested black and tan shepherds that rode in the back of each canine unit were officially considered members of the force, even if they did happen to be dogs.

Dean had gathered everyone in the lot. He stood before the collected officers, each of them standing with their partner and the shepherds sitting at attention, their ears perked and their eyes bright.

Dean's voice carried over the rush of passing cars on the nearby street. "Listen up. As you may or may not know, we've picked up a possible lead on the Tarot Card Killer. Evidence suggests he visited this arts and crafts shop behind us a few months ago. The materials he purchased may have been used in some of his murders."

The officers exchanged glances. There were hard looks and gritted teeth, as well as some murmurs. Apparently, their superiors hadn't told them what was on the line, but they looked determined to help.

"Obviously, tracking TCK's scent from that far back is impossible, even if we knew what to track," said Dean. "But we're not after his scent. We have reason to believe TCK lives nearby, and that he's been using these incense sticks at his home either before, during, or after the murders." He held up a package of the Fresh Escapes sandalwood incense sticks we'd purchased at Garland. "The murder of Lacy Breen occurred four evenings ago. It might be a long shot to think we can still catch a whiff of the scent, but we're not going to give up without trying. Maybe he uses them more often than we suspect. Maybe we'll get lucky."

There were nods amongst the officers, as well as some choice words about what they might do to him once they found him.

Dean put a kibosh on that and told everyone to stay focused. He lit one of the incense sticks and waved the first canine team forward. They had their dog sit as they waved the incense stick before the dog's nose. The animal flinched at the intensity of the smell, and then the team was off, walking into the neighborhood with their hound leading the way. Dean waved each team forward, and each one underwent the same procedure before heading off in a different direction. As the sixth team exposed their dog to the scent, Dean put out the stick and placed it in a sealed plastic bag before throwing it away, I guess to mask the scent so the dogs wouldn't double back. Then, Dean informed me we were coming with, and off we went with the final squad.

The canine unit led the way, though from my viewpoint it

wasn't immediately clear if the patrol officers were leading the shepherd or vice versa. The dog's leash wasn't taut, with him dragging the officers behind him in a rush, but neither was he stopping to sniff every signpost and bush. The pup walked a few steps in front of the officers, his tongue wagging out the side of his mouth as if he didn't have a care in the world, but the rest of him told a different story. His eyes were focused in front of him, darting from object to object, never resting for more than a half a second. His ears pointed up, twisting to and fro with the rumble of a passing engine or the whirr of a nearby window fan. It was his nose that never stopped moving, though, the tip wrinkling and his nostrils flaring as he pumped air in and out.

It was impressive to watch. It was one thing for the dog to understand what the officers wanted of him—they were intelligent creatures, even if they didn't understand language—but the even more impressive part was the ferocity and determination with which the shepherd attacked his duty. Officers of the law might vow to serve and protect, but the dog in front of me, with his chest heaving as he sniffed, might be the most dedicated member of the force I'd ever laid eyes on.

We headed east from Garland, working our way across a stretch of small shops before turning into a residential neighborhood. The homes there weren't anything special, little nicer than those where I'd been involved in the shooting. There weren't many people walking the sidewalks, though it was late enough that more than one home had people sitting on the front porch, enjoying a cold beer after a hard day's work. The individuals who saw us didn't approach or ask questions, they just viewed us from afar with apprehension and distrust. At first I thought we were traveling in a random direction, led neither by the dog nor his handlers, but as we cleared our block, headed further east, doubled back, and repeated the process, it became clear we were systematically walking the neighborhoods, as I'm sure the other teams were doing in other directions.

The sun dipped low in the sky. The shadows from trees and homes alike grew long, and still we walked. My feet hurt and I was losing hope, having lost track of how many streets we'd zigzagged up and down, but to his credit, Officer Pooch didn't seem discouraged. He kept going with that same dogged focus— no pun intended—as he'd started with, his eyes just as bright, nose just as active. Unfortunately, the fact that his demeanor hadn't changed since we started meant he hadn't caught any whiff of incense, and I couldn't imagine we'd keep going much longer. A glance at my watch suggested we had half an hour of sunlight left, if that.

Just when I thought Dean might call off the operation, I heard the far off wail of a siren. It grew louder, and within half a minute, a squad car appeared at the intersection of our street with the main boulevard. The tires squealed as it turned toward us. The engine roared as it accelerated, then the tires cried out again as the officer at the wheel put his weight on the brakes.

The windows were open. The officer in the driver's seat leaned out, face flushed. "Detective Dean. One of the dogs caught a scent. Still tracking it, far as I know. I came to find you."

Dean was halfway in the Crown Royal before the officer even finished speaking. I jumped into the back seat as Dean shouted at our canine unit to hustle back to the parking lot and call dispatch for further instructions. The officer at the wheel hit the gas, pushing me into my seat. I scrambled for the seat belt as we took a turn. Though Dean looked wild around the edges, he must've still had his wits about him. He asked the officer for directions on where the scent had been caught, then instructed him to swing past Garland so we could snag his Viper. The patrol car bounced as we pulled into the lot at too high a speed, but it only took Dean and me a few seconds before we were situated in his car and following our guide. Dean told me to call into dispatch and tell them to send Moss and Justice to Garland for backup. Turns out, we didn't have far to go. By the time the dispatch operator responded, we were already slowing, so I gave her the nearest street corner and hung the receiver back on the console.

Much to my surprise, the officer in the lead car wasn't pulling over in front of one of the area's many small homes. Instead, the car stopped in front of a stretch of undeveloped land. In a city the density of New Welwic, it was big enough to qualify as a park, though it clearly wasn't one. The grass within was mottled and varied, some high enough to come to my chest, some only to my ankles, some green and lush, some already brown in anticipation of winter. There were trees at the edges of the property, hiding the homes and businesses on the other sides, and next to the road was a steep drainage ditch. Could that be a coincidence, or were drainage ditches a necessity for every undeveloped property?

The Viper lurched as Dean put it into park. In the field, about forty yards past the edge of the ditch, two of the canine teams wandered about, the grass to their waists and almost obscuring the shepherds. Above us, the sky was turning shades of navy and royal purple, while the sky to the west still glowed with streaks of orange and magenta.

Dean held out a hand. "There's a flashlight in the glovebox."

I had one on my utility belt, but better to have more than not enough. I opened the compartment and gave the torch to

Dean. He got out, slamming the door behind him, and I followed him into the field. The ground squelched as we hopped across the ditch, then firmed up as we got into the thick of the grass. One of the officers in the canine unit waved as we darted through the brush toward them. It seemed as if they'd stopped moving.

"What is it?" called Dean. "What did you find?"

The nearest officer hailed us. "The shepherd caught the scent a few blocks from here, sir. Officer Johnston and Llewellyn's canine caught it, too. We met en route. Looks like the scent ends here." The officer waved to the object the dogs were sniffing at.

Dean pushed forward to get a look, turning his flashlight on to illuminate the area. I'd assumed if we were lucky enough to have one of the dogs catch a scent, they'd lead us to a home or a business. We were gifted no such luck, however. What the dogs stood before was nothing more than a rock. It was a large rock, to be sure, granite by the looks of it, weighing several hundred pounds and with a broad flat expanse on the top, free of moss or dirt or debris, but it was a dull piece of stone nonetheless.

"It's a rock," said Dean.

Let it never be said Alton Dean was immune from making inane statements like the rest of us. I don't think he said it to make me feel better, though. The look on his face suggested he was as surprised as anyone.

The officer shrugged as the dogs kept sniffing. "It appears to be, sir. Looks like there's a little black smudging on top. Could be soot from the incense."

Dean knelt low next to the thing. He shined his flashlight on it from several angles. "Could be." He pointed. "Is that blood?"

I turned on my flashlight and knelt down, too. There was a

spot on the top of the granite slab with a more rusty hue than the rest. It was in a depression, so blood might've collected there. Then again, granite spanned the gamut from gray to orangey-brown. It could've been the natural hue of the stone rather than dried blood. "We could call CSU. Have someone take a sample."

Dean stood. I was sure he'd heard me, but he didn't react. He gazed into the field, casting the cone of light from his flashlight into the rapidly deepening gloom of the overgrown brush. He turned, his brow furrowed as he gazed past the weeds and shrubs toward the trees at the edge of the property.

I joined him on my feet. "Dean? You want me to call CSU?"

His eyes were distant. He wet his lips with his tongue, and for a moment I thought he was going to ignore me again.

"No," he said eventually. "We'll have them come tomorrow. It's late, and we've done all we can. Officer Rourke? You and the rest of the canine units can head home. We appreciate your help."

The officer nodded. "Sure thing, Detective. Guys? Let's move out."

As the officers and search dogs headed back toward the street, Dean sat on the flat of the rock and sighed. His shoulders slumped, and he stared at the dirt underfoot.

I didn't think I'd ever seem him look so defeated. "Dean? Is this really it? Are we just going to pack it in?"

Dean glanced at me. Pain lingered in his eyes, a combination of disappointment and defeat. "We tried, Phair. The dolls, the incense? It was a shot in the dark. We took it, and we missed. We found a rock."

"A rock that could mean something," I said. "TCK could've been here. It could've been the site of a ritual. He could've—"

"Phair." Dean silenced me with another defeated glanced. "Go to the car. Call dispatch. Tell them Moss and Justice can head home. Grab some tape from the trunk, and we'll mark the stone off. Then we're heading out."

I didn't know what to say. Dean never gave up. To say he was dogged and tenacious didn't come close to depicting how determined he was. I couldn't say exactly what drove him. Maybe there was something in his childhood he hadn't told me about. A relative's death. Certainly his former fiancée's overdose played a part. But he didn't give up. At least, I'd never seem him do so—until now.

Part of me wanted to refuse. To tell him to get up and keep going. Something told me we were so close, and yet... maybe I should trust Dean's expertise. Night was upon us, and as much as I wanted to believe we'd stumbled upon something that would break the case wide open, it simply wasn't the case. He was right. We'd found a rock. Maybe it was a clue, but we'd found so many and all of them had taken us no further than an overgrown field.

In the end, I swallowed my pride and desire, nodded, and headed back toward the Viper.

CHAPTER THIRTY-SEVEN

D ean hadn't moved from his spot on the rock when I returned with the roll of yellow tape. His flashlight hung low in his hand, casting a bright yellow oval across a patch of dirt overgrown with grass that had gone to seed. I held my own flashlight in hand, using it to get an idea of what surrounded the rock. There weren't any nearby trees or even bushes for that matter, but some of the weeds looked tall and sturdy enough to withstand being looped with a thin strand of plastic tape. The other option was to lay it directly over the stone, but that would require Dean to move.

With the tape crinkling in hand, I glanced at Dean for guidance, but he didn't look at me. He stared forward, as if I wasn't there. In that moment, something inside me snapped. Seeing Dean so dejected, every one of his cues singing of defeat, I knew I had to do something. He'd claimed the TCK case wasn't about his career or his reputation. He'd said all that mattered was bringing TCK to justice, but there was more to it for me. Yes, I wanted to stop TCK and gain justice for the victims' families, too, but I couldn't sacrifice everything to get there. I couldn't let

Dean wring himself dry, put every ounce of his soul into the chase only to watch it shatter along the way. I had to build him back up. I had to support him. It's what friends did for one another.

I cleared my throat. "You want me to hang the tape over the biggest, sturdiest weeds?"

Dean gave a half-hearted shrug. "Sure."

I started with a lamb's ear that was over five feet tall. Based on the droppings underneath it, migratory birds had used it as a temporary perch. "You'll have to move, eventually. I'll fence you in, otherwise."

Still he didn't look up. "I will."

I wanted to help, but I didn't have any idea how to. How do you hype up a golden boy who everyone thinks is infallible? What do you say when the person who's the best at something doubts their own abilities?

I thought as I stretched the tape to the next giant weed and kept on thinking as I pulled the tape into the first half of a square. In the end, I figured it was best to speak from the heart. "Did I ever tell you about how I got my childhood dog, Dean?"

Though he looked despondent, his brain was still processing information. He looked up, confused. "What?"

I lightly looped the tape over a scraggly sunflower. "I think I first asked my parents for a dog when I was six. Maybe seven. My dad flat out refused. He didn't like dogs and he didn't want to care for one. Not surprising, really. He was something of an alcoholic. Later on, he'd become a full-blown one. As a result, responsibility wasn't exactly his strong suit, though I doubt it would've been even if he'd been sober. Regardless, I wasn't one to take no for an answer. So I'd beg and plead and cajole, and my dad would always give the same response. No, no, no.

"Well, there are only so many times you can get the same answer before you try a different line of attack, and mine was going after my mom. She wasn't as much of a hard-liner as my dad, but she was just as good at giving the same answer. Not unless your dad agrees, she'd tell me. So I'd go to my dad and ask again, he'd say no, and I'd ask my mom, and she'd ask what my dad said. I tried lying, but that didn't get me very far.

"That's when I started being creative. I tried to lure a dog in off the street. Got close a couple times before I eventually convinced a stray to come in. My dad wasn't happy when that happened, and neither was the neighbor from down the street whose dog it was. It went back to the neighbor, but my dad made it clear I wouldn't get to keep any mutts I found. All that taught me was that I couldn't let it be known I'd caught one. The next one I lured I kept in my room, but dogs aren't known for being quiet. That poor dog was shipped to the pound within a day of me finding him. So I tried a new tactic. I blackmailed my dad. I'll admit, it wasn't a great strategy, hiding his car keys and telling him I'd only give them back if he bought me a dog, but I was desperate and young and willing to try anything. Needless to say, it didn't work.

"Now, this endeavor to get a dog wasn't a couple week long thing. I was after it for a good three years, and during that time, the relationship between my parents deteriorated. That didn't help my chances to get a dog given all their efforts were spent fighting each other and any requests I had were met with spillover hostility. Eventually, they divorced. My mom moved out, my dad's alcoholism worsened, and soon my mom moved in with a new guy. I decided to stay with my dad for reasons too complicated to get into, but as a way to get me to visit more and acclimate to my new stepdad, guess what my mom got me? That's right. A dog. Took a few years, but I finally got one."

I finished hanging the tape over the fourth overgrown weed and turned back toward the first. I found Dean looking at me, his brow creased. "What message am I supposed to draw from this? That in their worst moments, you leveraged your parents' love for you into finally getting what you wanted?"

I snorted and shook my head. "The point I'm trying to make is... the things you want often don't come easy. There's always someone fighting you, someone with a goal diametrically opposed to yours. Sometimes it seems you'll never win, and you might get to a point where it feels like things can't get worse. When my parents divorced, that's how I felt. But there's always another dawn. Things change, and I got my dog. And in case you think the moral is purely about persistence paying off, it's not. I needed that dog. It was there for me when neither of my parents were. It was the best friend I had for years, and call me a little conceited, but I'm pretty sure it needed me, too. Because I persevered I got what I wanted, but I also cultivated a relationship that was warm and caring and heartfelt. That relationship saved me, Alton. It made me a better person in the long run."

Dean took a deep breath. "The hottest fire forges the strongest blade. I know that, and I agree for the most part. It's only when an adversary pushes you that you find out what you're made of. In a vacuum where just he and I were pushing our chips onto the table, perhaps I wouldn't mind matching wits with TCK. Perhaps I might even find it exhilarating. But as I've mentioned, this is about so much more than he and I. It's about all of us. You, me, Moss, Justice, the whole departments, and all the women who might fall under the swing of his executioner's axe. It's a tough burden to carry, Nell. You can argue it's not my burden alone, but that's how I feel. Every step I take I see him lurking in the shadows. Every time I get a phone call, I think I'll hear his mechanical voice. Every time I fill my lungs with air, I smell the stench of death thick in my nostrils." He breathed deep again, and his face twisted in disgust. "Gods. Don't you smell it?"

I stood with the tape in hand, waiting to complete the square. "I guess I haven't been as deeply affected by this as you have."

Dean stood, his brow furrowing. He took another deep suck of air. "No. I mean it. Something smells rotten. I don't think it's in my head."

I sniffed the air. If anything, it smelled cleaner than the usual New Welwic stink, probably because we weren't standing in an alley through which raw sewage occasionally overflowed, but then again, my sense of smell wasn't as finely tuned as Dean's elven one. "I don't smell anything."

Dean wandered into the field, his nostrils flaring. I dropped the tape where I stood and followed him, wondering if his mind was playing tricks on him. Dean walked slowly, turning his head to and fro as he crushed weeds and grasses before him. We'd walked about twenty feet parallel to the street before I noticed something in the air, too. A whiff of something sour and rotten, like trash left too long in the sun.

I frowned. "You're not crazy, Dean. I smell it, too."

He nodded, reoriented, and took a few steps toward the trees on the far side of the lot. Suddenly, he stopped and looked down, shining his flashlight onto the dirt.

I added my flashlight's power. There, in a bare spot between weeds, the earth had been disturbed. Not only had it been recently tilled, but it had been pushed into a small mound.

"Keep your light on that," said Dean. He flipped his flashlight around and knelt. He dragged the butt of his light through the loose dirt, then again, applying more pressure. As the smooth black metal passed through, it caught on something. Dean flinched.

"What is it?" I moved my flashlight to better illuminate the area.

Dean pulled a glove from his pocket. "It's carrion. Several days gone." The glove snapped as Dean pulled it on. He brushed some of the dirt away, revealing a mound of fur and flesh half eaten by worms. "I think it's a... rat."

My curiosity helped suppress my gag reflex. "*A rat?* Like the one we found near Lacy's corpse?"

"Well, it's not a mouse," said Dean as he poked the decaying corpse. "It's too large. Strange. You'd expect a field mouse in a field. Not so much a rat."

"Why didn't the dogs pick up on this?" I asked.

"I'm sure they did, but we hadn't asked them to alert us to the smell of carrion. They knew we wanted to track incense, so they had blinders on to everything else." Dean rubbed his chin. "This wasn't a natural death, otherwise it wouldn't have been buried. The body is too far gone to tell how it died, but TCK had to have been behind this, right? Why would he bother killing so many animals?"

Dean looked at me, as if I'd have an answer.

I shrugged. "I don't know. The witch I spoke with said black magic requires blood sacrifice, but maybe there's more to it. Maybe this rat's death created a link between it and the rat we found, or between Lacy. I couldn't begin to speculate. But... if that's why this rat was buried, there should be more. A bird, a squirrel, maybe something else."

Dean nodded, casting his torch around in search of more disturbed earth. Nothing was fresh like the spot we'd come across, but there was another mound nearby. Dean broke it up with the butt of his flashlight before clawing through the dirt with his fingers. After a moment, he came back up, eyes wide. There was a small bone in his hands.

"We did it." Dean's face was slack with disbelief. "The poppets, the incense, it all worked. TCK's been here, performing rituals. There's no two ways about it."

A chill ran through my spine, even as adrenaline rushed through my veins. "That means he's close by. He has to be."

Dean swung his flashlight, illuminating the grass and weeds around us. He swept the cone of light to and fro before stopping on a patch that to me looked similar to the rest. "There. That's a game trail... or a person trail."

Now that he mentioned it, a narrow path through the grass had been tamped down. "I think you're right."

Without a word, Dean set off through the field, and I had no choice but to chase after him.

CHAPTER THIRTY-EIGHT

Dean ran along the faint game trail, the yellow cone from his flashlight swimming through the grass with each of his loping steps. In no time at all, we'd reached the western edge of the undeveloped plot. There, the land sloped upward into a stand of centenarian trees, but as in most places in New Welwic, there wasn't much forest to go around. The grove was twenty or thirty feet thick at most, and we didn't need our flashlights to see past the trunks to the other side. There, at the top of the slope, the land flattened again into what appeared to be a cul-de-sac. Closest to us stood a two-story house, its back wall not ten feet from the edge of the trees. Its front half rested on the top of the hill while in the back spidery legs extended from its body to meet the dropping slope. A window upstairs glowed, a watchful eye of flickering light, while the downstairs windows yawned wide, dark and empty.

"Let's go," said Dean. He darted into the forest, bobbing and weaving through the trunks, once again leaving me to try and keep up. Dean killed his flashlight as he popped out of the trees onto the unkempt lawn on the other side, and I followed suit.

Dean held out a hand, motioning me to stay quiet and close. I followed him up the slope, trying to keep from stepping on any branches, though gods knew we'd made noise barreling through the forest. A single streetlight stood at the entrance to the cul-de-sac, its glow dying a good thirty feet from house before us. No porch light was lit, keeping its facade drenched in darkness. I couldn't even see the street numbers.

"This is it," whispered Dean. "We've found him, Phair. We've finally found him."

The streetlight's glow might've fallen short of us, but Dean's eyes were lit with an inner fire. They were the eyes of a man who knew what he was about to do. A man who'd suffered pain and defeat and saw redemption at hand. A man who'd eaten desperation and turned it into obsession.

"Dean, I don't think this is a good idea," I whispered back. "We haven't called for backup. Even if this is the right house, we don't have a warrant or exigent circumstances, and there's the issue of my psychiatric timeout. I shouldn't be here. I'm limited to office work and investigation, remember?"

Dean looked as if he hadn't heard me. He pulled his pistol from underneath his suit jacket and gripped it tight. He mounted the concrete steps to the porch and pressed himself against the house, eyeing the entrance.

He nodded to me. "The door's ajar. And..." He pressed his arm against the door, opening it another inch. His nose wrinkled, and his eyes widened even further. "Gods above. The incense. It's burning inside. I can smell it. He might be starting another ritual."

I swore under my breath. I might lose my job over it, but I'd be damned if I'd let my boss and friend, the man who put his neck on the line to pull me out of a toxic partnership and worked to build me into a competent detective, wander alone into the house of a suspected serial killer as he initiated deadly magics intended to kill innocent women.

I pulled my gun from its holster and joined Dean on the other side of the door. The woody, earthy scent of the incense tickled my nose, and I knew we were in too deep to jump back now. My heart hammered against my ribs. Sweat beaded on my brow and sprouted under my armpits. I might've been willing to go to war with Dean, but that didn't mean I wasn't scared pants-less about what awaited us. "What's the plan?"

"Stick together," said Dean. "Watch each other's backs. We'll do a quick sweep of the main level. If we don't see anything, we head upstairs. Move carefully. No flashlights. We don't want to give ourselves away. I'll stay in front. If anyone threatens us, I'll take the shot. I'm not putting you in that position again if we can avoid it."

My ears throbbed from the blood rushing through them. "I've got your back."

Dean nodded. "Let's go."

Dean pushed the front door the rest of the way open. He moved slowly and carefully. Thankfully, the hinges didn't creak. He crept inside with his pistol gripped tight before him, like a panther stalking its prey.

The home seemed to be a standard floor plan, with a central corridor down the middle, narrow stairs next to it, and living space wrapped around it. The lights were off on the main, as the windows suggested, but a warm, flickering light illuminated the top of the staircase. Given that my eyes had been adjusting as night fell, it was enough.

Dean whispered. "Check left side. I've got right. Stick close. Don't head in."

Dean took a couple steps through the open partition to his right, his eyes tracking everything in the room. I did the same on my side of the home, stepping into a living space. On first glance, the place didn't look like the home of a mass murderer. There was plenty of worn-in furniture, heavy drapes hanging from rods, and a floral wallpaper instead of paint. There was a musty smell in the air, not to mention the familiar scent of the incense, but the place didn't reek of death or decay. It seemed the sort of place you might find an elderly couple living in— except for the knickknacks.

There were oodles of odds and ends, on the coffee table, on bookshelves, hanging from the ceiling. I spotted a full skeleton of an opossum, mounted to appear as it might while alive. A painting of a moth surrounded by moons and stars and other mystic symbols I couldn't decipher hung from the wall, and on the table, I spotted a wooden bowl containing dice, shells, and small feathers. Next to it was what appeared to be a deck of oversized cards.

I backed into the central hallway. "Dean. *Tarot.*" I gestured toward the table.

He nodded. "Upstairs. Careful."

Dean paced to the stairs as the light at the top continued to flicker. He placed one foot on the lowest step near the wall, testing it with his weight. It didn't creak, but Dean didn't take that to mean none of them would. He went up slowly, methodically, and I followed him, step for step. I didn't know how old the house was, but it was a miracle the staircase didn't give us away. I took it as a good sign.

As we reached the top, we found a small central space around the stairs with a few open doors leading to bedrooms. All the doors were open, but the flickering light only came from

one. Suddenly, my mouth felt dry as a bone, and I feared the
sound of my breathing would give us away. Dean might've been
just as nervous. His knuckles looked pale as they clutched his
pistol, the force of his grip squeezing out the blood.

We didn't share a word. Dean moved forward, and I stuck to
him like glue. As we reached the door whose frame flickered
with an orange glow, Dean spun inside with his pistol raised. I
was right beside him, ready to cry out for whoever we found to
get on the floor, but the room was bare. No people, no victims,
not even any furniture. It was completely empty.

Well, almost. Against the far wall, underneath a window
with thick safety bars placed outside it, was a small shrine. A
lone pillow lay before it. On the shrine itself, in addition to a
pair of candles dripping with wax and a single stick of burning
incense, were a collection of dolls.

No. *Poppets.*

Dean closed on the shrine, and I felt myself similarly
drawn in.

Dean's face was drawn as he stared at the poppets. He saw
the same thing I did. There were four, and none were in good
condition.

My body coursed with adrenaline. I thought I might faint or
explode. Maybe both. "Dean." I spoke with the power of a
mouse. "We found them, but where is he?"

Before Dean could answer I felt a rush of air. I spun, my
pistol held high, and just caught the sight of the door slamming
shut behind us.

CHAPTER THIRTY-NINE

A roar split the air, cracking like a whip. Once, twice, thrice in quick succession. My ears stung as Dean's pistol sent three slugs barreling into the door that had slammed shut. Splinters flew, glimmering momentarily before vanishing as the light of the candles flickered and died, put out by the rush of air. A hint of sooty smoke joined the incense, the burning candles' last gasps.

If Dean's ears were ringing as mine were, he ignored them. He took a step forward, his body faintly outlined by the dim glow seeping through the room's sole window. "Give it up, TCK. We found you. It's over."

All I could hear was the fading echo of Dean's gunshots. After a moment, a low, staccato sound oozed my way, muffled by the wall. It took me a second to realize it was a chuckle.

"Detective. You seem to have misread the situation. Perhaps you'd like to reconsider your threats."

The voice was vaguely familiar: more of a bass than a baritone, lacking the muffle I'd heard over the phone, and strained with a touch of nervous insanity. It was infinitely more terrifying in person.

"I haven't misread a thing," said Dean. "You thought yourself too smart for us. You thought you could lead us by the nose without us becoming the wiser, that you could murder and torture innocent women with impunity. But you weren't as smart as you thought. You made mistakes. We tracked you. We're here. It's over."

The grim chuckle seeped through the wall again. "Really, Detective? I never thought you'd be one to resort to toothless bluster. You're too logical for that. Too grounded. Let go of your anger and accept the truth. You didn't catch me. *I caught you.*"

Dean's gun glimmered as he twisted in the near darkness, trying to get a bead on the source of the sound, but the wall muffled both the intensity and the direction. "I'm not bluffing, TCK. Your clock is ticking. You may have locked us in this room, but officers are en route as we speak. The longer we engage in this standoff, the more time you lose. You can give up now, or you can run, and how far do you think you'll get? We know where you live, and even though I haven't gotten a look at your face, it's only a matter of time until I know every detail of your life. There won't be a rock large enough for you to hide under once we start searching, so this comes down to how you want to go down. If you turn yourself in now, you'll get a trial. One last chance to crow and gloat, which we both know you love, otherwise you'll die from a hail of gunfire as every officer in the city chases you down like a dog."

The lie slid so easily off Dean's tongue that I almost believed it, but I knew better. I'd been the one to hail dispatch and tell the operator to relay to Moss and Justice they needn't bother coming. The canine units had headed home, and it was late enough no one would expect us back in the office until tomorrow. Moss would wonder where I was when I didn't spend the night at her place, but when would she start worrying? In the morning?

I heard a snort, and something told me TCK didn't buy the story, either. "The universe told me you'd be coming, you know. Leave the incense burning, it predicted, and you will follow. I looked deep into the abyss to make sure I wasn't reading it wrong, checked my bones and double played the cards, but always I came to the same conclusion. I would be in possession of you by night's end, and here you are. The divination told me you'd have another with you. Again it was correct, but it failed to show your friends arriving to save you. It showed only a terrible surprise for you, Detective, and this night ending in darkness. Then again, I suppose the divination could be a mirage. It did show us pitting wits, after all, and so far that has been a disappointment."

Dean didn't say anything, but I heard his teeth grinding against each other. My breath felt ragged in my throat, and the gun I held felt slick against my sweating palms.

"Regardless," continued the voice, the razor's edge of insanity as prominent as ever. "I will miss testing myself against you, Detective. I doubt anyone else in the department has half the brains you do, limited as they may be, but all good things must come to an end. As must you."

"And how do you plan to stop me?" said Dean. "You may have snagged us in this room, but you can't keep us locked forever. Officers will come for us, and that's if we don't escape first. You could always come in and face me, man to man, but I wouldn't recommend it. There are several bullets left in my magazine, and without a wall between us, I won't miss."

"Please, Detective," replied TCK. "As if I'd bother getting my hands dirty to commit murder. If the incense brought you here, then surely you know about the poppets. I bought twenty, remember? I'm sure you each shed a hair or two on your way upstairs, and a quick trip to your apartments will produce the other items I need. I have no doubt you'll have friends on the way sooner or later, but I work quickly. So enjoy the night, Detective. It'll be your last."

Dean growled. Not like a dog that had been cornered, but a deep, guttural snarl. A growl of unadulterated rage that rose from the pit of his stomach and flew through his esophagus like a dragon's flame. As the sound cut free of him, so too did more slugs from his pistol. The thing roared as he fired, over and over again into the wall. I lost track of how many times he fired, but as the cacophony of sound ended, a steady clicking replaced it, the sound of Dean's pistol failing to chamber a new round with each of his trigger pulls.

As the roar faded from my ears, I listened for cries of pain from the other side, but there were none. Instead, all I heard was a low, echoing laughter, malicious and jubilant and cruel.

I was fairly sure TCK left as soon as Dean fired his weapon, but that laughter stuck with me for long after.

CHAPTER FORTY

I couldn't have told you how long I stood in the darkness staring at that wall, imagining the bullet holes I couldn't quite see. All I know is it was long enough for me to cast doubt on every decision that had gotten me there. Fear rattled around inside me, too—how couldn't there be?—but the fear was a more distant concern. The doubt, on the other hand, escalated matters immediately. It grew and grew, gnawing at me, taunting me. Before I knew it, it had morphed into a festering ball of self-loathing that sat on me, crushing me under its weight and threatening to rob me of the very breath in my lungs.

My legs felt weak, and I stumbled toward the wall at my side. I managed to put out a hand before I thumped against the plasterboard. I felt nauseous. The room felt as if it spun around me, though with everything drenched in night I couldn't really tell. Somehow I holstered my pistol before resting my back against the wall and sliding to the floor.

Dean's voice split the air, thick with concern. "Phair?" It felt like the first words I'd heard in days.

My voice came out faint. Not out of caution but of a lack of conviction. "This is my fault, Dean. Moss warned me, but I didn't listen."

Dean turned toward me, his pistol hanging loosely from his hand. "Moss *warned you?*"

I nodded weakly. "We were talking over breakfast, the night after TCK first called. I'd shared my insecurities with her, that I wasn't sure if I belonged at your side. She told me... she told me that I needed to trust everyone. That if we worked together, it would work out in the end. But I didn't do that. I was too concerned about myself to think about the bigger picture, and I let you and everyone else down along the way."

Dean tucked his pistol into his holster. His shoes clacked off the hardwood floor as he stepped to me. "What are you talking about? How is any of this your fault?"

I swallowed, trying to find the right way to explain it. I think I knew, but admitting the truth wasn't easy. "Every time you speak about the cases you've closed, you emphasize justice, closure for the victims, seeing right beat wrong. Of course I want that, too, but I'd be lying if I said it was the only thing driving me. When you plucked me from the Williams Street precinct, when you pitched me on the good the department can do, I bought in, but I still wasn't sure if police work was right for me. I was just willing to give it a go if you were the one calling the shots. And then we solved a case. Stella Vernon's murder. Or, if I'm being honest, it felt as if *I* solved it. And it felt *good.* Not just because I'd done the right thing, but because it felt as if I was finally good at something, and I've never been good at much of anything."

I looked up at Dean, his pale eyes reflecting the room's dim glow. "That's the mistake I made with this case, Dean. I kept pushing because I wanted to feel important and smart and worthwhile. If it was about stopping TCK, I would've listened to Moss. I would've gone home when you and the captain and the psychiatrist told me to. If I'd trusted the team to find TCK instead of lusting after the rush of catching him myself, we wouldn't be here. I wouldn't have called my Nana and met with a witch. We wouldn't have tracked the smell of incense to an overgrown field, or even if we had, it would've been Moss and Justice with you instead of me. There would've been more of us. One of them could've called for help while the other stayed with you. Someone more experienced. Someone who would've noticed TCK creeping up on us at the top of the stairs. Gods, Dean, I didn't even hear him."

Dean was quiet. He took a breath. When he exhaled, it sounded ragged. He turned around and took a seat next to me. "You sure know how to cut straight to a guy's heart, don't you?"

This time, it was my turn to sound confused. "What?"

"Maybe you didn't do it on purpose. I think you're being honest about your motivations, but every criticism you made about yourself? I'm guilty of it, too. Except those same faults are less forgivable for me..."

I blinked. "I don't believe it. You approach every case with the best of intentions. With altruism instead of self-interest."

"Perhaps," said Dean heavily. "But you can have the best of intentions and still make missteps. You may have been seeking an affirmation of worth, but my sin was worse. I was filled with conceit. I thought I was the only one who could find TCK. I thought if I couldn't do it, no one else would. It's what drove my depression, thinking I'd failed and that he'd keep killing in perpetuity. But it's not true. I didn't find him. You did. You knew the dead animals were important. You wouldn't let it go. You're the one who figured out how they fit into the equation, and you're the one who thought to track the poppets. And what did I do? I pushed and pushed, my only focus on catching TCK. You told me you shouldn't be here, that we should call backup. I knew you were right, same as I knew it when we raided Cassman's place, but I didn't listen. I had to catch him. Me. It was personal, and it had to be now. I didn't trust anyone else to get it done."

Dean shook his head. He gave a heavy sigh, his head hanging low. "The sad thing is, this is why I brought you on. I needed help on my other cases so I could focus on the tarot card murders. Turns out *this* is the case I needed help with."

They say misery loves company, but I didn't feel any better knowing I wasn't the only one vulnerable to my personal flaws. I pulled up my knees and wrapped my arms around them, giving myself a tight hug. "Guess we both should've listened to Moss."

"Hey." Dean put a hand on my knee. "It's not too late."

I could barely see the hand in the darkness, but I felt the warmth of his touch. It felt nice. "What do you mean?"

"I mean we're both still here. You and me. It would be better if we had Justice and Moss at our sides, sure, but two people working together are still a team. If we can set aside our hubris, our self-doubt, and our fears, I don't think there's anything that can stop us. Not a locked room or a psychotic murderer or even black magic itself."

I put my hand over his. "You really believe that?"

He flipped his hand over to squeeze mine. "I know that every time I've succeeded, I've had good people helping me along the way. Come on. Let's figure a way out of here and get that son of a bitch."

CHAPTER FORTY-ONE

D ean stood and held out a hand. I grasped it, and he helped me to my feet. He pulled his gun from his holster, ejected the empty magazine, slid in a new one, and put it back on his hip. "Alright. Let's get an idea of what we're up against."

Dean moved to the door. He tested the handle, which rattled but didn't turn.

"Do you think TCK is still here?" I asked, wondering if the noise would alert him.

"He might be," said Dean. "But I doubt it. I think his threat of making poppets of us was a bluff, same as my assurance that we had backup on the way. Enchanting poppets can't be as simple a process as he or that witch acquaintance of yours make it out to be, otherwise I doubt he'd spend weeks between attacks. It takes planning for him to execute each murder, so I doubt he'd be able to put two poppets together overnight, not to mention he'd need to find animals to sacrifice. Besides, one of the few things we know about TCK is that he's intelligent. The smartest move for him right now is to flee. We still don't have any idea who he is, and it's possible that tracking the deed on this home won't lead us to him."

I suffered a pang of fear, not at the idea of being murdered but at losing TCK after everything we'd been through. "You think he's already slipped away?"

"It's what I would've done, but just because TCK is clever doesn't mean he's rational. He's an unstable sociopath. It's possible he's prioritizing our suffering and defeat over all else, which believe it or not would be a good thing. It would keep him blinded to the best course of action, just as our faults blinded us." Dean ran his fingers over the edge of the door where it met the frame. "The bad news is we're not getting through this door. This room was designed to keep people in, not out. The hinges are on the outside, the frame is reinforced, and the door itself is solid hardwood. A couple of my bullets punched through the wall, but not the door itself. If Justice were here, he might be able to kick this down, but we don't stand a chance."

I moved to the window, trying to keep the fear at bay. As I'd noticed upon walking in, there were thick iron bars over it. I'd seen them downstairs, too, so it hadn't struck me as odd. I figured the neighborhood dictated the choice, not the fact that the rooms might be designed as prison cells. "Window frame is reinforced, too. I'm not sure this window is even designed to open. We could break the glass. We couldn't sneak through, but if we shout for help, someone might hear us."

"We'd be shouting into the forest," said Dean. "The foliage will absorb our cries more than redirect them. Besides, if the gunshots I fired didn't attract attention, I'd wager shouting won't either. Let's consider that a last resort."

"If we can't get through the door, what other option do we have? Shine our flashlights out the window to attract attention?"

"We live in a three dimensional world, Phair. Doors and windows are not our only option." Dean brushed his fingertips against the wall at our side, then rapped his knuckles on it and listened. "Pretty sure this is lath and plaster. Makes sense in a building of this age. Drywall would be easier to get through, but lath and plaster isn't impossible. Studs are probably sixteen inches apart at least, so if we can smash our way through the plaster and wooden slats, we should be able to slide through."

"Smash though how?" I said. "Have you been working on your martial arts training?"

Dean unholstered his pistol, flipped it around, and grabbed it by the barrel. "Turns out these things work decently well as hammers in a pinch."

I glanced at the door. "That's going to make a lot of noise."

"Then let's hope TCK left," replied Dean. "Even if he didn't, we'll be safe as long as we work together. You cover the door with your sidearm while I work on the wall. We can switch when I get tired."

For the first time since the door slammed shut behind us, I started to feel as if we might get out alive. I pulled my pistol and nodded. "Got it."

"Here goes nothing." After removing the magazine and checking to make sure there wasn't a bullet in the chamber, Dean pulled back and slammed the butt of his pistol into the wall. The wall responded with a loud crack, and bits of plaster flew into the air. Again Dean pulled back, and again he smashed the butt of the pistol against the plaster. *Whack, whack, whack, crunch.*

I glanced at that last sound. An inky hole had appeared in the wall where Dean had been hammering. "That was easy."

"I'm not sure I'd go that far," he said. "This is murder on the hands. Pistols are meant to be held by the grip after all, and there's a long way to go. But it's progress. Keep an eye on the door. If TCK is going to come back, he'll be here soon."

Dean kept going, the butt of his gun hammering into the wall with the consistency of a metronome. Chunks of plaster sprayed over us. Despite the racket, the door didn't budge, nor did I hear any commotion in the moments Dean's pistol wasn't connecting. After Dean finished ripping our side open, I took a turn hammering the plaster-soaked lath on the other side of the wall while Dean watched the door. Soon my hand ached like Dean said it would, but I persevered, sweat beading my brow from the exertion. I guessed we'd been at it for close to ten minutes when Dean took over again.

"Should be almost through now," he said. "Stay aware."

Dean whacked the lath on the other side of the wall a few more times, resulting in a few ominous-sounding cracks. Dean reloaded and holstered his pistol, took a step back, planted his weight on his left foot, and kicked with his right. His first kick landed with a heavy thud, as did his second. The third blasted through the plaster, causing Dean to tip forward as his foot shot into empty space.

"You okay?" I asked, my pistol still trained on the door.

Dean pulled his foot back and shook some dust off his leg. "Suit's ruined, but I'm fine." He kicked a few more times, knocking more plaster-covered slats off the other side. From my angle, the room we'd broken into was as dark as our own, but there might've been a faint warm glow ours lacked.

Dean slid his body into the narrow gap and peeked his head out the other side. "It's a bedroom. Door to the hallway is open. Let's go."

I nodded. Dean stepped through cautiously, pausing to

glance at the room around him. He turned and extended me a hand. "Coast is clear."

I took Dean's hand for the second time tonight, reveling in the warmth and humanity of his touch as I angled my body sideways to make it through the gap. I wasn't as svelte as Dean was, so it was a tighter fit. As I poked my head out the other side, my body still in the gap, I got my first look at the room. There were two dressers, a bed along the far wall, and a bedside lamp on the adjoining nightstand, but it was the glow from the open doorway to the hall that drew me like a moth to a flame. There it was. Our path to freedom. We wouldn't become another statistic of TCK's black magic-stained hands. He'd really left, and yet... why would he turn on the light in the hallway before fleeing? The candles had been the home's only lights when we arrived.

As the thought crossed my mind, I saw motion in the hall. A figure appeared from around the edge of the open door, a hulking man with grayish skin, dark hair, and a face only a mother could love. A crazed sneer was frozen onto his face, and in his hands gleamed a long piece black metal, two barrels side by side.

I tried to shout Dean's name, but it came out as a terrified screech. I threw my weight into my hand, shoving Dean hard in the chest as the man brought the barrels up. Dean windmilled as he flew across the room, falling behind the bed. I barely managed to pull my arm back and tuck my body through the gap when the roar of the shotgun assaulted my ears. The smell of gunpowder filled my nose. Plaster dust flew. The mattress rippled and bits of down floated into the air. I fumbled as I swapped my pistol into the hand I'd used to push Dean, but before I could get it there, the shotgun roared a second time.

The lath in the wall splintered and cracked, crying out as it took the shotgun's punishment.

A voice in my head screeched in terror, but my quick thinking had done more than save Dean's life. He scrambled across the floor, using the bed as cover, before he popped up, pistol in hand. He fired two quick rounds toward the door before ducking back down. With my ears already taxed from the double barrel blasts, I couldn't hear where the bullets landed, but I didn't hear anyone cry out in pain. Apparently, these old houses were built to withstand wars.

"It's over for real this time, TCK," shouted Dean from the cover of his mattress. "You can come out of this house in hand-cuffs or a bodybag. Your choice."

If there was any doubt the beefy, gray-skinned monster with the shotgun was the same man who'd addressed us earlier, it was cleared as soon as he spoke. The same current of insanity laced TCK's speech, his voice as taut as a violin string and as thin as ice in early spring. "I really wish you'd played along, Detective." I heard a clack, then another, the sound of more shells being loaded into the barrels. "I don't like getting my hands dirty. Poppets are much more civilized, not to mention more fun. But I'm afraid you've forced my hand. I can't let you or your officer friend leave. Not alive."

Dean fired another round at the door, preemptively in response to the sound of TCK's shells. "Is this really how you're going out? Reduced to the level of a common thug? Is this the best you could do?"

As he spoke, Dean's eyes weren't on the door. He waved to me, trying to catch my eye. I caught the gesture, but I wasn't sure what was going on. Was Dean trying to bait TCK into another mistake?

The barrel of TCK's shotgun poked through the door, and I pulled back reflexively. "This is your fault, Detective. You're forcing me into it. Forcing me to behave like an animal. I'm not going to let you get away with it."

Dean caught my eye again. He gestured to his gun, then at me, then the door. "Are you kidding? This is all you are, TCK. A violent killer. Only seems fitting this is how it would end. In a mindless bloodbath."

Dean bored into me with his eyes. He nodded toward the door, urging me, and I knew what he wanted. There was a reason he was taunting TCK. To get his attention. So I could take the shot.

I took a slow breath and swallowed my nerves. I'd killed before—in self-defense, sure, and I hadn't confronted the emotions the incident wrought inside me—but this was different. This time, my choice to take a life was warranted. Not just to save ours, but countless others. I'd pay an emotional price, as well as suffer consequences within the department, but I had to do it. It was the right choice. For me. For Dean. For our team.

I poked my head through the gap in the wall, just enough to get a glimpse of the door. It would be hard for me to get a good shot while keeping myself safe given the narrow gap Dean and I had cleared. I'd have to move quick, but I could do it. I wouldn't miss. I gave Dean a nod, and he nodded back.

"Come on, TCK," shouted Dean, a nasty edge to his voice. "If you're going to kill us, get it over with. Come in here, guns blazing. It's all I'd expect of a pathetic moron like you."

I readied myself, my pistol trained on the opening. I thought TCK might howl in rage at Dean's insults, but instead he laughed. He burst out in a crazed cackle, his bellow echoing off the home's old walls. "Oh, I'll kill you, Detective, but it won't bother me. We all do what we must to live, after all. We debase ourselves when necessary. Make deals we later regret. But in the end, it's about survival. And I intend to survive."

I saw the flash of TCK's barrel and a sliver of gray skin. I pressed my finger against my trigger, ready to fire, but as TCK turned the corner, he hesitated. I heard an angry cry from the hall, a voice I didn't recognize. TCK turned toward the sound. His face went slack, and his eyes widened in surprise. His mouth opened, but he didn't get a chance to speak. The whip crack of gunfire spilt the air. One, two, five shots, one after another after another. Blood sprayed from TCK's chest. The shotgun slipped from his hand, clattering to the floor. He stumbled and fell out of view, then I heard a heavy thud as he hit the hardwood.

I slipped through the gap in the wall, taking cover behind a dresser as Dean poked up from behind the mattress. He called out. "This is the NWPD. Put your weapon down and show yourselves!"

"It's okay," said a gruff voice. "It's me. We're here."

I recognized the voice, but my brain didn't have time to match it to a face. The man in the hallway did it for me. Virgil Mason stepped into the open frame, smoking gun still in hand.

Dean's face relaxed at the sight of him. "Mason. What...?"

I heard the heavy thump of footsteps, and a moment later, Justice pushed through the door beside him. "Dean! Phair! Gods above, it's good to see the two of you."

"Justice!" I couldn't help myself. I holstered my weapon and gave the big guy a hug.

Dean came up, too, clapping Justice on the shoulder. Out of the corner of my eye, I saw Moss come in, pistol in hand. She cast a careful look down the hall at what I assumed was TCK's corpse before joining us in the bedroom. "Gods, Dean. Looks like we made it just in time."

"You bet you did," said Dean. "In body and in spirit."

Moss gave him a confused look. "Pardon?"

I let go of Justice. "You saved us before you even got here, Moss. It was your advice that helped us get our heads on straight and come up with a plan to get out of here. A plan to work together and trust in our team."

Dean gave a weak smile. "That's right. You guys pulled through for us, just like you always do."

I think Justice and Moss were too worried to look relieved, but Mason was chipper enough to take part in the accolades. He joined our group, a twinkle in his eye as he gave Dean and me a nod. "We're the NWPD. We're not a bunch of lone wolves. We work together to get the job done. *Always.*"

There was a moment of silence as we all looked at each other, varying levels of pride and relief etched on our faces.

Mason didn't want to let it linger too long, though. "There'll be time for drinks and reflection later. Now lets pull ourselves together. We've got a hell of a lot to do, and even more to sort out."

CHAPTER FORTY-TWO

I'll admit, it was difficult to establish a sense of normalcy after everything I'd been through that night. The adrenaline rush of finding the animal sacrifices and chasing TCK, getting imprisoned, then facing him in a fight to the death, one he ultimately lost. It was only because of the professionalism of everyone around me that I was able to hold it together. Nonetheless, I think everyone picked up on my fragile mental state. Moss was the first one to suggest that I sit out much of the wrap up process, something Dean agreed was a good idea. Justice offered to escort me outside, but as I took to the stairs, I couldn't help but cast a final glance at TCK's body. He lay there slumped in a corner, blood soaking his shirt and spattered across the wall beside him. He had that same look of shock from when Mason arrived frozen on his face, and there it would stay until the worms devoured him. I guess even serial killers can't plan for every eventuality.

Justice flicked lights on as we headed outside. Parked in front of the home was Mason's brown Crown Royal, but neither Moss's Hornet or Justice's Phantom joined it. Justice popped

open the door to the Royal and called in for backup. After he
was done, I asked about his car, at which point he explained
what I'd missed while imprisoned. After receiving my message
that we didn't need their services, Justice and Moss returned to
the precinct, but their interest was piqued. They'd heard about
our requisition of the canine units and they wanted to know
what we'd found. When the units returned and we didn't, they
got worried. I found that surprising, but when pushed Justice
admitted Moss was more concerned about Dean's mental state
following another failure than our physical wellbeing, proving
that Moss was smarter than anyone gave her credit for. They
tried to get dispatch to hail us. When that failed, they asked the
canine units where we were and headed out. When they found
our car abandoned in front of the empty lot, they grew
concerned. While they failed to find the half-buried carrion,
they did spot our trail of destruction through the brush after
some searching. They were able to follow it, more or less, until
the edge of the forest. That's when they heard the first of the
shotgun blasts.

They rushed through the forest and up the hill as fast as
they could, at which point they found Mason speeding toward
them in his Crown Royal. Apparently, he'd been trying to get in
contact with Dean after having an epiphany about the tarot
cards left on the victims, and when he found not only that Dean
wasn't responding to calls but Moss and Justice were in search
of him, he took off looking, too. Instead of ditching his car upon
finding Dean's Viper and Justice's Phantom by the empty lot, he
resorted to the age old police tactic of trolling the nearby neighborhoods in his cruiser. When he heard the shotgun blast, he
came tearing over as fast as possible. From there, I knew more or
less what happened. Mason rushed in like a bat out of hell—

which Justice thought was reckless—but ultimately it worked. He caught TCK off guard and saved our lives. Or at least, that was the narrative. Given how things were playing out, I think Dean and I would've made it out in one piece even if he hadn't shown up. Still, I was happy to have everyone there, Justice and Moss especially.

Justice stayed with me as vehicles poured in. Three cruisers arrived, sirens blaring, all within a minute of each other. A misting rain started to fall as the ambulance pulled up, at which point Mason exited the home and began going through the same steps I had in the aftermath of my shooting. Then Glenwell and Hawkins arrived, as did another pair of detectives from MCU. They went in the home, and after a bit, Dean and Moss came out. Moss gathered Justice, and together they corralled one of the many nearby officers.

Dean groaned as he settled onto the curb next to me. The light mist continued to fall, beading faintly over my uniform and his dusty, torn suit. Dean didn't seem particularly motivated to speak, a sentiment I could understand. After everything we'd been through, what was there to say? We'd reached the highest of highs before crashing to the lowest of lows. We'd each fallen down only to have the other catch us by the hand and pull us up. We'd stood side by side and stared death in the face, and it was only because we'd worked together that we both sat here now. After facing all that, words seemed almost superfluous.

Then again, sometimes it just feels good to hear another person's voice.

"Glenwell kick you out?" I asked.

Dean shook his head. "Not in so many words, but I played along. We'd already bagged the poppets and found TCK's stash of tarot cards. We've wrapped this case neatly for her. All she has to do is slap on the bow. Besides, I needed some fresh air."

I nodded, gesturing toward the receding forms of Moss and Justice. "Where are they headed?"

"Bringing up the cars," said Dean. "I gave Moss my keys, so she'll bring mine, too."

"Got it."

We sat in silence for another moment. Dean rummaged in his pocket and produced his package of Slowburn Lights. He stared at it for a minute before crumpling it between his fingers and chucking it in the direction of the nearest storm drain.

I lifted an eyebrow. "You're quitting?"

He sighed. "No better time to try." He wiped his hands against his slacks, whether to dry them or wipe off the thin sheen of mist, I couldn't tell. "I don't think I ever thanked you for saving my life."

I shrugged. "I reacted, that's all. I saw TCK out of the corner of my eye, and I shoved you. Anyone would've."

Dean shook his head. "Trust me, not everyone would've. Most people would've frozen. Some would've tried to save themselves. Very few would've had the wherewithal to save themselves as well as me. So thank you. For that and everything else you did for me tonight."

I swallowed, starting to feel emotional. "You're welcome."

Dean ran a hand through his hair, flicking away the moisture that accumulated on his fingertips. "How are you holding up?"

"Honestly? I feel like I've cycled through every emotion possible tonight. Excitement, disappointment, apprehension, fear, anger, hopelessness, determination, horror, shock, relief, joy, and finally, a strange sense of emptiness."

Dean snorted. "You and me both. Though to be fair, that's not *every* emotion possible."

Dean gazed at me, the mist making his hair sparkle and giving his dark skin a pleasing sheen. Though his eyes were the color of ice, there was a warmth there I couldn't remember seeing before. I thought back to when he'd squeezed my hand, how it felt to have his fingers pressed against mine and his body close. I'd felt comfortable. Safe, even, despite being trapped in the worst of conditions.

I felt my cheeks warm, and I looked down. "Yeah. Not quite every emotion, I guess."

I heard the rumble of more engines, followed by a squeal of brakes as cars pulled up. Dean swore under his breath. "Great. Chin up. We're not through this yet."

I looked up, the fanciful feelings I was flirting with disappearing in response to his warning. "What is it?"

"Not an it," said Dean. "A who. Maybe two."

There were so many cars in the cul-de-sac by now that the two arrivals couldn't get to the curb, but they parked as close as they could. One was a standard squad car, and the other was a sleek black coupe that made Dean's Viper look cheap by comparison. From the passenger side of the Crown Royal, Captain Ellison popped out, but I was more concerned with the black car. From that one, a tall bald man emerged, broad shouldered and barrel-chested. I'd seen him once before. Chief Cole.

Dean helped me to my feet, and Captain Ellison spotted us straight away. He rushed over, his face etched with ill-restrained fury. "Gods above, Dean, what the hell happened? What were you thinking?"

Dean's brow furrowed. "Sir?"

To be fair, I was confused, too. Wasn't the Captain pleased we caught TCK?

Even in the darkness, the color on Ellison's cheeks was obvious. "You went after the city's most notorious serial killer without backup? And with Officer Phair, who's barely supposed to be on duty much less confronting murderers? And this turns into a shootout? You're lucky you're not both dead!"

Ellison's voice dropped as a tall figure approached. We all turned as the chief joined our group.

Ellison gave Cole a curt nod. "Chief."

Even though they'd arrived at the same time, I got the impression it was by accident.

The chief returned Ellison's nod. "Captain. Perhaps you could head inside. Give Detective Glenwell a hand. I'll be in momentarily to check on things."

If Ellison was upset at being dismissed, he did a good job hiding it. "Of course, sir." He cast a narrow glance toward Dean and me as he left, though.

Dean waited until Ellison was out of earshot. "Chief. What can we do for you?"

The chief's face was a gruff mask. "Tell me what happened here."

"Where should I start?" asked Dean.

"When the canine teams left," he said. "I know everything until then."

Dean nodded and launched into a detailed account of what happened after I retrieved the police tape. He was thorough and precise enough that I didn't have to add anything, not that I would've even if he'd missed a point. I hadn't been asked to speak, and it was the chief of police himself listening.

Dean didn't embellish anything as he recounted our escape

from TCK's lockbox, but neither did he pull any punches. He told it the way it happened, giving credit to me and Mason alike where credit was due. As he finished, the chief pursed his lips and gave a slow nod. He didn't look pleased, per se, but men in his position rarely did.

"Well," said the chief after a pause. "It may not be the ending I wanted, but it's an ending nonetheless. Good work, Detective. The city is in your debt. And don't worry about the aftermath. We'll clean this up."

"Thank you, Chief," said Dean.

Cole turned to me. "Officer Phair."

I straightened. "Yes, sir?"

"You were involved in the shooting the other day."

It wasn't a question. I swallowed. "Yes, sir."

The tall man cocked his head. "I can't say I agree with you being on duty alongside Detective Dean tonight, but it's hard to argue with the results. It sounds as if the two of you wouldn't have gotten out unscathed if you hadn't been there to back each other up. Given everything you've gone through, I want you to clear a second psych eval, but don't worry about any long term fallout. I'll make sure this doesn't stain your permanent record, despite what Captain Ellison might feel about it."

I took a deep breath. "Thank you, Chief."

"Speaking of the long term," he continued, "how long have you been with us on the force?"

I swallowed again, suddenly nervous. "Ahh... about a month, sir."

"Hmm." The chief lifted an eyebrow. "Detective Dean, if I recall correctly, you had one of the quickest transitions from officer to detective in the history of the department. How long did it take you?"

Dean also lifted a curious eyebrow. "About a year and a half, sir. And it wasn't *one of* the quickest transitions. It was *the* fastest. I took the exam the first day I was eligible, the day after I completed my probationary rookie year."

"There are always regulations standing in the way, aren't there?" The chief looked at me and smiled. "Still, records are made to be broken, aren't they, Officer? You might want to start studying for the exam sooner rather than later, just in case the rules happen to get bent down the line."

I blinked, totally caught off guard. "Uh... yes. I will. Do that, I mean. Thank you, sir."

The chief gave us both a nod. "Detective. Officer. We can handle it from here. Go home. Get some rest. And good work out there."

I stood, dumbfounded, as the Chief walked up the steps into TCK's home. Meanwhile, Dean stared at me, an amused grin on his face.

It was too much for me. "Are you laughing at me?"

He shook his head, but the grin didn't disappear. "Not at all. I'm just happy that if my record gets beaten, at least I can gloat I was the one who picked the person who eventually went on to break it."

I still wasn't sure I'd misheard things. "The chief wasn't serious, was he? Besides, I hate studying. I'm good at a lot of things, but not that."

This time, Dean did laugh. He nodded as another pair of cars entered the cul-de-sac, his own and Justice's Phantom. "I don't think you need to worry about that tonight. Come on. Let's get out of here."

CHAPTER FORTY-THREE

For the first time since crashing at Moss's condo, I woke up feeling fully rested and refreshed. The relaxing effect of knowing a psychotic killer was dead and gone had made me sleep like a newborn babe. Better, really. More like a teenager without anything to do the next day. I wondered what the psychiatrist would make of that. Shouldn't I be emotionally scarred from my close encounter with TCK? Death was death, after all, and his shooting probably should've shaken me more than it had. Maybe my sense of right and wrong made me feel justified in the outcome, violent though it may have been. I was sure I'd find out soon enough. By the chief's own command, I needed to schedule another session with Dr. Nelson, but hopefully there would be time for other activities today, as well. It was high time I started searching for my own apartment and got out of Ginger's hair.

I think Ginger slept well, too, as she didn't stir until almost eight-thirty. It was well past nine when the two of us rolled into the Fifth, heading to the third floor. Dean and Justice weren't at their desks, which would've made me suspect everyone had slept in if not for the presence of a tailored jacket over the back of Dean's chair. As we settled in, I asked Moss if she had any assignments for me, but she said she had some administrative work to take care of and suggested I look for Dean.

I took her advice and succeeded soon enough. I found Dean in the war room, which hadn't yet been emptied and converted back to a conference room. If anything, there was more stuff in the room than the last time I'd visited. Dean sat at the table with pieces of evidence from TCK's home spread before him, all of it tagged and contained in clear plastic baggies. Currently, he had one of the poppets out of its bag. With a magnifying glass in hand, he inspected it closely.

"Morning, Dean." I came in and took a seat.

He looked up from his work, at which point I realized he must not have slept as well as I had. He had a bit of a haggard look. There were bags under his eyes, obvious despite his dark skin, and his hair didn't look as if it had been washed. He gave me a tired nod. "Morning, Phair."

"You look like you've had a busy morning." It was the kindest way I could think of to say he looked like death warmed over.

Dean shrugged. "I didn't sleep well. Too much on my mind. Too much evidence to examine."

I pointed at the doll he held. "You mean the poppets?"

"There's more, but at the moment, yes."

"What are you trying to determine, exactly?" I asked.

Dean shook his head. "I'm not sure. Everything there is to know, I suppose. How they worked. How TCK built them. What elements he used in their construction. Because of how they were used to kill the victims, we don't have any smoking guns tying TCK to the murders. If we had to use this evidence to prove the case against him in court, we'd be screwed. We found the tarot cards at his place, sure, but the pieces on the victims didn't have any prints. And have you ever tried to convince a jury that magic is both real and can be used to kill people from afar? I doubt the prosecutor would even let us introduce these poppets. We'd have to rest the whole case on our testimony. We would've convicted TCK on false imprisonment and attempted murder of a police officer, but we never would've gotten him for the tarot card murders."

I was quiet for a moment as I considered how to phrase my question properly. "I guess I'm confused. Why are you so concerned with hypotheticals? Sure, the case against him might've been dicey, but we don't need to present a case against him. He's dead. It's over."

Dean screwed up his face. "I don't know. Maybe it's my inquisitive nature. There are elements here that don't make sense. That's why I couldn't sleep. These niggling inconsistencies kept bouncing around my head all night." He sighed. "I know. I'm hopeless. I can't even take the win when it's handed to me on a platter."

"I don't think you're hopeless." I wanted to reach out and take Dean's hand, but I didn't. As much as I might want it to be a harbinger of things to come, I couldn't treat the spark I'd felt the night before as anything but a fleeting moment. "You're a detective who thinks everything through. That's part of what makes you great. If you have concerns, they're probably valid, so share them. What's on your mind?"

That elicited a shy smile from Dean, and I had to remind myself the spark was in my head. "It's the poppets. You mentioned what was needed to make these—an element from the body, a piece of clothing, a memento from the dead—and

TCK seemed to confirm it last night. Regardless, the elements are here. Each of these poppets has a single hair woven into it, not to mention a scrap of clothing sewn to it and something else tucked inside. Two of them have bits of photographs, one has a locket, and another a ring. So fine. Let's accept that TCK used these poppets to kill his victims and that there was a blood magic ritual involved requiring the sacrifice of small animals, both near him and the victims. Without learning black magic ourselves, I doubt we'll ever understand the details of how it worked. We're probably better off not knowing, but how did TCK get the elements for the poppets?"

I saw what Dean was getting at. "You thought from the start TCK might've been breaking and entering into the victims' homes, either to scout the women or to tack the cards onto their clothes preemptively. Now we know he was there for different reasons, but the result is the same. We know he was there, yet he never left a single piece of physical evidence. CSU swept every apartment, and they didn't come up with a single set of prints. Not one hair. Nothing."

"It goes beyond that," said Dean. "TCK, whose real name is Zulkis Yetu, is at the central morgue so Glenwell can oversee the autopsy. I got some measurements from the coroner in charge. Yetu was six foot six inches tall, and his weight upon arrival was over three hundred pounds. That gray skin of his suggests troll heritage, and I don't know how well you looked at him, but his face was distinctive, to be kind. How is it a guy that big, who probably stuck out like a sore thumb even in a city this diverse, managed to break into four apartments without a single neighbor noticing?"

I frowned. "Maybe the divination magic had something to do with it. Maybe he was able to predict when his victims wouldn't be home and when his victims would be alone so he could strike. He might've also been able to predict which clothes they might wear, if we assume he tacked the tarot cards on ahead of time."

Dean lifted an eyebrow. "That's hand-waving away a lot of questions with magic. I'll admit I don't know the first thing about divination, but your source suggested it wasn't that precise. I mean, Yetu was wrong with his predictions just last night. He said the divinations showed us coming, but they never predicted the arrivals of Moss, Justice, and Mason."

The frown on my face was now lodged firmly in place. "Maybe he didn't use magic. Maybe he was an adept criminal, after all. He could've broken into the victims' homes the old fashioned way. He probably cased their apartments, got a feel for when the women and neighbors would be around. It's not that bizarre. We know TCK was meticulous and careful. All the murders were executed with pinpoint precision, except the murder of Ellowyn Farview."

"That's another thing," said Dean. "Not Miss Farview, although I still have questions about her murder. TCK's profile. Yetu doesn't fit it. Trust me. I've tracked and caught two professional assassins before. They were every bit as meticulous and precise as TCK was, and do you know what their apartments looked like? Clean. Perfectly organized. Weapons placed strategically around the home in case they had to defend themselves from attack. Each place had multiple escape routes. Was that what you saw at Yetu's home?"

I shook my head. "It looked like my grandmother's home but less pricey and with more animal bones."

"Right," said Dean. "It's not the home you would expect of someone like TCK. It doesn't fit the profile. And speaking of profiles, remember how Mason outlined who we should be looking for? Someone with a violent past? Perhaps former military or a bodyguard? And coming from a broken home? We're still working on unearthing Yetu's past, but he has no priors, and as far as we can tell, he never worked in a violent profession."

As the conversation progressed, the feeling of calm I'd woken up with had gradually drained out of me, replaced with an uneasy dread. "Dean, what are you saying? Do you think we found the wrong guy?"

Dean waved a hand. "No. There's no way last night was a setup. Not like Cassman. There's no way someone could've predicted everything we went through to track Yetu to his home. Besides, Yetu all but admitted to being TCK."

The mention of the informant Cassman wrinkled my forehead. I'd mostly forgotten him, to be honest. "Speaking of Cassman, how did TCK plant the tarot cards at his place? More importantly, Cassman *did* fit the profile for TCK, but how would Yetu know that?"

Dean lifted a finger. "I almost don't want to say it out loud because I don't want it to be true, but if I consider the evidence... I have to believe TCK wasn't a single person. I think Yetu had a partner."

"A partner?" The thought sent a shiver down my spine. It couldn't be true. We'd stopped TCK. We'd killed Yetu. I'd stared into his pale, dead eyes, that look of shock frozen on his face. Perhaps his divinations had predicted our arrival, but in the end they'd failed him. He said our friends wouldn't show, but Mason arrived, gunning him down.

Unless... his divination had been right. The night did end in darkness—for him, not us. The divination was accurate, but not precise. What if he *did* foresee Mason's arrival, but he didn't think Mason was our friend. Perhaps that's what froze his face in shock. Not Mason's arrival but the fact that he shot him. That could've been the terrible surprise he foretold.

As clear as dawn, I saw Mason in my mind. The twinkle in his eye as he'd joined us in Yetu's bedroom. I heard his voice, gruff as always. *We're not a bunch of lone wolves. We work together to get the job done. Always.*

My eyes widened. *"Oh, shit..."*

CHAPTER FORTY-FOUR

D ean's brow furrowed as he stared at me. "What is it?" Though I'd been through stressful situations in my life, it wasn't until that moment that I experienced a panic attack. The edges of my vision went dark. My body filled with vibrating energy, and I couldn't breath. I tried to fill my lungs with air, but no matter how hard I tried, I couldn't get more than a mouthful. Every interaction I'd had with Mason flashed before me. The way he'd stared at me with his flat gray eyes when we first met. How he'd stayed behind to help me collate files for MCD when everyone else left. How he'd pumped me with theories of what the tarot cards meant, then met us at the home of Maggie Richards and stuck by my side. It wasn't that I'd been alone with him so many times that made me want to scream. It was that he'd been grooming me. He'd picked me out from the start. A rookie officer. A young, impressionable female. He'd pushed his narrative through me from the beginning, using me as a pawn.

"Nell? Are you okay?"

Dean's voice was at my ear, and I realized he'd come around

the table to my side. A cone of darkness constrained my vision to a spot in front of me, but I could feel the touch of his hand, his fingers squeezing tight against mine. I focused on that. Focused on the warmth of his touch as I tried to get my breathing under control.

"That's it. Breathe, Nell. It's going to be okay."

His voice helped soothe me. I closed my eyes and thought of nothing but his touch and his smooth tenor. Within a minute I felt my breathing return to normal, and the tingle started to fade from my extremities. I opened my eyes and faced Dean, who'd pulled a chair close beside me. Gone was the exhaustion I'd seen earlier, replaced with heartfelt concern.

"Close the door," I whispered.

He stood and shut it before returning to his seat. "Nell, what's going on? Are you okay?"

I met Dean's eyes and held them. "It's Mason."

"What do you mean, it's Mason?"

"I mean he's the second half of TCK," I said. "He fits the profile to a T. He's not former military or a bodyguard, he's a cop instead. While I don't know if he had a troubled childhood, I'd bet if we start digging, we'd find a glaring red flag. Mason is neat, organized, precise, calculating. The sort of person who'd know how to break into a home without leaving a trace because he knows exactly what we'd look for. He's perfectly average look-ing, the kind of person who can blend into a crowd without sparking suspicion. He knows the mind of a killer perfectly—because he is one."

"Whoa, Phair," said Dean with a wave of his hands. "Let's pump the brakes. Just because someone fits the profile of a killer doesn't mean they are one. Maybe Mason adheres to that philos-ophy, but we're both better than that."

"It's not just his profile, Dean," I said. "There are way too many coincidences. Take last night when he showed up. He told Justice and Moss he discovered something critical he had to share with you, and when he wasn't able to contact you he came looking. Does that make sense? What would be so critical he had to share it with you last night instead of this morning? Besides, how did he know where to find us? He claimed he heard the gunshots and followed them to Yetu's house, but how plausible is that? Moss and Justice would've heard them, been able to track them. They were close by, on foot. Mason wouldn't have been as close, and he was in his car, with the engine running. Isn't it far more plausible he was on his way to Yetu's house already when he ran into Moss and Justice? Heck, Yetu could've called him for backup!"

Dean's face tightened. "Moss also told me he rushed in before they could formulate a plan of attack. Some might justify that by thinking we were in immediate danger—which we were —but not Mason. He's as shrewd as they come. He's not reactionary."

"But he needed to be the first one in," I said. "Because he couldn't risk Yetu being taken into custody. He had to kill him, right away, to keep him quiet. Yetu said we all make deals we later regret. He could've been referring to Mason. I mean, you saw the look of shock on Yetu's face as he was shot. What if he wasn't shocked at Mason's arrival but at his treachery?"

Dean chewed on his lip. "There are other explanations that fit the course of events. Your theory is still just that."

"There's more," I said. "Someone planted the tarot cards on Cassman, right? It had to be someone who had access to the police reports, someone who knew Cassman was involved in the robbery. Someone who would've had access to Cassman's permanent record and would've known he fit the profile Mason himself put together for TCK. At the same time, it would have to be someone who *didn't* have access to top secret knowledge that Cassman was an informant in a sting operation. Mason checks all those boxes. Beyond that, it makes sense Mason is the one who planted the stolen necklace in Maggie Richard's apartment. He told me exactly what sort of item we should look for, and he showed up to help Justice and me in the search. He was smart enough to let Justice find the necklace, but he made sure to steer me away from the romance novels I found. And as soon as Justice found the necklace, Mason was *adamant* we'd found the right clue.

"But even that doesn't tell the full story. When Glenwell came by after the Cassman interrogation and pulled you and Mason aside, you came out angry and stormed off, so you didn't see Mason's face. He was shook, Dean. It's the only time I've seen him that distressed. Now I know why. Because he thought he'd been found out. He knew he'd screwed up by planting the evidence on Cassman—but he didn't freak out. He excused himself and disappeared. I suspect he called Yetu, and together, they came up with a new plan of attack. I don't think it's a coincidence Mason showed up in the war room with me, and within a minute or two of him arriving, TCK called. Mason wanted to make sure he was in the room when it happened. To make sure no one would suspect him."

Dean didn't say a thing. His face was drawn, his eyes looked haunted and angry.

I leaned in, letting anger seep into my voice. "Dean. He used me. He targeted me from the start. I know it! The way he looked at me when I met him at HQ? He was sizing me up. He didn't think he'd be able to influence you to come to the conclusion he wanted, so he used me instead. Shared his theories about the tarot cards with me. Suggested I continue to search the homes of the victims, even after I'd shot a man and should've been off duty. Pushing Cassman on us. It was him. I know it was."

"He could've been stalking the women, too," said Dean. "Keeping an eye on them for Yetu. He could've called Yetu from his two-way radio to tell him when to initiate the rituals. Maybe they screwed up during Ellowyn Farview's death and learned from it, tightening up their operation."

Dean blinked. He shook his head, and his eyes lost a little of their cloudiness. "All right. Consider me convinced. But we don't have any evidence. All of this is conjecture. A judge wouldn't even grant us a warrant to search a crack house on this, much less search the home of a renowned police consultant and former detective. Not that there's any evidence of these crimes at Mason's home, in all likelihood. He's the cunning, conniving half of TCK. We know how careful he is, as evidenced by the total lack of physical evidence left at the victims' homes."

I almost jumped out of my seat as inspiration struck. "You're right. He wouldn't leave evidence behind. But Yetu might've."

Dean cocked an eyebrow at me. "CSU has been combing his home since last night. We've found an abundance of evidence. Not just the poppets and tarot cards but the incense he bought from Garland's. The tools he used for animal sacrifice. The voice modulator he used while calling us. It was all there."

I shook my head, feeling jittery with equal parts fear and excitement. "That's not what I mean. Mason knows all that. But he doesn't know what he doesn't know. What if Yetu had a backup plan. Incriminating evidence he'd saved in case things between him and Mason went sour?"

A knowing look conquered Dean's face. "You want to flush him out. Let Mason incriminate himself..." He frowned. "It could work, but there's a problem."

"What?" I asked.

He looked at me, that same look of concern in his eyes. "It won't work unless you're the bait. He'll suspect me or Moss or Justice. But you? He thinks you're a rube. That he's successfully manipulated you from the start. He'll feel safe if you're the one leading him."

The fear and excitement within me bubbled into a frothy mess. "You're saying I need to *allow him* to continue to manipulate me."

Dean nodded. "I'm not going to lie, Phair. It won't be without risk. But it's our best shot. Maybe our only one."

Despite the fear and nervous energy, I didn't hesitate. "Let's do it. Let's nail his ass to the wall."

CHAPTER FORTY-FIVE

To say I had butterflies in my stomach as I rode up the police HQ elevator to the fifth floor would be a lie. It was more like a swarm of ravenous locusts had taken flight inside me, and they intended to mount an escape at any moment.

And by the latter, I mean I might vomit.

I took a deep breath and forced it through my nostrils as the bell dinged and the door opened. I kept telling myself I had nothing to fear. Mason wasn't one to show his cards or get his hands dirty. It's not as if he'd bash me over the head before gutting me like a fish in the middle of police headquarters. He'd act calm, cool, and collected as he welcomed me with open arms, all while sharpening a knife behind his back. I had to act the same way if I was to be successful.

I stopped by the restrooms first, straightening my uniform in the mirror and getting a cool drink of water from the nearby fountain before heading in search of Mason's office. I found him at the end of the hall, in a corner office that afforded him a good view of downtown. The door was open, but I paused as I reached it regardless. I knocked upon the wood as I poked my head inside, summoning every ounce of will I had.

"Excuse me? Mason?"

Virgil sat at a desk on the right side of the office. As expected, the room was immaculate. Two bookshelves of dark, glossy wood occupied the wall behind him, filled with thick tomes wrapped in leather and decorative paperboard. There weren't any baubles on the shelves though, and the desk itself was bare except for an inbox and an outbox for mail on opposite corners. A single chair faced his desk, small and made of metal. It didn't look forgiving on visiting behinds.

Mason looked up at the sound of my voice. One of his eyebrows inched upward. "Officer Phair. This is a surprise."

I tried to act casual. "I hope I'm not interrupting."

"Not at all." He waved to the metal chair. "Come in."

I sat down. The chair was as uncomfortable as it looked. It was probably a ploy on Mason's part. Make whoever he talked to as uncomfortable as possible to give him an edge. "Have you already met with Dr. Nelson?"

Mason sighed. "Yes. I had a session with him this morning after spending almost all day yesterday in the gentle care of IA."

I nodded. "I'm intimately familiar with that process. I've got another meeting with Dr. Nelson scheduled for tomorrow, myself. I'm a little worried what his recommendation will be, but we'll cross that bridge when we get there, I suppose."

Mason jutted his chin toward me, a gesture that seemed both sharp and dismissive. Strange how his mannerisms hadn't triggered me before, but knowing the truth of someone's character makes all the difference. "What brings you in?"

"Right," I said. "It's about TCK. You know CSU has been

tearing through his home, practically taking the place down to the studs. They found something interesting."

Mason didn't flinch. "Interesting how?"

"One of the techs found a hidden panel in the floor. Inside the hidey-hole was a journal. There's writing in it, but unfortunately, it appears to be in code."

Mason pursed his lips. "That *is* interesting."

I resisted the urge to lean in. *Act casual,* I told myself. "Detective Dean thinks it's meaningful. Even though TCK is dead, he's convinced there's more to this case than meets the eye. Honestly, I think he needs to accept that TCK is dead, but this has become an obsession to him. He can't let it go. Regardless, Dean was hoping you could take a look at the journal."

Mason played his cards close to the vest. He gave me a curious look. "I'm always happy to help, but I'm not a cryptographer. And I don't want to encourage Dean in continuing this obsession."

Sure, act coy asshole. "Dean thinks the presence of this journal changes things. Now we're dealing with secret codes, hidden messages. He thinks there might be a network of killers working together, sharing secrets, reveling in their kills. Even if he's wrong, whatever's in the journal must be important, otherwise TCK wouldn't have encoded it. Either way, it changes what we know of him. We need to refine his profile. Use that to figure out if TCK had any associates."

"Detective Dean is like a dog with a bone. He won't give it up easily, if at all." Mason shrugged nonchalantly. "He's probably making much ado about nothing, but I suppose I could take a look. Is the journal in evidence lockup?"

Funny you should ask, I thought. "We've got it in the war room. We haven't reverted the place to a conference room yet."

"Fair enough." Mason tapped the papers in front of him. "I need to finish up a few things, but I can head your way in fifteen to twenty minutes."

I thanked everything that was holy he hadn't asked to ride with me. So far, I'd managed to keep it together, but being alone with him in my squad car might've broken me. "No problem. See you there."

I forced myself to walk at an even pace as I left the office, headed down the elevators, and back to my assigned squad car. I didn't encounter much traffic as I drove to the Fifth, and in short order I found myself in the war room. The file boxes were still stacked in the corners and the evidence was loaded into similar boxes on the table, but nobody else was there. I headed to the far side of the table, opened the lid of one of the boxes, and lifted out a clear plastic bag. Inside was a book with a greenish cover and dark brown binding. The edges of the book were gilded, but time and wear had taken their toll, dulling the shine to more of a bronze.

I drew latex gloves from a box and pulled them on. Carefully, I extracted the book from the bag and sat down with it. There weren't any markings on the outside, just those from years of wear. As I opened it, I was confronted with a musty smell, the one you find in used bookstores and libraries, the smell of old glue and chemicals used to treat paper. The pages in the journal were yellowed but not brittle. On them were scribbled a series of incomprehensible cyphers, each of them written in black ink by a hand that was uniform but rough.

I couldn't understand what was written, but then again, no one could. It was all gibberish, put together by a cryptographer in conjunction with members of the counterfeiting gang we'd booked a few days prior. All in all, I couldn't believe we'd been able to craft such a convincing fake in twenty-four hours. The book itself looked as if it had been stuffed in a cobweb-infested corner of Yetu's attic for two decades, and the handwriting was identical to his based on samples we'd unearthed from his home.

I just hoped it was enough to fool Mason.

I sat there with the book open in front of me, taking notes on the frequency of the symbols used and checking the clock every few minutes. The waiting was difficult, but the more nerve wracking part was knowing from here on out, I couldn't follow a script. We didn't know what Mason's play would be, so I'd have to play it by ear. Dean had expressed his full confidence in me, though, and I think he meant it. That made a big difference.

Fifteen minutes ticked off the clock, then twenty. Officers and detectives alike passed by, heading to meetings or the break room. Almost half an hour after I arrived, I again heard footsteps. This time, they stopped at the war room.

Mason appeared in the doorway. His eyes scanned the space before darting to the book in front of me. "Where's Dean?"

I felt as if I was being watched by a jungle cat. His every move was careful. Practiced. Precise. "I'm not sure, to be honest. There was another murder last night, so we're back to juggling cases."

He eyed the aged tome. "That's the journal?"

I nodded.

Mason closed the door behind him and started around the conference table toward me. A voice inside me screamed, but I slapped it down. I was as safe in the middle of the Fifth as I'd be anywhere.

He settled into a chair next to me. "Mind if I take a look?"

I pushed the box of gloves toward him. "By all means."

He gloved up and cracked the cover. Mason's brow was furrowed as he took in the first page. He spent close to a minute on it before moving to the second.

I tried to smile. "I don't suppose you've already cracked the code."

Mason didn't chuckle, nor even snort. "As I mentioned, I'm not likely to be able to help you with that. But it doesn't surprise me you found this. It fits TCK's profile."

I lifted an eyebrow. "It does?"

Mason gave a stiff nod, his eyes glued to the page. "We already know TCK liked to play games. The tarot cards he left on his victims as clues. The fact that he contacted Detective Dean directly on more than one occasion, or at least tried to. How he diverted attention away from himself toward Gregory Lloyd Cassman. This journal fits with all of that. Pages filled with secrets, protected by a cypher, are exactly the sort of thing I'd expect from a serial killer, more so out of one like TCK. It's another game."

"But he didn't leave it for us to find," I said. "We found it hidden in his home after his death. How could it be part of his game?"

Maybe there was a spark in Mason's eye, or maybe I imagined it. "That's the thing about serial killers. They're obsessed with death. They plan for it. Embrace it. They don't let it stop them."

Even though I was trying my best to control myself, I couldn't help but swallow a little harder than normal. "So what do we do with it? How do we unravel the secrets within?"

"For that you need a cryptographer. There's a good one at the University of New Welwic. I met him a number of years back. He helped me on a case. As I mentioned, cyphers are a common fascination of serial murderers. I'd go to him. He'd be able to give us a starting point."

With that tidbit, I saw clearly what was about to happen. Mason would offer to take the journal to the professor. Maybe he'd make the journal disappear along the way, or he'd swap it for a different one. Maybe the cryptographer was a buddy of his and would offer a false translation. Thank goodness the cryptographer we'd used to help put the thing together wasn't affiliated with the University. Regardless, I knew exactly what Mason was planning.

Except I didn't, because at that very moment, the fire alarm sounded.

CHAPTER FORTY-SIX

Mason looked up in surprise. "Is that...?"

"The fire alarm," I said. "Yes."

Mason frowned. "It's got to be a false alarm, right?"

"I don't know." Gods above, was Mason going to *burn down the building* to destroy the evidence?

"We need to evacuate." Mason grabbed the plastic baggie and slid the journal back into it. Once again I thought I knew what his plan was, but instead of claiming we needed to keep the journal to make sure it stayed safe, he grabbed the evidence box, pulled it over, and tossed the book inside. "Come on. Let's go." He waved toward the door.

I nodded and headed around the table, Mason following me. As we exited the room, Mason barked at me. "Lock the door. We don't want to take any chances."

Luckily, Dean had given me a key when we first started using the room. I locked the door and proceeded alongside Mason to the stairwell, where everyone on the third floor was congregating. I hadn't taken part in a fire drill since joining the

Fifth Street Precinct, but everyone proceeded down the stairs in an orderly fashion without panicking. Then again, the building was only four stories high, and everyone who worked for the department was used to accepting a certain measure of risk as part of the job.

As we reached the lobby, there were several officers ushering people outside. There, another pair of officers directed people across the street. In the distance, I could hear the wail of fire engines, but when I looked at the Fifth, I didn't see any flames or smoke pouring from any windows. I assumed that was a good sign.

The sidewalk was packed as we reached the other side of Fifth Street. As I looked for a spot to stand, Mason gave me a nod. "I'm going to try and find Dean or Captain Ellison. See if anyone can tell me what's going on."

Mason stomped off, and soon I lost him in the crowd. The police presence on the sidewalk thickened, slowing traffic, but despite that, within a minute a pair of fire trucks arrived. They screeched to a halt in front of the precinct. A half dozen fire-fighters poured out of each truck. They waited in their heavy coats and oblong hats as the last of the officers and staff exited the building before hustling inside. Around me, officers murmured in discontent, wondering what was going on, but based on the snippets of conversation I heard, no one was any more informed than I was.

I waited for about five minutes, shifting my weight between the balls of my feet until finally Mason returned. He scowled and shook his head. "I couldn't find anyone. What a mess."

I gave a halfhearted smile, but inside I seethed. *You're behind this,* I thought. *What's your plan, Mason? Clearly the building isn't burning down, so what? Do you have more accom-*

plices? Have we underestimated how many people comprise TCK? Maybe it was more than just Yetu and Mason. Maybe it was a trio or an entire team.

I stood there in a state approaching agony for another ten minutes before finally the firefighters exited the building. There was a conversation between them and the officers closest to the building, and then those same officers shouted to everyone that it was safe to enter.

Mason snorted. "Must've been a false alarm."

I didn't bother responding. The throng of officers slowly shuffled toward the entrance, and within a few minutes, we were back on the stairs heading to the third floor. As I headed toward the war room, I considered what I was supposed to do. As we'd shuffled outside while the fire alarm sounded, I'd half expected Dean or Justice or Moss to find me, but none of them did. That suggested I needed to continue to play my part, but I didn't know how to. I didn't know what to expect at all.

I surreptitiously tested the handle of the conference room to make sure it was still locked. As I unlocked it and opened the door, Mason waved me in. "Where were we?"

"Ah..." I felt off my game. Surely if Mason hadn't suspected anything yet, he'd pick up quickly. "You were telling me about your cryptographer friend."

"Right. He's as good a place to start as any." Mason nodded toward the box. "Get the journal and we'll find your boss. With Dean's approval, we can get this ball rolling."

I nodded and opened the evidence box—only to find the journal missing. I half expected it to be gone, but I was nonetheless shocked. How had Mason pulled it off? The door had been locked. Who else had a key?

Then again, perhaps my sincere shock was a good thing. I looked up, gobsmacked. "It's gone!"

"What do you mean it's gone?" Mason scowled as he reached across the table, pulling the box toward him. His eyes grew wide in shock, though I don't think his response was as real as my own. "What the hell? Someone stole it!"

He had a hard glint in his eyes as he looked up. "It must've been one of the firefighters, or maybe one of the other officers in this building. Good gods... Dean was right. This *is* a network. This goes deeper than any of us thought..."

"Morning, Mason."

Mason and I both jumped. In the open door stood Dean, hands in his pockets, looking as cool and collected as I'd ever seen him.

Mason composed himself almost immediately. "Detective! I've been looking all over for you. First I couldn't find you while the fire alarm went off, and now—"

"Now, what?" Dean interrupted, his gaze never straying an inch from Mason. "Don't tell me evidence has gone missing?"

Mason must've picked up on his patronizing tone, but he pushed ahead as if he hadn't. "The journal CSU picked up from TCK's home is gone! It was right here in the evidence box when we evacuated the building. Officer Phair saw it, too, unless..." He turned his vile gaze on me. "She's the one who locked the room. Or rather, was *supposed* to lock the room. She might've pretended to, and then while we were outside, I lost track of her."

My jaw dropped. I couldn't believe he was going to try and shift blame onto me.

Before I could defend myself, Moss entered, followed closely by Justice. "Nice try, Mason, but we had eyes on you the whole time. We tracked you through the crowd to the alley behind the bagel shop. We saw you stash the journal behind the dumpster."

So Mason had pocketed the journal himself? How? I'd had eyes on him the whole time... or had I? He followed me out of the war room. It's possible he could've filched the journal in the split second I had my back turned. It would explain why he was so adamant I lock the door. To establish that he couldn't have been behind the theft, same as he'd made sure Yetu called while he was in the room with us.

Mason scoffed as he stared down the trio of Dean, Moss, and Justice. "Stash the journal? What are you talking about?"

Dean had been resting against the edge of the door frame. He pushed himself off and drew himself to his full height. His eyes were cold and bright, and they burrowed into Mason with the strength of an electric drill. "Give it up, Mason. We know it's you. We know you're Yetu's accomplice."

"Yetu's accomplice?" Mason frowned. "You mean TCK?"

"You were his right hand man," said Dean. "Or maybe he was yours. It does seem as if you were the brains of the operation, after all. I'm assuming he came up with the idea to use effigy magic, letting him do the killing while you watched from close by. It does make me wonder what he got out of the experience, though. Did he not revel in the violence the same way you do?"

Mason's face hardened. "What is this? Some sort of desperate power play? You've lost it, Dean. TCK is dead. I don't know what you intend to gain by claiming I'm the one who stole this journal, but it's not going to work. It's your word against mine."

"Not exactly." Captain Ellison pushed into the room alongside a particularly burly patrol officer. I don't know if he'd been lurking there, waiting for the right moment to walk in, but either way, the war room was starting to feel quite crowded.

Ellison looked at Mason with raw disgust. "This isn't the word of Detective Dean against yours. He cleared this operation with me from the start. He shared with me his thoughts. How everything pointed to you being involved. I was skeptical, to be sure, but I agreed there were questions in need of answers. So I agreed. We lured you here on false pretenses, Mason, and it wasn't just Dean's squad keeping tabs on you. I've had officers tracking your movements from the moment you stepped foot in this precinct. We saw you go into the bathroom. We know you set the fire. A slow burning fuse to light a tinder bundle. Plenty of smoke, little fire, and it would give you enough time to get up here and pocket the evidence. Nicely done."

Dean smiled. Not the smile of a man who was happy but the smile of a man who knew he'd finally won. "Why'd you do it, Mason? Why'd you kill those women? You gave us the profile. What abuse did you endure during your childhood that led to this?"

Mason's jaw muscles bulged as he ground his teeth against each other. He had to know he was beat. He was too smart not to, but he'd never admit it. I doubted he'd ever admit to anything.

He spoke through clenched teeth, his eyes ablaze. "I did go to the restroom when I arrived, but I didn't set a fire. You can't prove I did. And as far as that journal? It's your testimony against mine. What do you even plan to charge me with? Mishandling of evidence? That's a far cry from murder. If I'm disciplined at all, it'll be internally. There won't be a trial.

Maybe I'll get suspended for a week or two for poor judgement. Is that your end goal, Dean?"

Dean took a step toward him. In his shoes, I would've been quivering with rage, but Dean remained calm. Proud. Confident. "What we have, Mason, is probable cause. Cause to believe you were working with Zulkis Yetu and involved in the murder of four young women. Enough probable cause to get a judge to issue a warrant to search your office, your home, your car. To dig into your every relationship, every interaction, every movement. To dig into your life until we find the truth. And we will find it. Trust me, Virgil. I don't stop once I find the killer. I see things through to the end."

If Mason had a retort, he kept it to himself. He scowled, defiant to the end as Justice and the patrol officer put him in handcuffs and dragged him down to processing.

CHAPTER FORTY-SEVEN

D r. Nelson sat in the same oversized blue suede chair I'd last seen him as I arrived at his office. Again, he wore a sweater vest over a shirt and slacks, though the colors had changed and his vest was plaid rather than solid color. He looked up as I reached his door, perhaps hearing the sound of my approaching feet. "Good morning, Miss Phair. Come in."

"Good morning, Doctor." I closed the door and sat in the greenish chair opposite him. Light streamed through his open windows, and a crisp breeze followed it inside.

Nelson smiled. "You seem to be in better spirits this morning than last."

"I suppose I am," I said. "It's hard not to be given everything that's transpired in the past few days."

Dr. Nelson lifted an eyebrow. "Indeed. It would appear you've had a few full days, despite my recommendations."

I grimaced. "I guess news gets around pretty fast in the department."

"Not just in the department. In the *actual news*. Have you picked up a paper in the last two days?"

I sighed. "Look, Doctor, it wasn't on purpose. I tried to stick to investigation and stay out of stressful situations, but some of the circumstances were out of my control. My superior needed backup. I couldn't abandon him. What was I supposed to do?"

Nelson lifted a hand. "I'm not accusing you of being a terrible person or even of making a mistake. I'm simply stating that, from what I know of the events that transpired, you've had anything but a relaxing period in which to decompress. But I would like to hear your perspective on everything."

"You mean how I felt during our chase and confrontation with TCK? And during our entrapment of Mason?"

Doctor Nelson snorted. "No. In this case, I'm actually curious to know what happened, not how you felt through it all. It's fine if we run long. I don't have any other appointments until after lunch, and the department is footing the bill."

I smiled. "Fair enough." I wasn't sure where to start, but I figured our chase with the canine team was a good enough spot. I told Doctor Nelson about finding the animal remains, which in turn led to an aside about effigy magic and divination, before telling him about our trek to Yetu's house. I told him how we were lured inside and captured, then how Dean and I overcame our fears and worked together to get out. I told him about the standoff with Yetu, about his death at Mason's hand, then about my revelation regarding Mason and our efforts to bring him down. I even told him about the raid on Mason's home we conducted last night, where we unearthed a secret cache containing four slim envelopes. Each was neatly labeled and contained hair presumably pulled from the hairbrushes of the victims, something

Emmett had later been able to confirm. Apparently, even someone as careful and conniving as Mason suffered the same addictive impulses that drove other serial murderers. While the raid hadn't provided us with everything we'd hoped for, such as answers to how Yetu and Mason had known what their victims would wear or where they'd be, it had given us enough to ensure Mason would go down for the crimes he committed.

Doctor Nelson listened intently throughout, looking surprised at times and curious at others, but never interrupting, letting me tell the story in my own words. When it was clear I was done, he pursed his lips. "That, my dear, is quite the adventure."

I nodded. "It was hard to appreciate it in the moment. Even now it's hard to accept it's really over, but given time, I'm sure I'll look back and feel proud about not only the outcome but how I got there."

Nelson steepled his fingers. "Speaking of feelings, I think it's time we discuss how all this has affected you. The last time we spoke, it was obvious to me you were repressing your mind's normal reaction to an incident as jarring as taking another person's life. Now you've been involved in another, though under a different set of circumstances. You didn't pull the trigger this time, though from what you tell me, you would've felt justified if you had."

I didn't have to think too hard about that. "Yes. I would've."

"Why do you think you would've made that decision so easily? Because you were so convinced of Mr. Yetu's guilt?"

That question took a little more thought. "In part. He imprisoned us. Threatened to kill us. All but admitted to his role as part of TCK. But it goes beyond that. It was one thing when I was being threatened, but when Dean almost got shot?

When he would've died if not for my actions? That solidified it in my mind. Yetu went after my friends, and I couldn't let him succeed."

Nelson rubbed one thumb across the back of another. "So your biggest motivation was to protect the people you care about. About having your team's back."

I snorted and shook my head. "You know, it's funny. When I joined the force—just a few weeks ago, though it feels like more —I was stuck with this awful TO by the name of Stonefist. He tried to ram into my head that the department is a brotherhood. That we always stand up for each other, no matter the adversary, and that protecting each other is a greater priority than protecting anyone else. I hated him for that. It went contrary to everything I'd been taught about protecting and serving the community. Yet here I am, practically spouting the same nonsense."

Nelson's brow furrowed. "I wouldn't say that. You're making the argument that it's more important to protect people you care about than yourself. These are people you chose to protect. Who grained your trust by their words and actions, not as members of a club. It's a more nuanced take."

I took a slow breath. "I suppose. Though at the same time, I can understand why reliance on those around you is important. I've been trying to do too much, same as Dean was. It was wearing me out, isolating me, and forcing me into bad decisions. In the end, recognizing I needed to rely more on my team made the difference. It's what helped us catch Yetu and Mason. I couldn't have done it without everyone else in the department. Not just Dean or Moss or Justice. The other patrol officers. Captain Ellison, who I thought was at odds with Dean. Everyone played their part. I guess it's because at the end of the day, we're all on the same side. We might squabble and have differences of opinion, but we all want to see justice done."

"Well, not everyone," said Dr. Nelson. "Mason was a member of the police, too, more or less."

I frowned, feeling confused again.

"My point is the world isn't black or white," said Nelson. "Everything around us is painted in shades of gray. There are good people who do good things, and bad people who do bad things. Most are a mix of good and bad. All sorts are distributed among us in all walks of life, and you can't always tell who is who from afar. But the important thing you've realized is that you're better off surrounding yourself with the good ones, supporting them, and letting them support you. Because we all need a helping hand every now and then."

"Yeah. I suppose that's true."

Nelson and I sat in silence for a moment. Nelson picked up a notebook from the small table beside him. "So in regards to the shooting incident from our previous session, have you reflected on how that makes you feel?"

I took a deep breath, then let it out. "Not really, Doctor. If I'm being honest, I feel burnt out emotionally. I know it's something I should confront, but I haven't yet. Maybe I should take a break. It's not as if the work would miss me right now."

Nelson gave a small smile. "That, at least, is progress. Once you accept you have a battle awaiting you, you can prepare." He plucked a pen from the table and scribbled a note in his pad. "I think a break would be an excellent idea. At least a couple days, but you could take more if you think you need them. During that time, I'd encourage you to allot time for self-reflection. Take a long walk in a park, or sit on a bench and watch the sunset. Don't fill your days with errands and activities. The whole point of the exercise is to let the feelings inside you come out, because only then can you address them."

I nodded. "I think I can do that."

"Good." Nelson stood and held out a hand. "It's been a pleasure, Miss Phair. My door is always open, unless I'm with another patient."

I stood. "I'm cleared then?"

"You're on the path to recovery," said Nelson. "But feelings can change. They're tricky beasts. If you need me, I'll be here."

"Thank you, Doctor." I shook his hand, and headed out.

Upon reaching the ground floor and exiting onto the street, I headed toward where I'd parked my squad car, but as I approached it, I noticed a distinctive emerald green Howardson Viper parked in front of it. Dean leaned against the hood, a smile on his face, legs stretched out before him, and his jacket flapping in the breeze. He wasn't smoking, though. Maybe he really was making an effort to quit.

I wasn't entirely sure what he was doing there, but I couldn't help but let his positive aura seep into me. "Don't you look chipper."

Dean's smile grew as I stopped beside him. "What's not to be chipper about? It's a lovely fall day. Yetu is dead, and Mason is behind bars, where he's going to stay for good. I had the first good night's sleep I've had in ages. Feels like the weight of the world has been lifted off my back."

I snorted. "You're not the only one."

Dean's face lost a little of its cheer. "I'm sorry if I failed to see how badly the case was affecting you, by the way. I was so wrapped up in it, I couldn't even see it was tearing me apart, much less anyone else."

I shrugged. "I don't think it was the case, so much. Don't get me wrong. It was creepy at times, anxiety-inducing at others. But it wasn't the case that was choking me. It was..." I paused. Old me wouldn't have wanted to share everything with Dean, but whether because of Dr. Nelson's guidance or my new rapport with Dean following our life and death adventure, I felt more at ease around him. "I guess I wasn't comfortable with who I was yet. With this position. Being around you and the rest of the team. I didn't know my place, but I do now. I know my role, and I like it. I'm good at it. And I know I can't do it all myself, but that's okay."

Dean stood. "I'm glad you're finally comfortable in your role. That's no small thing, but if what the chief told you the other night is true, your role might be growing in short order."

Suddenly, a pang of fear struck me. "Wait... Is that why you're here? Are you interviewing for a position at HQ? Is that why the chief wants to fast-track me to detective? So when Moss or Justice takes over we'll still have three on the team?"

Dean placed his hands on my shoulders. He looked me in the eyes. "I'm not going anywhere, Nell. I just came by to take you to lunch."

I blinked. "You did?"

"I did."

The fear disappeared as Dean's hands dropped away. "Well... thanks, I guess. You want to hit that taco truck again?"

Dean headed to the driver's side of his car. "I was thinking someplace more relaxed where we could go inside and not eat in the car. A place where we could talk and get to know each other better. If I'm being honest, we've been through more in the last three days than most people go through in a lifetime, yet there's still so much I don't know about you."

I cocked my head. *Dean wanted to get to know me? At a*

restaurant? I'd been on my fair share of dates. I knew that if something looked like a duck, swam like a duck, and quacked like a duck, it was probably a duck. Still, there wasn't any reason to call Dean out on it. Why not enjoy it for what it was, and see where the wind blew us?

"Alright, Alton," I said. "Let's get some lunch."

ABOUT THE AUTHOR

Hi. I'm Alex P. Berg, author of *Divination and Rot*. Things are looking up for Penelope Phair at the moment. The Tarot Card Killer is behind bars, Phair is comfortable with her role in Dean's team, and there might even be a hint of romance in the air. But as good as life is now, a bumpy road lies ahead. To make sure you don't miss Phair's next big adventure, be sure to sign up for my new release mailing list.

Can't wait for the next Penelope Phair novel? Well, have you read my Daggers & Steele series? It features Nell's great-grandparents and homicide detectives extraordinaire Jake Daggers and Shay Steele, back when New Welwic was just going through the industrial revolution. The complete ten book series is available now, so what are you waiting for! Read it today! You can even buy the complete series in a single low-priced omnibus volume.

Word of mouth is **critical** to my success. If you enjoyed this novel, please consider leaving a positive review on Amazon or your retailer of choice. Even if it's only a line or two, it would be a *huge* help. Thanks!

Want to connect? Visit me at www.alexpberg.com or contact me on social media.

For a complete list of my books, please visit: www.alexpberg.com/books/.

www.ingramcontent.com/pod-product-compliance
Lightning Source LLC
Chambersburg PA
CBHW021203250626
47155CB00008B/2651